inVincible

CHRONICLES
of NICK

invincible

SHERRILYN KENYON

St. Martin's Griffin ≉ *New York*

INVINCIBLE. Copyright © 2011 by Sherrilyn Kenyon. All rights reserved. Printed in the United States of America. For information, address St. Martin's Press, 175 Fifth Avenue, New York, N.Y. 10010.

www.stmartins.com

The Library of Congress has cataloged the hardcover edition as follows:

Kenyon, Sherrilyn, 1965–
  Invincible : chronicles of Nick / Sherrilyn Kenyon.—1st ed.
    p. cm.
  ISBN 978-0-312-59906-5
  I. Title.
  PS3563.A311145I58 2011
  813'.54—dc22

                            2011008850

ISBN 978-0-312-60327-4 (trade paperback)

First St. Martin's Griffin Edition: March 2012

10   9   8   7   6   5   4   3   2   1

To my boys,
who wanted a book to share with their friends.

For my husband,
who has always been the wind beneath my wings.

And as always, to you, the reader,
for taking these fun journeys with me.

ACKNOWLEDGMENTS

To all my paranormal investigating friends and col-
leagues, thanks for all the fun and memories. In particular thank you to Mama Lisa and Tish, the best
exorcist and two best psychics I know. Keep to the
light, my sisters. Keep to the light.

CHAPTER 1

They say when you're about to die, you see your entire life flash before your eyes.

They lied.

The only thing Nick Gautier could see flashing was Kyrian Hunter's vampire fangs. That horrifying sight froze him in place on the elegant mahogany staircase at the front of Kyrian's sprawling antebellum mansion.

I'm going to die. . . .

Again.

Yeah, since he'd attempted to go to school about twenty-two hours ago and found out his principal had been eaten by a zombie, everything and its brother had been after him.

Now his friggin' boss was a vampire.

It figured. So much for his paycheck—unless the devil could cash it, Nick would never see a nickel of it.

Would this day *ever* end?

Dude, right now, you're the one who's about to end. That thought finally shattered the terrified fog in his head, which had held him immobile.

Run, dude, run!

He couldn't go downstairs, 'cause that was where Kyrian stood. The only place to run was upstairs, after his mother—who'd already gone into the bedroom Kyrian had loaned them for the night. She was completely oblivious to the fact that they were in mortal danger and that their blood was about to be drained. He spun around to warn her.

"Nick! Wait!"

Wait, my gluteus maximus. Vampire was shy a few quarts of blood if he thought Nick had any intention of not going Casper on him.

I'm too young, too smart, and too good-looking to die. Yeah, and then some. The world needed him to improve the gene pool. Not to mention, at fourteen he hadn't even had his first date yet. He'd only just, this night, had his first kiss. He should have recognized that alone as a sign that the apocalypse was coming and that his death was imminent.

As Nick neared the top of the stairs, Kyrian jumped straight up from the floor twenty feet below and flipped over the shiny railing to land gracefully in front of him and cut off his escape. Kyrian's black eyes flashed in the shadows. Dressed all in black and at over six feet in height, Kyrian made a deadly, impressive sight, even with his boyish blond curls.

There was no way to get past him.

Crapola . . .

Nick skidded to a halt. What should he do now? His mom was in a bedroom a few feet behind Kyrian. He'd yell for her, but the last thing he wanted was for Kyrian to kill her, too. Maybe if he kept quiet, Kyrian would only drain him.

"It's not what you think, Nick."

Yeah, right. "I think you're a bloodsucking demon vampire who's going to kill me—that's what I think."

Before he could so much as blink, Kyrian reached

out and grabbed Nick's neck with some kind of Vulcan death grip. He wanted to fight, but he was as helpless as a pup being held by the scruff. With the inhuman strength you'd expect from the undead, Kyrian hauled Nick past his mother's temporary bedroom and into Kyrian's upstairs office.

As in the rest of the house, the floor-to-ceiling curtains were drawn shut to protect against the dawning sun—something that should have clued Nick in that Kyrian was a ghoul from the first moment he stepped into the mansion. The dark wood of the desk blended in seamlessly with the dark green walls. Without breaking stride, Kyrian flung Nick into a dark burgundy leather chair.

When he started to run, Kyrian slammed him back into it. "Stop a minute and listen. I know I'm asking the impossible from you, but for once in your life, shut your mouth and open your ears."

"I'm not the one talking."

Kyrian snarled at him. "Don't get smart with me."

"You want me stupid?"

"Nick . . ."

Nick held his hands up. "Fine, just don't eat my mom, okay? She's had a bad enough life without becoming the Bride of Dracula."

"I don't drink blood."

He arched a brow at that. "Yeah, right."

"Yeah, right. I don't. I'm not a vampire."

This from the one with the long freaky canines? "Then what's with your peculiar dental problem, huh? And don't even try to tell me they're fake, Mr. Armani suits and fancy car, 'cause you ain't the type to have false ones, and all that also says you have the money to fix them if you wanted to. Not to mention the fact you don't go out in daylight, and how did you ninja-flip up the stairs just now if you're not one of the undead?"

"I'm gifted."

"And I'm gone." Nick tried to escape, and again, Kyrian body-slammed him into the chair hard enough to get his attention.

"You know about Acheron, and you accepted him. Why don't you trust me?"

Acheron Parthenopaeus was a giant immortal . . . something. But even so, he'd been nothing other than nice to Nick and his mom. And most important . . . "He don't got no fangs."

"Yes, he does. He's just better at hiding his than I am mine. He's also my boss."

Nick would argue he was full of cow manure, but that explanation actually made sense in a weird way. Ash was more than eleven thousand years old and had seemed a peculiar friend for Kyrian to have. But if the immortal giant was Kyrian's boss . . .

That explained it.

Still, Nick wasn't a fool, and he accepted nothing at face value. For all he knew, Kyrian was lying his fangs off. "What line of work are you in?"

"People protection."

"Like saving punk kids getting beat to death by people who're supposed to be their friends?" *I.e. me getting shot by Alan and stomped into the ground by Tyree and Mike a couple of weeks ago.* That had been how the two of them had met and what had led to his working part-time for Kyrian after school.

Kyrian inclined his head to him. "Exactly."

Nick relaxed a degree as he reminded himself how

much he owed Kyrian. But for Kyrian, he'd be dead right now. "So you're not going to attack my mother or suck my blood?"

"Good gods, no. I don't need the indigestion. You've caused me enough of a headache for one night. I don't need any more."

Nick sat in Kyrian's chair, staring up at him. If Kyrian wanted to kill him, he'd had plenty of opportunities. Instead, he'd protected both Nick and his mother and allowed them to spend the night in his mansion.

"If you want to know the correct term for me, I'm a Dark-Hunter."

Nick digested that word slowly. "Which means what? You hunt darkness?"

"Yes, Nick. That's exactly what I do. There's just not enough of it." Now, there was some sarcasm you could cut with a knife.

Nick wasn't amused by it. "So you going to explain it or not?"

"We're immortal warriors who sold our souls to the goddess Artemis. For her, we fight and protect humanity from whatever stalks the night, trying to prey on them. For the most part, that means we track and slay Daimons."

"Which are?"

"To put it in terms you can relate to, they're vampires who live on human souls. Instead of blood, they take your soul into their body, and once it's there, it starts to wither and die. We have to kill the Daimon before the soul is completely used up."

"I don't understand. Why take souls?"

Kyrian shrugged. "It's what nourishes them. They have to keep a living soul in them or they die."

That was harsh. For them and especially for the person they killed to get it.

"How do they take souls?" Nick asked.

"No idea. I asked Acheron that question once, and he refused to answer. He's good at that."

"So did he teach that to you, too?"

Kyrian smiled, not the tight-lipped smiles of the past, this was a full-blown one that showed off his fangs. "He did, indeed."

"I give you an A-plus, then."

Kyrian cocked his head, watching him as if waiting for Nick to run again. "Are we good?"

Nick considered it. He probably should be terrified and bolting for the door, but Kyrian had been there with him, fighting zombies and protecting his friends tonight. He'd opened his house to Nick's mom.

He seemed okay. . . .

You can trust him. For the first time, Nick knew who that weird deep voice in his head belonged to.

Ambrose—his whacked-out uncle who swore he was here to help him. Strange, how everyone kept claiming that. But—

"Nick?"

They both jumped at the sound of Nick's mom in the hallway, calling his name.

Kyrian went to the door and opened it. "We're in here, Mrs. Gautier."

Stepping into the room, she looked around suspiciously, as if she expected to catch them doing something illegal, unethical, or unnatural. Tiny, petite, and beautiful with bright blue eyes, his mom had always reminded him of an angel, especially when she wasn't wearing makeup—something he hated on her. Her blond hair was rumpled and she was dressed in a black T-shirt that went all the way to her knees. It looked like Kyrian had loaned it to her to sleep in. At twenty-eight, she was really young to have a kid his age. But that had never mattered. It'd always been the two of them against a hostile world.

"Nick? Is everything okay?"

"It's all good, Mom."

She gave Kyrian an arch stare that said she didn't believe Nick's answer. "You sure, boo?"

"Absolutely. Mr. Hunter was just telling me that I have tomorrow off since I worked so late tonight. Isn't that right, Mr. Hunter?"

There was an amused gleam in Kyrian's eyes as he realized Nick had manipulated the situation to his advantage. "Yes, that's correct."

"Couldn't you have told him that outside?"

Kyrian pressed his lips together in an effort not to smile and expose his teeth. "Nick came in here to get online and play. I was just telling him he needed to go on to bed."

Oh, the rat . . .

Pulling the parental censorship card? That was just rude. Unconscionable. If Nick weren't the victim, he'd applaud the quick thinking. But the last thing he needed was for his mom to have yet another reason to ground him.

She leveled an angry stare at him. "Nicky . . ."

Nick held his arm up in surrender. "Mom—"

"Don't you 'Mom' me, boy. I can't believe you'd do this when you know better. Get your butt in bed. Right now. March!"

Rising from his chair, Nick growled low in his throat and cast a warning snarl at Kyrian. He'd get him . . .

Eventually.

Kyrian let out an evil closed-lipped laugh. "I'll show you to your room."

His mom was having none of that as she blocked the doorway. "He can sleep in my room. With me."

Kyrian released a tired sigh. "I wondered where Nick got his suspicious nature from. You've taught him well."

His mom smoothed a stray piece of blond hair

back from her face and tucked it in behind her left ear. "Yeah, well, I've seen the ugly side of people too many times. No offense to you, Mr. Hunter."

"I assure you, I've seen an even uglier side of them than you have. Many times, myself. Call me Kyrian, please."

That seemed to embarrass her. She gestured to Nick. "Come on, babe. The sun's already up. You need to get some sleep. You're still getting over that gunshot wound."

What she didn't know was that it had healed, courtesy of some powers he didn't want her to know about. If she did, with his luck, she'd report him to the authorities and he'd end up naked in a lab somewhere as an experiment. "Do I have to go to school?"

"Since it starts in less than two hours, no."

"It won't be open today anyway," Kyrian said, drawing their attention back to him. "The police are still investigating it."

His mom frowned. "How do you know?"

"I talked to one of Nick's teachers."

"Which one?" Nick was dying to know who on the

faculty to avoid for fear of them ratting him out to his fanged employer.

"Ms. Pantall."

Great. Just great. She'd never thought much of him, anyways. She was one of the lead faculty members who wanted him expelled. But there was nothing he could do about that tonight.

Nick yawned as his exhaustion caught up with him.

His mom *tsk*ed. "See how tired you are?"

He hated when his mom asked stupid questions. It took all his restraint not to smart off. But he'd already skated past one restriction tonight. No need to court another one.

So minding his tongue, he followed her back to their room. Like Kyrian's office, it was huge. Bigger than their entire itty-bitty condo, which he loathed. And it had a king-sized bed, so his mom wouldn't kick him in her sleep. She spun around in bed like a rotisserie chicken, and he despised anytime they had to share sleeping space.

But the four-poster bed looked like it could easily hold a family of ten in it. The neatest part to him was that the blue and gold comforter matched the wallpaper. Even the gold-foil-looking stuff, which was really cool on the walls. He'd seen that on TV shows . . . and horror movies.

His mom turned to him. "How's your arm doing? You need any more medicine?"

Nick had to force himself not to react to her question. He'd already forgotten about that again. Crap. He better remember; otherwise, everyone would want to know how he healed it so fast.

"It's okay."

"Good. Now hit the sheets."

Nick went to the other side and slid in. The moment he was settled, she pulled him against her and started playing in his short brown hair. He cringed and squirmed, trying to escape her. Unfortunately, she was like quicksand. Once you were dumb enough to get into its reach, it was over. "Ma! What are you doing?"

"Can't I hold you?"

He screwed his face up in distaste at the mere thought of it. "I don't know why you worry about Mr.

Hunter when you're the one who's always sexually harassing me, Mom. Gah, can't I even go to sleep without you groping me?"

She popped him on the butt. Not hard enough to hurt. Just enough to get his attention. "Stop saying that. Showing my baby affection with a hug is not sexual harassment. You know, there are a lot of moms out there who have no sense of maternal instinct at all." Those who threw their kids out of the house and into the gutter because of a single mistake, like keeping a baby they didn't want her to. His mom didn't say it, but he knew when she ranted on this topic that it was a tirade against her own parents, who'd abandoned her when she was his age. "Be glad you have a mother who loves you."

He *was* glad of that. A lot, since she was basically the only person on earth who did. But now that he was a full head taller than her, it was weird when she tried to cuddle him like he was a baby. He could be almost seven feet tall like Acheron, and she'd probably still try to pull him into her lap. "Sorry, Mom. I'm just really tired."

"I know, precious." She leaned over, brushed his hair back from his face, and kissed his cheek. "Good night. Sleep tight."

"You, too."

Without another word, she turned over. Then scooted so that she was touching him with her icy cold feet. He would protest that, too, but it might hurt her feelings again.

I can't wait until I'm grown and have my own place. . . .

I know you hate it now, Nick, but savor it. I promise you, you'll spend many more years of your life wishing you could see her again than you'll spend wishing she'd leave you alone.

Nick frowned at the intrusiveness of Ambrose in his head. *How is it I hear you?*

One day, I'll teach that power to you. You'll be able to project your thoughts to anyone, just like I can.

Will I be able to read other people's thoughts like you do, too?

Yes, you will.

That was cool. He could definitely get used to knowing what other people were thinking. It sure would make asking a girl out a lot easier if he knew going into it that she thought he was a total loser dork.

When can I learn it?

Ambrose laughed in his head. *Patience, boy. You still haven't learned everything about controlling the dead that you should have. Or what you need to. Your buddy caused us to accelerate learning that power. And even though you survived, you really didn't learn much other than how to run from things out to kill you. Before something gets a lucky shot in, I think we should take things a little slower. Learn to crawl, and then I'll teach you to fly. Literally.*

Nick's eyes widened at that last bit. *I'll be able to fly? Really?*

Kid, you have no idea what powers lie within you. What powers I'm going to teach you. But be warned, you are going to have many enemies come at you. Parthenopaeus being one of them.

Nick frowned again. *Ash?*

Yeah. He's not what he seems, and if you have any brains in your head—and I know you do—you'll cut him a wide berth . . .

Before it's too late.

But he really liked Acheron. Surely someone who was so cool to be with and respectful to *his* mother couldn't be so bad. Everyone had problems. Because he and his mother had been rudely misjudged by so many, Nick hated doing that to others. He believed in liking, not necessarily trusting, everyone until they personally gave him a reason not to.

Like shooting me when I decide that I don't want to live a life of crime.

He heard the sound of exasperation from his uncle.

Go to sleep, kid. Tomorrow will begin a new life that you can't imagine.

With people trying to kill me?

Yes. And that includes your mother.

CHAPTER 2

Nick came awake to the sensation of his mother strangling him. Dressed in the black T-shirt she'd slept in and jeans, she was on her knees beside him, wringing his neck. "Ma! What are you doing?"

She tightened her grip. "I'm killing you. Do you understand? Dead. Dead. Dead."

He coughed, trying to twist away from her. "What did I do?"

Growling, she released him and moved back, then popped him on the butt. "Because of the stunt you and those moron friends of yours pulled last night, I'm fired. I hope you're happy. I can barely afford to feed and shelter us now. What am I supposed to do without a job at all? I didn't graduate high school, and I have no experience except as a dancer."

She looked like she was about to cry. "You have no idea how awful some of the other clubs treat their people. I know you hated my job, but it was the only thing I could find that paid above minimum wage for someone with no skills or real job experience. I can't even work a cash register, never mind run a computer or do anything else. Peter won't listen to an apology. He said that he doesn't care what happened or how it happened. I'm fired and not to even come back for my check—he'll mail it to me 'cause he never wants to see me again. Oh, God—what am I going to do?"

"Mrs. Gautier, I hear there are places online where you can sell children for a good price. Nick is still young enough, he should fetch enough to tide you over for a bit."

Nick gaped at Rosa's voice from the other side of the door as she walked past their room. Normally, he loved the sound of her thick accent, but right now . . . "Thanks, Rosa. 'Preciate it."

"De nada, m'ijo."

Nick scooted across the bed, trying to get away from his mom before she started choking him again. "Kyrian said he knew some people who could hire you."

She stared at him as if she really could kill him. "That doesn't get you off the hook, mister. Are you and Bubba going to waltz in and tranq me again and cause me to lose another job? You know most employers tend to frown on their sons bringing in a brute to carry them out over their shoulders when they're supposed to be working."

"But it was for your own good."

"So's the spanking I'm about to give you."

Nick leapt back onto the bed, rolled across it, then ran for the door and into the hallway, where he hoped it would be safer. "I'm too big to spank."

"Fine, you're grounded until your grandkids are old."

"Kind of hard to do. How am I supposed to have grandkids if I'm grounded?"

"Precisely my point, you demon spawn. You're never going to get off restriction. Ever!"

The door at the end of the hall opened to show an

irritated Kyrian. Dressed in a pair of black pajama bottoms and no shirt, he glowered at them. His hair was tousled and he had a good shadow on his face. More than that, he had a build Nick would kill for. Dang, no one at school would ever pick on him again if he was ripped like that.

Kyrian pinned them both with an angry scowl. "People, I really need to sleep. Can you go downstairs to shout at each other? Or better yet, outside in the yard?"

His mother immediately calmed down. "I'm sorry, Mr. Hunter. We didn't mean to disturb you."

Kyrian raked his hand through his blond hair, which made it stand straight up. Nick would laugh or mock it, but Kyrian wasn't as attached to him as his mom was. His boss might actually kill him. "No problem. Now, if it'll help stop this fighting and save Nick's life before he can pay me back, put a call in to Sanctuary on Ursuline. Ask for Nicolette Peltier. She's the owner and I've already spoken to her about you. She said to call her anytime and they'd be more than happy to add you to payroll."

"But—"

He held his hand up in an imperious gesture that actually silenced Nick's mom. Wow, to have those evil Jedi tricks. Had Nick done it, his mom really would have spanked him. Hard.

"No *buts*. Give her a call. I assure you, you'll love working for them." And with that, he vanished back into his pitch-black room and shut the door.

Nick let out a relieved breath. He might survive the morning yet.

"Oh, don't even." His mom turned her nasty gorgon face back at him. "You're still not off the hook. Get your butt dressed. You have five minutes."

"For what?"

"Don't back-talk me or argue. Not if you want to live to see noon. Get in there and shower. Now!"

Fetch. Heel. Bark, Fido, bark. He really hated when she talked to him like he was nothing but a dog with no other purpose than to obey her every whim. "You know, I don't ride the short bus, Ma. I can understand you."

"Apparently you can't, because you now have only

four minutes and thirty seconds before they start playing your dirge."

With a juvenile desire to stick his tongue out at her, he walked back into the room and into the adjacent bathroom so that he could obey and not stay grounded any longer than was necessary.

Though at this rate, it seemed like she was looking for reasons to ground him.

Empty-nest syndrome. She was afraid of him leaving home, so she clung to him all the tighter. Okay, that's probably not what it was called, but that's what he was calling it.

Sighing, he stripped his clothes off and started the shower.

Of course, it took him longer than five minutes to finish and dress. And when he opened the door that led back to the bedroom, he found his mother on the bed, staring furiously at him.

"What? I hurried."

"Sure you did." She slid off the bed. "You didn't even shave."

"You told me to hurry, so I didn't bother looking for a razor. Besides, I have only three hairs. Not like anyone can see them except you." He kept hoping they'd grow longer and multiply, but so far . . .

They were just enough to be emasculating and aggravating. Something else for his mom to nag at him to do.

She made an annoyed sound that always reminded him of a tea kettle letting out steam. "C'mon. We have to catch a streetcar."

"Where are we going?"

"You heard Mr. Hunter. We need to go to Sanctuary."

"He said to call."

She rolled her eyes—something that would also have got him grounded if he'd done it to her. "You don't apply for a job that way, Nick."

"But—"

"Go!"

He didn't want to go across town for no reason. Why did he have to watch her apply for a job, anyway? He'd rather have his eyes gouged out than sit there bored and watching the fluorescent lights flicker. "Can't I stay here?"

"No. We don't take charity, and you know that.

Mr. Hunter was nice enough to put us up for the night, but you should never overstay your welcome."

"But—"

"Nick, do what I say."

Grinding his teeth, he headed for the stairs. He might as well take the *but* out of his vocabulary, since all it seemed to do was act like a nuclear accelerant that caused her temper to explode.

No sooner had he reached the bottom than he smelled something delicious. . . . Something that smelled like real, juicy, delectable, make-your-mouth-water-and-arteries-harden bacon. Not those bacon bits packets his mom saved from condiment stands and added to his powdered eggs in the morning.

Yum!

Without conscious thought, he beelined for the kitchen.

His mother grabbed his arm. "Where are you going?"

"Food. I'm following my nose." And his rumbling stomach.

"No," she whispered to him. "What part of 'no charity' have you missed?"

The part that said he couldn't eat.

But he knew better than to argue, especially when she had *that* look on her face. "Fine." He headed for the door.

Rosa came around the corner of the wall and frowned at them. "Nick? Mrs. Gautier? Do you not wish to eat before you leave?"

He looked at his mother, hoping she'd change her mind.

"Thank you, Rosa, but we have an appointment to keep."

Rosa's frown melted into a kind smile. The same height as his mother, she was a beautiful woman with black hair she kept in a bun and bright brown eyes. "Then let me get it for you to go."

His mother released his arm. "No, thank you. We don't want to put you to any trouble."

"Is no trouble," Rosa assured her. "I made the food for you. I have already eaten, and Mr. Kyrian won't be up until much later today. If you no eat, I just throw it away."

Nick gave his mom his best begging stare and pouty lip. It was a look that had gotten him away with many things that didn't have a moral dilemma attached to them.

He saw the reluctance in her eyes. She really, really didn't like to take anything from anybody. *People always expect something back when you do. Nothing in life is free, Nick. Don't take and you won't be beholding.* He knew her litany well.

But he didn't view this as the same thing.

"You always say we shouldn't waste food, Ma."

She took a deep breath before she relented. "All right. Thank you, Rosa."

"My pleasure. You want me to—?"

"We'll eat at the table. I don't want to put you to any more work."

Nick all but ran to the kitchen, where Rosa had two plates already made and sitting on the center island. The warm smell made his stomach cramp even more. "Oh, my God! We have pancakes and bacon!" It smelled so good, he was already salivating.

Rosa laughed at his eagerness. She had no idea how rare a meal like this was for him. "Don't you want syrup?" she asked as he grabbed one of the pancakes and took a bite.

Nick swallowed the delicious-tasting food. "We have syrup, too?"

She pointed to the counter behind him, where a huge bottle of Log Cabin waited. *Oh yeah, that's what I'm talking about. . . .*

He grabbed it, popped the top, and proceeded to drown the plate.

His mom was much more sedate as she took her food. "Nick, don't use so much syrup. You won't be able to taste your food."

That was the idea. "Ma, it's real good syrup and it's not watered down." Something she did to make it last longer for them whenever they were lucky enough to get some.

Her face turned bright red.

Rosa patted her on her hand. "It's okay, Mrs. Gautier. I understand what it's like to have to struggle to feed my son. Miguel and I had many lean years before I come to work for Mr. Kyrian. You eat as much as you want. Mr. Kyrian's policy is that no one goes hungry in his home."

"Thank you."

Rosa inclined her head, then moved a plate full of

pancakes toward Nick. "But you go a little easy and leave some for your mother. Too many, and your stomach will hurt."

"Yeah, but so worth the pain. These are delicious. Thank you so much for making them."

She smiled as she handed him a napkin. "I'm glad you enjoy."

"I more than enjoy. It's like all the taste buds in my mouth are singing and dancing. I bet if you listen close, you can even hear them."

And it got even better when she handed him a glass of freshly squeezed orange juice. Oh yeah, he was in heaven.

By the time his mom was finished eating, he'd plowed through most of the pancakes.

Shaking her head, his mom took him by his "uninjured" arm and pulled him away from his empty plate. "C'mon, boo. We need to get going."

He licked the syrup off his fingers.

His mom screwed her face up in distaste. "Nick, you have a napkin. Please use it."

"Yeah, but I don't want to waste it. It's good."

She let out a sigh of exasperation as she met Rosa's gaze. "I swear, Rosa, I have taught him better. It just hasn't taken yet. Not from lack of effort on my part."

She laughed. "I know. Believe me, my Miguel is the same way."

Ignoring them, Nick took one last bite before he followed his mom out of the house and down the street to the station. They didn't speak much as they made their way from the fancy, high-end Garden District, where Kyrian lived, to the other side of the French Quarter, where the bar and restaurant called Sanctuary stood at 688 Ursuline. Something that involved their getting off the streetcar at Jackson Brewery and hoofing it a few blocks over toward the Ursuline's convent that had given the street its name. Sanctuary was only one block up the street from it and not that far away from his high school.

He'd been by the place more times than he could count. His mother said the crowd in there could be rough and she didn't want him getting hurt, so he was technically banned from it. And that statement always made him wonder how his mom knew what the crowd was like, since she'd never been inside it either to his knowledge. However, he'd never asked her.

It fell into the category of "don't ask, 'cause you'll only get a stupid parent answer." *If all your friends jumped off a bridge . . . Because I said so. So long as you live under my roof . . . and so on.*

Sanctuary aside, Nick had always loved coming to the Quarter as an escape from their run-down condo and neighborhood. There was something about it that soothed every Cajun root inside him—the history, the beauty, the mixture of cultures, smells, food, and people. No place else on earth like it. Not that he'd ever been anywhere else except Laurel or Jackson, Mississippi, whenever they'd had to evacuate for hurricanes—and then he'd seen only the parking lots of whatever store or mall where they'd made temporary camp in their rusted-out Yugo.

He paused as they came even to the Café Du Monde that sat at the edge of the French Market and the smell of chickory coffee and beignets hit him. It was the first time in his life the sweet smell didn't cramp his stomach with hunger pangs. Today, with his stomach completely full, he appreciated and savored it.

Until he realized he was being left behind.

Even though he was taller than his mom, he had to hurry to catch up to her. For a little woman, she could seriously haul whenever she wanted to.

Luckily, she was so intent on her destination that she didn't even notice he was trailing.

She cut down Dumaine to Chartres. And as they went up to the corner of Chartres and Ursuline, she finally slowed down, as if suddenly apprehensive. Not that he blamed her. Almost a city block in size, Sanctuary was not only huge, but legendary as well. Everyone in New Orleans knew about the place that was opened from eight A.M. to three in the morning. It was said to have some of the best food in the world and some of the meanest patrons.

The three-story redbrick building had a huge sign that hung over saloon-style doors. It was black with a motorcycle parked on a hill and silhouetted by a full moon. The word SANCTUARY was white with a hazy purple outline. And on the lower right-hand side of the sign, in a much smaller font was the slogan, HOME OF THE HOWLERS.

But that wasn't what made Nick hesitant. Standing

just outside the doors was a huge mountain of a man who leaned against the wall. Even taller than Kyrian, he had arms like two tree trunks and long curly blond hair that was pulled back into a ponytail. And as he stared at him, Nick saw a flash in his mind of the bouncer turning into a big, angry bear.

He was one of the shape-shifters Alex Peltier had told him about last night. . . .

Nick had no idea how he knew that, but he did.

His mom pulled him across the street to where the werebear was standing.

As if he sensed Nick feeling his preternatural powers, the bear narrowed a pair of glacial blue eyes on them. "You two lost?"

His mom swallowed audibly. "Um . . . Kyrian Hunter told me to speak to a Nicolette Peltier? I believe she owns this establishment."

He met Nick's gaze with a curious frown before he pulled a walkie-talkie off his belt and pressed the button. "Aimee? Is Maman in her office?"

"Yeah, why?"

"I have two humans out here who want to see her. Kyrian sent them."

His choice of words amused Nick. While his mother would dismiss it as eccentric, he knew better. The guy in front of him was warning the rest of his family that new humans were entering. Nice code. In your face and at the same time innocuous enough to fly below the radar of most people.

"Be nice to them, Rémi, and don't bite their heads off. Maman will be right out," the woman on the radio said.

Rémi opened the swinging door for them. "If you two want to go on in and wait . . ."

His mother smiled. "Thank you."

Nick paused at the door to look back at the bear. "Is Alex around?"

Rémi narrowed his gaze on him. "How you know Alex?" Could there be any more suspicion or challenge in that tone?

"We go to school together."

"Ah . . ." And that was all he said.

Okay . . . Obviously the bear wasn't a morning person and had no desire to tell him where to find his classmate. Deciding not to irritate someone who wasn't human and who could probably break his spine in half,

Nick went inside and joined his mother, who was standing in front of the first round table that was set with four chairs. Since it was still an hour and a half before lunch, there weren't many occupants in the room. Two men . . . no, a werepanther and werehawk, stood at the bar, restocking and cleaning. There was one person at a table with a laptop and a cup of coffee. Two women eating a late breakfast and an older man reading the paper and making notes of some kind.

His mom handed him a dollar. "Go play a video game while I talk to the owner."

Thinking it was odd, but too grateful for the rarity of having money to waste, Nick went off to the rear of the restaurant, where pool tables were set out and arcade games were placed against the wall. As he neared them, he caught sight of a boy a few years older than him who was cleaning tables. It wasn't the matted blond dreadlocks that made him pause so much as it was the small monkey sitting on the boy's shoulder, eating a banana. The monkey bared its teeth at Nick before it made noises at him. The busboy reached up to soothe the monkey, and it settled right down.

Nick wanted to go and investigate the primate, but

something about the busboy warned him to keep his distance.

No, not boy.

Weretigard. A very vicious and antisocial one.

How can I tell that by looking at him?

Yesterday, he'd been normal.

Today . . .

He was a freakfest as images of the shape-shifters around him flashed in his mind. He didn't know their names, but he knew what they were even though they were masquerading as humans.

What is going on?

His head was spinning from an overload of information. But with all of that was an overwhelming sense of safety. He didn't feel threatened by the animals around him. It was as if they were guardians of some sort. Protectors, not predators. Something that sounded as far-fetched as a restaurant and bar owned by a family of shape-shifters.

Ambrose? He silently summoned his uncle, needing someone who could help him understand. *What's going on here? I'm seeing some scary things. People who aren't people . . .*

Remember what I told you, kid. You have the power of perspicacity. The ability to see what's hidden.

So no one will ever be able to lie to me again?

No. That's a different power. Perspicacity allows you to see most preternatural beings who are trying to blend into the human world.

What do you mean "most"?

There are some demons who are powerful enough to hide. As well as upper-level gods and those who are possessed. In time, you'll be able to see them, too. But that will take a lot of training and discipline.

For now . . . it was like living in some bad psychedelic hallucination.

Just relax, Nick. Go play a game.

He felt Ambrose leaving him alone again. With nothing better to do, he went over to the Galaga machine. Wow, he hadn't seen one of these in a long time. Some old-timer here must have caught a liking to it. Pulling out his dollar, he converted it to tokens, then put one in and listened to distinctive music. He'd just started playing when a shadow fell over him.

He looked up and froze instantly. *Holy Mother . . .*

This dude had to be over seven feet tall. An older version of the guy at the door, this one had the most merciless expression Nick had ever seen.

I'm going to die. . . .

"Who said you could play my machine?"

Nick knew it was a man saying it, but he saw Grizzly Peltier in his mind. A huge bear with blood in its eyes. "Uh . . ."

The man laughed and playfully shoved his arm. "Relax, kid. Don't wet my floor. I was just teasing you."

Easier said than done, since his heart was racing like Richard Petty at Daytona.

He shook his head. "I'm Papa Bear Peltier. You have a name?"

"N-n-nick."

"Nice meeting you, N-n-nick." He pulled a token out of his pocket and held it out to him. "Sorry I ruined your game. But I love the look of shock on people's faces the first time they meet me. It's a thing of beauty."

Nick took the token, but still wasn't sure what to think.

He's a good guy, kid. Thank him for the token.

"Um, thanks."

Papa Bear patted him on the shoulder, then walked over toward the stage so that he and another guy who was an exact copy of Rémi could run electrical cords on the ground.

"Close your mouth, sug. Papa only bites those who bare their teeth first."

He turned at the soft, lightly accented voice to find what had to be one of the most gorgeous women he'd ever seen. Tall, blond, and built with the kind of curves men dreamed about, she wore a black Sanctuary T-shirt that was tight enough to make him really uncomfortable.

"I'm Aimee Peltier. You must be Nick."

Man, she had better powers than he did. "How do you know my name?"

She leaned in to speak into his ear as if she were imparting a great secret to him. "Your mother told me in the back room," she whispered.

Oh yeah, duh. He felt epically stupid with that.

"C'mon and let me introduce you to the crew that is currently awake and functioning."

Unsure about that, Nick hesitated. "Why?" Was she going to feed him to the bears or something?

"Since your mom will be working here and your school is just down the street, you'll probably be hanging out a lot in the near future."

"Oh." Finally relaxing, he allowed her to lead him to the busboy with the monkey.

"Wren, say hi to Nick."

The busboy didn't respond other than to glare out from under his mop of gnarled hair.

Aimee took it in stride. "Wren doesn't really speak. But he's a nice guy, and he lives next door in our house. You'll see him a lot, since he has no personal life or outside interests. He basically works all the time." She scratched the monkey on its head. "And his furry little friend is Marvin. Marvin, say hi to Nick."

The monkey jumped from Wren's shoulder to Nick's, startling him. Nick grabbed him and held him close while Marvin mussed his hair and stuck one leathery little finger in his ear. *Ew!*

"He likes to mess with people's hair." Aimee held her hand out, and Marvin allowed her to pull him into her arms and hug him. "Marvin's a little beggar. Keep some snacks handy, and he'll be your new best friend." She nuzzled his nose before returning him to Wren.

Wren didn't say a word as Marvin perched on his shoulder. He merely went back to work, wiping down the tables.

Aimee led Nick away. "You met Rémi when you arrived. My best advice to you on that is to learn which of the quads he is."

"Quads?"

She gestured to the stage, where Papa and the Rémi look-alike were working. "I have four brothers who are identical quads. Quinn!" she called.

The younger werebear looked up.

She smiled and waved him back to work. "That's obviously Quinn. I thought so, but sometimes, rare though it is, I can't tell him from Cherif. They have the same exact haircut, which they occasionally do to mess with us. It's normally a little shorter than Rémi's and Dev's. Dev you can spot pretty easy because he's always laughing and cracking sarcastic jokes—your mom said that that's right up your alley. He also has a double bow and arrow tattoo on his arm, and he's most often the one at the door. He took the day off to run over to Kenner to pick up a motorcycle he had on order." She drew up short and gave him a sinister look. "If you approach one of them and he growls or doesn't speak, assume it's Rémi. He has perpetual PMS and will tear your arm right out of its socket. You don't really have to do anything other than breathe to piss him off. Word to the wise."

He made a mental note of that as she took him to the bar.

"The blond is Jasyn. Jasyn, say hi to Nick."

The werehawk inclined his head to him.

"The other charming bartender this morning is Justin."

Black hair, tall, and with an aura of *I'll kick your butt so hard, you'll be burping my shoe leather.* Another one Nick intended to avoid.

An older version of Aimee came out from the door next to the bar. She paused as she caught sight of him.

He felt like he was under a microscope as she eyed him from head to toe.

Finally, she held her hand out. "Good day, Mr.

Gautier. I am Nicolette. But please, call me Mama
Lo."

"Mama Lo."

Her glower melted into a kind expression. "Welcome to our family. I hear you work for Kyrian."

"I do. Until he fires me."

She laughed. "No need to give him reason to. Besides, he doesn't fire his people. He kills them."

"Maman!" Aimee said with a laugh. "The poor boy
doesn't know you're kidding."

"Nick? What are you doing here?"

He turned at the call that came from Alex's sister
Kara, who also went to school with them. Even in
height to him, she had the same blond hair as Aimee
and Mama Lo.

Aimee explained his presence before he had a
chance. "His mother will be working for us, Kiki.
Why don't you take him to the kitchen? I'm pretty
sure Morty's cookies are done."

Cookies? Dang, if they kept this up, he was going
to be huge.

But it would be worth it.

Nick took a step toward the kitchen, then paused as a cold chill went down his spine. Something was here and it was evil.

He searched the room until his gaze found the source of his discomfort. The man stepped through the door behind the women, carrying a silver tray. Dressed in a black T-shirt and gray hoodie, at first glance, he appeared like any guy around the age of twenty.

Until Nick locked gazes with him. It felt like electricity jolted him. There was no denying the intensity of this creature's presence.

He was Death, and he'd ridden in on a pale horse. . . .

CHAPTER 3

Okay, Death wasn't exactly *on* a pale horse. He was carrying it. . . .

Nick wanted to run for the door, but he couldn't get his feet to obey. It was like every joint in his body was locked by some invisible force.

"Morty!" Kara said excitedly. "Your ears must have been burning. I was just going to come and find you."

His gaze never left Nick's. "Really? No wonder I knew to come out, then. Must have heard all of you screaming for cookies of Death."

Nick watched as the pale horse, which was no bigger than his hand, reared up on the stack of cookies. Its color was like nothing he'd ever seen before. A strange mixture of blue and white, the color seemed to be a living entity all its own. The miniature horse snorted fire from its nostrils before it ran down Morty's arm and vanished inside the pocket of his hoodie.

WTH?

More than that, was the image of Morty dressed in black armor, brandishing a sword. His black hair whipped around his face and shoulders, while his eyes glowed a fierce, vibrant red and his skin glinted like it was bronze and not flesh.

Nick glanced around to see if any of the weres had noticed. If they did, they gave no indication.

"Would you like a cookie, kid?"

It took him a second to realize Death was speaking to him. "What?"

"Do. You. Want. A. Cookie?"

He could have done without the tone that said Death thought he was a moron.

When Death offers a cookie, or anything else, refuse.

Yeah, that definitely seemed like the wisest course of action.

Nick shook his head. "I just ate. A lot, and I'm still burping syrup. Thanks, but no thanks."

The corner of Death's mouth quirked up in wry amusement.

Kara frowned at him. "You should try them, Nick. They're delicious. No one makes cookies that taste like this."

Probably because arsenic was a key ingredient.

He patted his stomach. "Have to watch my girlish figure. 'Cause if I don't, no one will."

Death laughed as he handed the tray to Kara. "C'mon, Nick, let me show you around."

"I think I'm good."

Completely oblivious of the fact that Nick was highly disturbed by their stygian cook, Aimee grabbed a cookie off the plate. "That's a good idea. You two have fun. I need to get back to payroll, anyway."

Mama . . . , Nick silently whimpered.

Morty grabbed his arm and all but hauled him through the swinging door that led to the kitchen, where two giant brutes were cleaning. One was humongously tall and bald, with dark eyes that missed nothing. He had a tattoo at the base of his neck that looked like some kind of angry bird. The other was not much taller than Nick. His brown hair was cut short.

Death clapped the tall one on the shoulder. "Nick, meet my two companions. Pain and Suffering." Pain was the big one, and Suffering the smaller of the two. "You'll have to ignore Suffering, since he's mute."

"Mute?"

"Mmm . . . You know, you should always suffer in silence."

Nick would laugh, but he was afraid Pain might hit him for it, and since he was Pain, best to leave him be. "Nice meeting you two . . ." He looked around nervously. "Oh, wait! I hear my mom calling. I better go see what she needs." He turned to leave, only to find that his legs were locked again.

Death sauntered over to stand in front of him. "Don't play coy, Cajun. We don't like that."

Yeah, and he didn't like being stuck in the kitchen with ghouls either. Sometimes you just didn't get what you wanted. "What do you want from me?"

"Normally, it'd be your life and your soul." He sighed heavily. "Unfortunately, I can't take either right now. Sucks to be me today." He slapped Nick so hard on the shoulder that it made him stagger. "I was sent here to teach you."

"Teach me what?" Dying painfully in a back alley somewhere?

"How to understand augury."

Nick scowled. "Ahhhga . . . who?"

"Augury," Death repeated. "The art of divination."

Okay, that made absolutely no sense to him. "But you're Death."

Death gave him a droll stare. "I know, kid. Believe me, it's not something you forget. But there are many agents of death, messengers as it were. I am only one. In my opinion, I'm *the* best one. However, there are plenty more out there able to do the job. Poseurs mostly, granted. But enough that Death can sometimes take a holiday." He winked at him as he mentioned the title of a movie Nick's mom loved to watch.

Yeah, Death was a few quarts shy of a gallon. "I take it the death business doesn't pay too well, so you moonlight as a cook here in this place."

"You would think that, right?" Death stepped out of his body. Literally.

Where there had been one person, there was suddenly two. Only, one of them now had short black hair, a white apron, and tattoos running down both arms. That person ignored them while he went to the oven.

"Where are my cookies?" He looked around and then scowled as he caught sight of Nick. "Who are you, and what are you doing back here? Only staff is allowed in the kitchen. Rémi!"

Nick opened and closed his mouth like a fish. He pointed to Death.

"He can't see me, kid. He just thinks you're nuts for pointing at nothing."

Great. That was all he needed. One more person who thought he was on drugs. "Morty?"

The cook drew up short as he was headed for the door. "Yeah?"

"I'm Nick. Aimee told me to come back here and introduce myself to you. My mom will be working here."

Morty held his hand up in warning. "Stay right there. Don't you move." He went to the door and pushed it open only enough for his head to vanish while he spoke to the others. Nick could hear his muf-fled voice, but couldn't understand the words.

Death laughed evilly. "I love making humans think they're losing their minds. Nothing else is quite so satisfying . . . other than listening to them try to bargain with me for their lives. You know, I was once offered my own private island with a harem of virgins and three camels. Tempting, but a ghoul has to do what a ghoul has to do." The look on his face said he was savoring that memory. Then he hit Nick on his "injured" shoulder. "Watch this. . . ."

Morty returned with a stern frown on his face. "How did I get my cookies out there without knowing it?"

Death snickered. "Look at his face. I *love* it."

Nick cleared his throat. "Meth is death, dude. Lay off the crack."

"What?" Morty looked at him as if he'd forgotten he was there. "Um, anyway, Aimee said you're legit. I still don't remember meeting you. I just don't remember."

"It's all right. We all have—" He slid his gaze to Death, who was still laughing, and had to wonder if he wasn't imagining things, too. "—our issues. Tell you what, I think I've met enough new people for the day. I'm going to go chill for a while." *And have my head examined, 'cause obviously, I'm having a hallucination probably brought on by finding out my boss is a freak of nature.*

Now I'm seeing freaks everywhere.

"Good idea." Morty headed to the stove.

Death slung his arm around Nick's shoulders. "Call me Grim or master. I prefer master, but Grim works since it reminds you of who and what I am and what will happen to you if you get under my skin. *Capisce?*"

"Got it."

"Good. By the way, did you know the word *capisce* is actually from the Latin word for 'seize'? As in *carpe diem* or, in the case of your nocturnal boss, *carpe noctem.* Seize the night."

Nick wasn't sure what to make of any of that.

"Close your mouth, kid. The cook already thinks you're crazy. Remember, right now only you have the privilege of my company."

"Okay."

"Hmm. The correct answer should be *capisco*. 'I understand.' So I say *capisce*, and you say . . ."

Nick hesitated before he answered. *"Capisco."*

Grim patted him on the cheek. "Beautiful. You *can* be taught. Makes my job so much easier when you're actually intelligent. You'd be amazed at the idiots I've come across. As George Carlin so eloquently put it: Think of how stupid the average person is, and realize half of them are stupider than that."

He had a point. "I try to keep my stupid to a bare minimum, since my mom's always telling me it can be fatal in large doses."

"Oh, she's right. Believe me, I know. For that matter, it can be fatal even in small measures. Remind me sometime to tell you about the woman I claimed who was vacuuming her cat."

"Who are you talking to?"

Nick felt his face go hot at Morty's question. "Still in the kitchen, aren't I? Guess I need to keep walking. Oh, look! Yonder is the door, which I'm going to make use of right now." He quickly made his exit.

The small group he'd left earlier had dispersed. No

one was there except the two bartenders who'd gone back to restocking behind the bar.

Nick paused beside them. "Where's my mom?"

Before they could answer, she came out of the restroom area dressed in a black Sanctuary T-shirt that matched Aimee's. Thankfully, hers was on the large side and kept her completely covered. Her face lit up the moment she saw him. She practically danced her way over to him.

"Hey, boo!"

He started to ask her if he was forgiven for getting her fired, but decided that might not be in his best interest. "You look happy."

"Oh, baby, I am. They are so nice here. *All* of them." She slid her gaze to the door. "Well, Rémi's a little distant, but I'll take that any day over some of the people I worked with at the club. They're even going to give me a day schedule so that I can be home with you at night. And, best of all, they feed me free while I work and you, too, and not just scraps. We could eat steak if we wanted to."

"I'll settle for the cookies."

"Yeah, I know you would." She squeezed his cheek. "I'm technically on the clock already. I should have left you at Mr. Hunter's."

"I tried to tell you that."

"Don't sass me." She let out a sigh. "I know you'll be bored here. I mean, they have things to do." She glanced over to the game area. "But it's probably best not to press our luck the first day."

"I can go hang at Bubba's. It's just down the street."

All the joy evaporated off her face. "That is one name I never want to hear again. I swear, that man and his antics . . . He's ridiculous."

He'd also saved both their lives last night. But for Bubba and his epic fighting and driving skills, they'd be dead today.

That thought made him glance past his mother's shoulder to where Grim watched them with a bemused expression. He tapped his watch.

"Bubba's all right, Mom. He was trying to help."

"Yeah, well, for his own personal safety, you better keep him away from me—or you'll have two parents in prison for murder." As soon as those words were out of her mouth, she slapped her hand over her lips and looked around frightfully. "Let's not talk about that here, okay?" she whispered.

"I don't talk about that man's unfortunate and eternal incarceration to anyone. Ever." No offense, but he hated the sperm donor who'd spawned him. Speaking of people he didn't want to talk about, his father was a cold-blooded killer who'd knocked them both around the few weeks he'd been out of jail. If Nick never saw him again, it'd be too soon.

"Go stay with Bubba. I'll check with you later."

"All right. Do you have my new cell number?" That'd sounded infinitely better in his head than it did coming out of his mouth, as it invoked an image of him in prison orange, sitting on a bench doing time in Angola like his dad.

"Not with me." She pulled a pad and pen from her pocket and handed it to him.

He jotted his number down and gave it back to her. "If you need me, shout."

She kissed him on the cheek. "Be safe. Be good."

"Always." Nick turned around and headed for the

door. Luckily Grim didn't speak to him again until they were on the street and away from Rémi.

"Aww, Nicky, that's so sweet. Your mama loves you so."

Nick froze instantly. "You don't mock my mother. You don't speak of her in anything but the most reverent of tones. I don't care if you are Death, I will open a can of Cajun whup-ass all over you, boy."

Grim arched one brow as his two companions took a step back, as if giving him space to beat Nick into a bleeding pulp. "Normally, I'd be handing you the can opener and daring you to go for it. Be glad I owe a debt that precludes me from killing you right now. But don't push it. While you have a predetermined death, your own free will decisions can override that. Put that in the bank and think about it before you try to make a withdrawal."

Nick frowned at him. "What do you mean I have a predetermined death?"

"Did I stutter?"

"No."

"Do I look like Webster's?"

Nick frowned. "No."

"Then you should understand what I said, since I didn't speak in code. Every mortal creature is born with an expiration date. Some immortals, too. Set by the big clockmaker. But excessive stupidity and moronic tendencies can shorten it. Pissing me off is one really good way to cut yours down to three seconds from now."

The ice in his voice as he spoke went a long way in making Nick back down. Not that he made a habit of that. Far from it. His mom often called him Snapper after the snapping turtle. *Because anytime you sink your teeth into something, you won't let ago until lightning strikes you.* It was sadly true.

However, his survival instinct won out. "So what are we doing, anyway?"

Grim gave him a droll stare. "We're going to Bubba's. Isn't that what you told your mom?"

"Yeah, but I thought—"

"For the first lesson, I can train you anywhere. Just remember, I won't be seen. *You* will be."

Nick considered that. "Bubba's it is." He was the one person who wouldn't even bat an eyelash that Nick was talking to an "imaginary" friend. Heck, he'd probably bring one of his own out to play, too.

"So who sent you to train me, anyway?"

Grim grinned. "I'm not at liberty to say."

"Then how do I know I can trust you?"

"You're still breathing, right? If an MOD comes to you and you see them and you live through it, obviously we're here for your good and not your demise."

"MOD?"

"Messenger of Death." The moment Grim spoke those words, Nick saw an image of him standing with his wings extended, his eyes flashing red, and his face a glowing purple skeleton.

"You like to freak people out, don't you?"

Death grinned. "Absolutely. I love the sounds of fear they make. Music to my ears."

And on that note, Nick decided it would be best to continue on. No, he wasn't sure he could trust Grim, but . . .

It wasn't worth angering him. So he turned down Royal and made his way to the Triple B—the only computer and gun store in the world—at least that

Nick knew about. And that said it all about Bubba, whose logo was him standing over a shot, smoking computer with a gun slung over his shoulder.

1-888-CA-BUBBA
IF I CAN'T TAKE CARE OF YOUR
COMPUTER PROBLEMS ONE WAY . . .
I'LL TAKE CARE OF THEM
ANOTHA'

Yeah, Nick knew all kinds of people.

"Triple B?" Grim asked as they approached the sign that hung above the door. "What's that stand for?"

Nick scratched the back of his neck. "There's some debate on that. Some think it's for Big Bubba Burdette. Others believe it stands for Big Balls and Brains."

"What does Bubba say?"

"He changes it every time someone asks."

Grim smiled. "I like him already."

Nick slowed as he saw the damage from the night before. The main window had duct tape over the broken panes. The front door, which had been blasted off its hinges, had been chained in place, and there was soot from the flamethrower all over it.

Yeah, last night had been fun. It was a wonder they weren't all in jail.

Grim crossed his arms over his chest as he surveyed the mess. "Reminds me of the apocalypse. Shame I missed whatever went down here."

"It was a zombie invasion, and we barely escaped with our lives."

Grim scoffed. "What are you? Arthritic? Zombies don't move fast enough to be a threat to anyone. They do, however, make great targets when you're bored."

"These weren't undead zombies . . . at least not all of them. There was a group of Mortent demons after me. They found a video game that a friend of mine made that could reprogram the human brain and turn a person into a mindless killing machine. They were using my football team to come after us, and trust me, them boys can move and move fast. We didn't want to kill them, because it wasn't their fault."

Grim screwed his face up as if Nick's words caused him pain. "Let me give you free advice, kid. Whenever something is coming for you, snap its neck or double tap. Never, ever hesitate. It's infinitely better to be judged by twelve than carried by six."

He had a point, but Nick wasn't his father and he didn't want to take anyone's life. Especially not one of his classmates'. He was pariah enough without adding that to his résumé.

Grim pulled against the padlocked chain that was holding the unhinged doors across the storefront. "Any way in?"

Nick pulled out his phone and dialed Bubba's number.

"Yell-oh?" Because of Bubba's thick Southern drawl, most people thought he was stupid when they first met him. But Bubba was a summa cum laude graduate from MIT and was without a doubt the smartest man Nick had ever met.

A little . . . no, a lot crazy, but highly intelligent.

"Hey, Bubba, it's Nick. My mom started a new job at Sanctuary and wanted me to lie low until she gets off work. Since you're the reason she got fired, I was wondering if I could work in the shop today?"

"Oh, hell yeah, get your Cajun hide around to the back door pronto."

"I'm right outside." Nick scooted around to the rear door that was usually reserved for deliveries.

Bubba already had it open as he eyed him. "How you doing?"

"I'm alive, so no complaints."

"Wish Mark thought that way. Boy ain't done nothing but cry like a girl all morning long."

"I'm not crying. I'm in pain, you heartless Cro-Mag."

At six-four and with a full black beard and short black hair, Bubba was the epitome of what most people would call a redneck. But the one thing Nick had learned in his short life was that people seldom fit whatever stereotype others wanted to give them. Case in point, while Bubba loved his truck, his mom, and his guns and flannel shirts, he was also a huge horror movie fan and a sucker for foreign girl movies. In fact, Bubba's favorite show was *Oprah,* and he watched it faithfully every single day. Woe or, more to the point, death to anyone who came between Bubba and his TV at four. His music of choice was punk or alternative, and he was never caught with a pair of Doc Marten's boots.

Just like Bubba, Mark Fingerman wasn't what he seemed either. Yes, he wore a lot of camouflage, but that was to keep the zombies from seeing him.

Don't ask.

Mark believed in all paranormal creatures. Even the tooth fairy.

Again, don't ask.

Mark could try the patience of Gandhi.

Only a handful of years older than Nick, Mark was Bubba's sidekick. With shaggy brown hair and bright eyes, Mark stood in the store with a mop and bucket. Currently, he was choking said mop and kicking the bucket so much, it sloshed water onto the floor.

Nick scowled at them. "What's going on?"

Mark came forward to hand him the mop he so obviously hated. "Clean up, my friend. Welcome to the party. I'm so glad you could make it."

Groaning, Nick took the mop. He'd argue, but Bubba might shoot him—as he'd done the last four computers that had irritated him. The guts of the most recent one were still spread out over Bubba's worktable in back.

"Look." Mark held up his hands for Nick's inspection. "They're all pruny and wet. I'll never have my soft sweet hands again."

Nick snorted. "You're not right, are you?"

"Oh, please. If I were right in the head, do you think I'd be working for Bubba? Especially given what the cheap bastard pays. How hard did you hit your noggin last night?"

Nick dodged Mark's hand as he tried to touch his hair. "Dude, don't do that." He glanced over to Grim, who rolled his eyes.

"I know this clown," Grim said in an evil tone. "He keeps teasing me with these near death experiences. One day, I'm going to take his butt down even when I'm not supposed to. You can't keep knocking on my door and then slamming it in my face. It's just not right."

"Nick?" Bubba called. "Why don't you clean the front of the store while Mark and I pick up back here?"

"All right." As he left the back room and headed to the store area, he realized how much the two of them had already done. All the debris was picked up and most of the shattered glass. They must have been cleaning for hours.

For a full minute, Nick saw the events of last night play through his head. It'd been horrible. But the one good thing had been the fact that they'd accidentally found a way to fix the human zombies and return them to normal.

The other kind . . .

Those had just been gross and nasty to take out.

Grim wandered around looking at the shelves of computers and laptops, as well as peripherals and accessories that were set in the middle of the floor. The walls were lined floor to ceiling with one of the largest gun selections in the Southeast. Glass cases separated the guns from anyone who might wander in and pick one up.

Bubba's first rule.

No one handles a gun in my store without direct supervision.

Nick's gaze involuntarily went to the picture of Bubba's mama that hung on the wall. A portrait that had a huge gunshot in it, right between her eyes. His stomach slid to his feet. Yeah, that had been a close call.

"So what are you going to teach me?" he asked Grim in an effort to avoid thinking about how he'd shot Bubba's mama in the head. He was lucky he was still breathing after that.

"How to open your mind and pay attention. The universe is always speaking to us. Sometimes the signs are in our faces, and other times, they're very, very subtle."

"Subtle how?"

Grim pointed to the picture of Bubba's mama. "Let's use that for an example. When you look at that, you see nothing but a hole in a painting. When I look at it, I can tell exactly when and how you're going to die, and I don't mean Bubba coming after you in anger over defacing his mother's image. It shows an integral part of your future . . . and its end."

CHAPTER 4

Nick's throat tightened as he walked to the picture that hung about three feet over his head on the wall. He stared at the powder burn marks and hole. While there was a Rorschach-esque quality to it, it didn't look like much. Tilting his head, he squinted and treated it like a *Where's Waldo?* puzzle.

That showed the date of his death? Forget meth was death. Death was *on* meth. It just looked like a big mess to him.

He scowled at Grim. "You're pulling at me, right?"

"Maybe. Maybe not. You'll have to play with me for a while to see."

Nick wasn't sure he liked the way Grim phrased that. "Why is it when you say things like that, I feel like I'm gambling with my life?"

"Probably because you are. I never gamble for anything less."

Now, that just made him feel all warm and fluffy inside. "Oh, goody."

"Did you say something?" Mark stuck his head through the curtain that separated the front of the store from the back room.

"Uh, yeah. I said, 'Oh, goody.' As in I get to clean this mess up."

Mark gave an evil laugh. "I had that same reaction. I even tried to quit when I showed up this morning, but Bubba wouldn't let me. Told me if I tried to leave, he'd shoot my butt full of buckshot. He's the only SOB I know who's crazy enough to actually do that. So here I am. Ticked off, but alive. It's a good day." He vanished behind the curtain to return to whatever he and Bubba were working on.

Nick went back to Grim. "Don't you have any friends you could hang with?"

"I do. But the problem is when I hang out with my friends, it usually gets ugly for the rest of you. Especially when we're bored. Nothing entertains us more than plagues, famine, war, and bloody massacres."

"You play D&D, too, huh? Who's your DM?"

Grim *tsk*ed at him. "The difference between my group and yours . . . our toys are real." All of a sudden, the horse ran out of his pocket and up his arm to rest on his shoulder.

Neat trick. Creepy, but neat.

"So . . . that's like your pet monkey?"

The tiny horse snorted flames and whinnied at him.

"Easy, girl." Grim stroked her mane to calm her down. "You'd do well to show her respect. She can understand you, and she doesn't take well to insults."

"Sorry, Flicka. Didn't mean to rattle your bridle." Nick started straightening.

Grim dogged his steps. "The key to what I have to teach is that the universe and its beings speak to you constantly. But much like the little book you received last night, they seldom speak overtly. You have to figure it out on your own and hopefully before it's too late. The power of divination is a way for you to listen to the warnings the universe gives."

Nick stiffened as a chill went down his spine. "How do you know about my grimoire?"

Grim snapped his fingers, and the book appeared in his hand. Small and black with a funky red symbol on the front that was supposed to be Nick's personal emblem, it contained riddles that had helped Nick survive the attacks from the night before. All he had to do was ask it a question and release three drops of blood on it—something he still thought was gross, but . . . His blood would circle and move to form words and pictures on the page and give him clues.

That being said, the book was a snarky little slug. It didn't like answering questions anymore than Nick did, and it answered them with a venom Nick wished he could get away with and not stay grounded for life.

Narrowing his eyes on the book, Nick slapped at his back pockets to see if the book in Grim's hand was a duplicate.

It wasn't.

His pants were empty. . . .

Well, wait a minute, *they* weren't empty, 'cause that would imply something that definitely wasn't the case, but his pockets were. That was definitely his book, and Death was tainting it. He glared at Grim for the theft.

Normally he'd reclaim it, but snatching something out of Death's grasp didn't seem particularly intelligent.

Unless it was your own life.

Oblivious of and impervious to Nick's anger, Grim tapped the book with his fingertip. "Let me get back to the fact that the universe speaks to us constantly. And this little puppy barks loudly." He shoved it against Nick's chest. "Guard this with your life because in the right hands, it is your life and your death. You've bled in this book, and it is the most personal of possessions you'll ever have. A master wizard, witch, upper-level demon, or any number of other entities can use it to control or destroy you. In fact, guard *every* possession you have. Every stray hair. Every particle of skin and clothing. Let no one near anything you have ever owned or will own. You're special, kid. In ways you can't conceive, and you will have to guard your back every second you want to keep breathing."

He definitely didn't like the sound of that. "Aren't you just Mary Sunshine?"

"There's a reason they call me Grim."

Yeah, no kidding. Nick returned his book to his back pocket. "So how does this divination junk work, anyway?"

"Think of it as the cold chill you get down your spine whenever someone walks on your grave. That niggling sensation that tells you not to do something, and when you disregard it, you wish you hadn't."

"Kind of like getting out of bed this morning."

Grim rolled his eyes. "Frik. Frak," he snapped at his two skulking minions. "Get started cleaning this place while Nick and I work."

Without a word or hesitation, Pain took the mop from Nick. Suffering moved to pick up glass.

"Wow. Where have you two been all my life?"

Pain quirked an eyebrow as he mopped the floor. "Walking hand in hand with you. Haven't you noticed?"

Nick fell silent as he realized the truth of that

statement. He had walked hand in hand with Pain and Suffering since the hour of his birth. Bitter poverty and the worst sort of bullying. Heck, he'd even been shot by one of his best friends, who'd intended to kill him dead in the gutter.

Yeah, they'd definitely been his constant companions.

He looked back at Grim. "Come to think of it, can we leave them behind?"

Grim appeared offended by his question. "No. They're my best friends."

"Yeah, but I don't want to be in pain, and I definitely don't want to suffer."

"Well . . . The only way to avoid them is to die." Grim gave him a hopeful smile.

That chilled him all the way to his soul. "Okay, let's change the topic now." He pointed to the wall behind Grim. "Oh, look! A chicken."

Grim made a sound of extreme frustration. "Fine. Let's begin with something even you can't screw up."

"Way to build up my crappy confidence there. You should volunteer for the suicide hotline."

"What makes you think I don't?"

Nick screwed his face up. "Ah man, that's wrong on so many levels."

"Je suis ce que je suis."

Nick took a step back. Last night had taught him to be wary of any foreign words. "Is that a spell?"

Grim shook his head. "It's French, Nick. Means 'I am what I am.' Sheez, kid. Get educated. Read a book. I promise you it's not painful."

"I would definitely argue that. Have you seen my summer reading list? It's nothing but girl books about them getting body parts and girl things I don't want to discuss in class with my female English teacher. Maybe in the boys' locker room and maybe with a coach, but not with a woman teacher in front of other girls who already won't go out with me. Or worse, they're about how bad all of us men reek and how we need to be taken out and shot 'cause we're an affront to all social and natural orders. Again—thanks, Teach. Give the girls even more reason to kick us down when we talk to one. Not like it's not hard enough to get up the nerve to ask one out. Can you say inappropriate content? And then they tell me my manga's bad. Riiight . . . Is it too much to ask that we have one book, just one, on the required reading list that says, 'Hey, girls. Guys are fun and we're okay. Really. We're not all mean psycho-killing, bloodsucking animals. Most of us are pretty darn decent, and if you'll just give us a chance, you'll find out we're not so bad."

Grim let out a bored sigh. "Are you through ranting?"

"Maybe."

Grim slapped him on the back so hard, he stumbled. "Puberty is embarrassing. That's the point of it. Get used to it. And look on the bright side: Once you survive the teen horrors and degradations, adulthood is easy."

Great. Just great.

Nick scoffed. "And for the record, I do read. Lots of things, which is how I know it can be painful. Very, very painful."

Grim rubbed at his forehead like his head was starting to hurt. Then he pulled at the gold chain around his neck to expose a strange hematite pendulum that had a gold skull securing it to the chain. He held it out toward Nick.

Nick hesitated before he took it. He ran his hand

down the cold stone, noting that the skull had eyes made of bloodred rubies. The point of the hematite was so sharp, he could probably use it to stake Kyrian should his boss ever get too frisky with him.

Epically cool.

He could also use it to prick his finger if he needed to ask his book a question. Yeah, this thing had a lot of uses.

"What you hold is one of the keys to the universe." Grim's voice had dropped an octave. "You can use a pendulum to answer questions, locate things and—"

"What sort of things? Can it find my mom's keys when she loses them?"

"Yes," Grim said between clenched teeth. "It can also locate people you seek."

Okay, now *that* was handy. Nick swung it back on forth on its chain. "How does it work?"

Grim captured it in his hand and used the sharp tip to point at him. "It allows you to get in touch with your higher consciousness. In time, you won't need it to do that. You'll be able to access that part of your-self anytime you need to. But for now, you'll require a tool to help you channel all the teenage hormonal

ADD that's bouncing around and through you." He touched the tip to Nick's nose. "The best part of this one is that the stone will change to meet your needs."

"What do you mean?"

"For simple questions, it won't matter what the stone is. You can use any kind of pendulum, made out of any substance. A ring, a stick, even a pen or pencil. But as we progress to other tasks, the material it's made out of will matter exponentially. This one is currently hematite because that's the strongest stone of protection. It limits and deflects negativity. Something you need, kid. And it will protect you. Evil and negativity gravitate to the hematite, and if you're attacked badly enough, the stone will shatter and warn you while it deflects those powers away from you."

Yeah, Nick could be pretty negative most days. And that was without trying. Once he put his mind to it, he could be really pissy.

Grim gave it back to him. "Pull your book out."

Since Grim had already bogarted it from his pocket without touching it, he knew better than to delay. Nick grabbed it and handed it over.

Grim flipped to a blank page.

Nick frowned as words and letters magically appeared with arrows. In a weird way, it reminded him of a Ouija board. The two arrows intersected, forming a square cross with the words *Yes* and *No* highlighted.

No, wait. They were *glowing*.

"What's it doing?" he asked Grim.

"This is your pendulum map. It'll answer any yes or no question you ask. All you have to do is focus your mind on the question and hover the pendulum over the page. In time, you'll be able to ask more complicated questions and it'll spell out the answers."

"Duly awesome." Nick did as he suggested and hovered the stone above the words. He carefully kept his hand steady as he focused on the most important question he wanted an answer to. "Will I lose my vir— Hey!"

Grim snatched it from him. "Stop being stupid and take this seriously."

Nick glared. "Can't work with it if you snatch it out of my hands."

He grudgingly gave it back.

Nick wrapped the chain around his forefinger. "What's wrong with asking that, anyway?"

"It's a stupid concern."

Bull crap on that. It was the primary one he'd had for the last year. . . . Well, that and if he'd ever be able to afford a car. "What are you? Asexual or something?"

Pain laughed, then stopped abruptly as Death jerked his head in his companion's direction.

"My libido is fine, Nick. However, it takes a distant second place to my need to kill people who annoy me."

Normally, Nick would have mocked him for that, but he knew better. "Fine." He returned the pendulum and stated his second-most-often-asked question. "Will I ever be rich?"

At first, nothing happened. But after a few seconds, it began to swing along the *yes* line. Something that made his blood rush. "Really rich?"

It swung even harder.

Oh yeah, he definitely rocked to this. "Like Rockerfeller rich?"

Grim snatched it away from him again. "Yes, kid, you'll have money. Can we move on?"

"I suppose, but I'd really like to investigate the future of my not being broke a little more. I like that thought. A lot."

Grim sighed heavily. "I swear I'm getting a migraine."

"My mom suffers from those a lot, too."

"Being around you, I imagine she does."

Nick cupped the pendulum in his palm. "What else can this do?"

"Right now . . . nothing. Learn one technique, and I'll teach you others. You can't do geometry until you understand one plus one equals two. Besides, you two need to get acquainted with each other."

Nick scowled. "What? Are we dating?"

Grim stared at him with a blank expression for several heartbeats. "And now that my blood pressure and patience have breached their safety valves, I'm going to take a break and leave you here to clean your mess." He snapped his fingers. "Pain. Suffering. Come."

Like two dutiful pets, they vanished right alongside him, leaving the mop to fall on the floor with a loud slap.

Dang . . . couldn't they have finished first?

It's what you get for running your stupid Cajun mouth, boy. His mom always said that 90 percent of intelligence was knowing when to shut up. One day, he'd learn to heed her wisdom.

Sighing, he went to the mop and picked it up to finish. But he'd barely gotten back on it when he heard someone knocking at the front door.

He turned to tell them the Triple B was closed, when he saw it was Caleb. Up until yesterday, he'd thought Caleb was just another overprivileged jackweed at his high school. Well, not entirely true—Caleb had never been mean to him, so he didn't really qualify for jackweed status, but he had ignored Nick.

During the chaos of last night, Nick had learned that Caleb Malphas, captain of the football team and Mr. Popularity, was actually a high-level (he forgot the proper term 'cause it just wasn't that important to him) demon who'd been sent to serve as Nick's bodyguard.

How cool was that?

Nick held his hands up and gestured, letting Caleb know there was nothing he could do to let him in.

Caleb looked to his right and then to his left before he disintegrated on the sidewalk. He turned into a filmy red smoke that slid through the crack of the doors. It snaked across the ground like a weird mist and reassembled into Caleb in front of Nick.

He arched a brow at Nick. "You keep using that arm, boy, and everyone's going to know you ain't right."

Nick handed him the mop and returned his arm to the sling. "I'm working on that."

Always dressed impeccably in designer threads, Caleb had dark hair and intelligent eyes. He also possessed the kind of body and face that Nick would kill for. Muscled and Hollywood good-looking. While Nick wasn't ugly, he was still gangly and awkward, like most guys his age. His body was growing so fast that he never seemed to know where his limbs were, so he was always banging into something or busting his knees. The worst part was that at school he constantly stepped on girl feet whenever he took a seat in the cafeteria.

Yeah . . . no wonder he couldn't get a girlfriend.

"So how are you feeling this morning?" Nick asked.

"Like I got my ass kicked by a bunch of psycho demons. How 'bout you?"

"Slightly better than that. But only slightly. What brings you here?"

"I tried to call you and got no answer. After last night, it worried me. I was afraid something might have eaten you the few hours I dared to try and heal, so here I am, making sure you're still breathing and that I continue to do so."

Weird. His phone hadn't rung at all. Nick pulled out his phone and checked it. Sure enough, he had a missed call. Hmmm . . . Grim must have blocked it. Evil death troll. But it made sense. Death wouldn't want to be interrupted.

Caleb jerked his chin at Nick. "What are you doing here?"

"Bubba and Mark have me cleaning."

Caleb rolled his eyes. "Pah-lease." He snapped his fingers, and everything went back to the way it'd been before the fighting.

Nick gaped, impressed by his friend's psychic demon powers. "Man, I've got to learn how to do that. But I should probably mention that this will out us faster than my using an arm that's supposed to be injured."

Caleb grumbled before he returned the broken doors and enough of the damage that it would look like normal cleaning. "By the way, I got a strange call this morning."

"From?"

"New football coach."

Nick scratched his chin at that news. "Dude, that was fast."

"Tell me about it. He said it was because of the state finals that the school called him up and offered him the job yesterday afternoon."

Nick let out a low whistle. They'd barely allowed the old coach to get booked for killing their principal before they'd hired his replacement. That was so cold. "What else did he say?"

"He asked me if I knew you. Since we're down about half the team due to the zombie attack, he needs replacement players." Caleb inclined his head to Nick's arm. "I told him you were injured and couldn't play. He said at this point, he'd take a couple of benchwarmers just to fill out the roster and jerseys so that we wouldn't have to forfeit the play-offs."

"I can definitely warm a bench. It's what my mom says I'm best at anyway."

"What the—? How you get in here?"

They both turned to see Bubba staring at them from the curtain.

Caleb indicated Nick with his thumb. "Nick let me in."

"In how?" Bubba rushed to the doors to make sure they were still chained closed.

"I squeezed in through the opening. I'm like a mouse. Doesn't take much room for me."

Bubba gave him a suspicious grimace. "Don't do that again. You could have broke something, and then your parents would have sued me."

"Sorry."

Bubba glanced around the cleaned-up store before turning his attention to Nick. "Good job, snotnose. Looks great in here."

"Caleb helped."

"Way to pitch in and get things done. Now, if I could get Mark to put down his phone and stop taking breaks, we'd be able to finish up before *Oprah* comes on."

Caleb exchanged an amused grin with Nick. "Bubba, what are you going to do when they cancel her show?"

"Shut your mouth, boy. That's sacrilege in this store. You talk like that, and I'll toss you through the window like an old-timey hobo in a Western."

Caleb took a step back. "Given that I was almost roasted alive in your SUV last night, I don't want any more injuries for a while if I can help it."

Bubba pointed at him. "Remember that." Then he turned around and left them.

Caleb shook his head. "That is the strangest man."

"Tell me about it."

When Caleb moved closer, the pendulum began to heat up. So much so that Nick hissed in pain. He pulled it out.

Caleb's eyes flashed to their bright yellow orange demon snake form. "Where did you get that?"

A cold lump settled deep in Nick's stomach as he

contemplated what that reaction meant. "I was told it would protect me from evil. Why did it react to you, Caleb? What are you not telling me?"

No sooner had he asked the question than he saw an image flash through his mind.

It was a vision of Caleb killing him.

CHAPTER 5

W hat are you doing, Ambrose?"

Ambrose moved away from his black scrying mirror that he'd been using to watch the past unfold in an entirely new direction. With the flick of his hand, he laid it down on his ornately carved black desk and covered it with a black silk cloth as he confronted the last being he wanted to deal with.

Savitar.

Born to be a fail-safe to the gods who might abuse their powers, Savitar was one of the very few creatures taller than Nick. Dressed in a pair of white cargo pants and an open light blue cotton shirt, Savitar smelled like a sunny day at the beach. Normal for him, since he lived on a vanishing island, where he spent the better part of his days surfing. His dark hair held highlights from the sun, and his face had at least three days' growth of whiskers around his goatee. Because of his ancient age—he was born not long after the dawn of time—and his omnipotent powers, Savitar was used to people wetting themselves the moment he entered a room.

Ambrose wasn't most people, and it'd been centuries since Savitar had frightened him even a little. Stepping away from his desk, he went to pour himself a drink.

Not wine or water, but rather the chilled blood of a perityle demon. Vintage age and packed full of the nutrients he needed to live.

That was if anyone was dumb enough to qualify his current existence as living.

Ambrose took a drink and savored it. Not quite as satisfying as when the demon had begged to have his life spared, but still fresh and heady. A slight smile quirked his mouth as he remembered killing the demon. He'd never understood how creatures who were so brutal and merciless to others expected someone else to show them the pity they'd been unable to dispense to their victims. A peculiar hypocrisy, to be sure. "Since when do I answer *your* questions?"

Savitar's expression would have terrified the gods themselves. But since Ambrose was their scourge, it had no effect on him whatsoever. "You are tampering with powers you don't understand."

Ambrose raked a glare from the top of Savitar's windswept hair to the bottom of his bare feet. "I find that funny as hell coming from *you*."

"Yeah, and when I did it, I almost destroyed the world."

The irony here was that Ambrose was actually trying to save it. He already knew how the world would end. The date, the moment. The screams of the humans as they realized it was all over and everything they'd once valued was now completely worthless . . .

That no amount of begging or bartering could help them.

Time was drawing close. He could feel the last of

his humanity leaving him with the tick of every passing second, and when it did . . .

The world was doomed. There was no longer anyone who could stop him.

Not even Savitar.

"I know what I'm doing."

Savitar ground his teeth. "No, Nick, you don't."

Nick. Savitar was the last of those who used his real name anymore, and the Chthonian did so only when he wanted to get Ambrose's full attention.

Ambrose glanced back to where his black mirror lay covered, and he remembered how things had been when he was a boy. If he could just go back . . .

For one tiny nanosecond.

The smallest decisions made had such profound repercussions. One ten-minute wait could save a life.

Or end it.

One wrong turn down the right street or one seemingly unimportant conversation, and everything was changed. It wasn't right that each lifetime was defined, ruined, ended, and made by such seemingly innocuous details. A major life-altering event should come with a flashing warning sign that either said ABANDON ALL

HOPE or SAFETY AHEAD. It was the cruelest joke of all that no one could see the most vicious curves until they were over the edge, falling into the abyss below.

As Ambrose started away, Savitar grabbed his arm and pulled him to his side. His lavender eyes flared to a deep red. "You are awakening powers and bringing new players into your past. Players whose actions none of us know. You asked me yesterday about Nekoda. . . . You don't remember her, because she wasn't originally in your past. It's your meddling now that took her to your door when you were a kid. And she's not the only one. Don't you understand? Your father was supposed to die before you hit puberty. That is the natural order, and that event was imperative for your growth and safety. Now he's alive when he shouldn't be, and you're amassing powers at an age when—"

"I wasn't supposed to have an older brother either. Was I?"

Savitar looked away.

Exactly . . .

Life-altering events. Unseen disasters. Little things that became . . .

Best not to go there.

Ambrose curled his lip. "You, Acheron, Artemis, my father . . . all of you kept your little secrets from me. Now I am trying to repair *your* mistakes."

"And in the process, you're making entirely new ones. Ones we can't foresee yet. *I* can't foresee yet. Do you understand what I'm saying?"

He did. And there was one thing he saw clearest of all. "Then you don't know if what I'm doing is wrong."

Savitar cursed. "You can't rewrite the past. No one can. Not without terrifying consequences."

"I am the Malachai." Nick sneered at him. "I don't take orders from you, Chthonian." Designed to be the police of the natural order and protectors of man, Chthonians had been bestowed powers that would allow them to kill a god if need be.

But those powers didn't work on creatures like Nick. Born of the darkest part of the universe, the Malachai were immune to all but one.

And that one wasn't here to stop him from the destiny he'd been born to.

Ultimate destruction.

Tick . . . tock . . .

Savitar took a deep breath. "Fine. Hang on to that ego." He pointed to Ambrose's mirror. "What you've done is tapped your powers at an age when you were most vulnerable. Why do you think they were hidden in the first place? What you have done is unleashed the hounds of hell all over a young kid who's incapable of fighting them."

But Nick would learn. He knew himself and his survival instincts. Nick wouldn't go down. Ever. "I sent him a protector."

"Yeah. Good luck with that. Ask Acheron what happens when people tamper with the fates of others, even when all they were trying to do was protect them. . . . Oh, wait, I forgot. You can't do that anymore, can you?" Savitar's gaze seared him with an accusation he didn't even want to contemplate. "Right now, in New Orleans, a fourteen-year-old kid is being stalked."

"By?"

"You know the answer. They're there to shut you down and make you bleed. You think you've suffered now? Just wait and see what you've unleashed on yourself. And this time, you have no one else to blame. *You* did this with all of us trying to stop you." Savitar flicked at the talisman around Ambrose's neck. "You think you understand those powers because of what you are and the centuries you've lived. You don't understand shit."

He was wrong about that. Ambrose understood fully. Most of all, he knew what was about to happen if he didn't change it.

Honestly, would it have been so bad had he died as a kid?

Part of him wondered if that was all it would take to stop the wheel from turning. To keep the end from coming.

Saddest of all was that every time he'd tried to kill himself, something had prevented it.

Except for the one time that was most important. Nothing he'd tried yet had prevented that from happening.

One shot.

And all because of Acheron's curse.

There had to be some way to break that.

He stroked the medallion. This was his last chance. After centuries of mistakes and miscalculations, if it didn't work this time, it was over for all of them. He didn't care that his life would end. As far as he was concerned, his life had ended when he was twenty-four.

It was all the others who would pay. They were the ones he was trying to save. The ones he'd once loved. The innocent who didn't deserve what was coming to them.

Help me.

He was slipping, and it was getting dark. Cold. Terrifying. Right now, he didn't see an alternative ending. Not even with his meddling. Every road seemed to lead him back to this time and place.

Back to what was coming.

A war the world wouldn't survive.

Trying not to think about the future he saw so clearly, Ambrose poured himself another drink. "You never answered my original question. Who and what is Nekoda?"

Completely stoic, Savitar shrugged. "The truth? I don't know."

I don't know. Those words echoed in his head. The one thing he'd learned over the centuries of dealing with Savitar. Whenever the Chthonian said that, it meant one thing.

And it was never good.

Batten down the hatches. Things are going to get even bloodier.

CHAPTER 6

Caleb let out a deep sound of supreme annoyance as he tried to keep Nick from wetting on the floor. "Calm down. I'm a demon, Nick. Hematite doesn't like my genetics. It doesn't mean anything other than I have really bad parentage."

"Then why am I having flashes of you killing me?"

"What'd you eat this morning?"

Nick didn't care for that answer. Not one little bit. "I saw it happen. You were choking the life out of me."

Caleb rolled his eyes. "Oh yeah. That is definitely a figment of your overactive, over-Hollywood-stimulated imagination. I assure you. I don't kill people that way.

Takes too long. I'm not into torture. I prefer a quick death so that I can move on to something more satisfying."

Strangely enough, *that* he believed. Patience wasn't a virtue Caleb practiced. "You sure?"

"Dude, look at me. You think I'd have let the demons pound all over me last night so that you could escape if I had any intention of killing you? Really? I've had enough pain in my existence. At this point, I'd like to avoid any more. Get your head out of your sphincter, and use your three brain cells to think it through."

Nick raked his hand through his hair as he finally calmed down. Last night, Caleb had gone above and beyond. He was right. Nick had no reason to doubt his loyalty. "Sorry. I don't know what to think anymore. I have all this weirdness inside me."

"It's called puberty."

"Besides that," Nick said drolly. "Actually, I miss that being my only problem. I just don't know what to think anymore." 'Cause every person around him wasn't who or what he thought they were.

"It's all right. I don't blame you for not trusting me. I'll be honest. I'm not above betrayal. However, if I betray you, I don't want to face that demon. So you're safe until I figure out a way to get out my slavery."

Well, that said it all about their relationship. "Appreciate the honesty."

"You should, since it's a rarity for me." Caleb yawned. "Glad to see you're still breathing."

"Glad to be breathing." Especially since he'd spent the last hour before Caleb's arrival entertaining Death. Not too many people could make that claim.

Caleb chucked him on the arm. "Don't forget about your sling."

"You leaving?"

"No need in my being here. You're not under threat, and I'm still exhausted. I'm gonna rest. Not as young as I used to be."

"How old are you?

Caleb laughed. "That many zeros and you just get tired of counting. Old enough to know better. Young enough to do it anyway." He winked at him. "Catch you later." He literally vaporized in front of him.

"I have so got to learn those powers." What would it be like to do anything he wanted? To have all the money and time and powers he could dream of? He couldn't imagine anything more awesome.

Closing his eyes, he conjured an image of himself as an adult. Only he didn't see him. He saw Ambrose in his mind. And he didn't look happy.

Weird. Ambrose stood in front of a giant ornate hearth, where a huge fire blazed. The flames flickered in a pair of eyes that were inhumanly green. With one hand braced against the stone mantel, he stared into the fire looking lost and sad. Heartbroken.

Don't become me, Nick.

It wasn't Ambrose's voice he heard. It was deeper, sinister, and it sent a chill down his spine.

I'm losing my mind. He had to be. There was no other explanation.

"Hey, Nick. Need a hand."

He blinked at the sound of Mark's shout. Pushing everything out of his mind, he went to help them.

Hours went by as they put everything back and repaired the plaster walls. Just after three, Nick left them to walk over to the Café Du Monde. Nekoda had promised to meet him there after school. Even though school had been canceled, he hoped she'd show, and in case she did, he didn't want her to think he'd stood her up.

It didn't take long to reach the covered pavilion that was bustling with tourists and a few locals. World famous and a New Orleans tradition since the mid nineteenth century, the Café Du Monde was a must-see for everyone. Open twenty-four hours a day, seven days a week except on Christmas and during hurricanes, this was one of Nick's favorite haunts. The menu was reasonably priced (okay, it was cheap, which was why he could afford to come here for a rare treat) and extremely limited—basically water, milk, soft drinks, orange juice, and chicory coffee. But the real reason to be here was for the powdered sugar beignets. French doughnuts that didn't have holes in them. Messy as all get-out, they were the tastiest thing he'd ever eaten. Forget cookies. Beignets ruled.

As he stood on the corner of St. Ann and Decatur, waiting for the light to change so that he could cross the street, he saw three musicians playing in front of the café.

"Hey, Nick," the trombone player called to him as he made it across and neared the entrance.

Nick smiled at the older African-American man who'd been playing jazz and zydeco on the street as far back as he could remember. At night, he played in several of the clubs around town too. "Hey, Lucas. How you doing?"

"Just fine. Hope your mama's well."

"You know I take good care of her. How's your daughter doing? She settling into school okay?" Lucas's wife had died of cancer four years ago, leaving him alone to raise Kesha, who'd graduated last spring. Now she was up at LSU taking classes, wanting to be a cancer researcher one day.

"She loves it so much, I'm having a hard time getting her to come home to visit. Can you believe it? Never thought she'd leave. Now I doubt I'll get her back."

Nick laughed. "I'm sure she'll be home soon. How could she not?"

Thomas, the drummer, tapped his drumsticks together to let them know it was time for another song. Lifting his trombone, Lucas inclined his head to Nick before he joined in with them to play "Iko Iko."

Nick cringed. While he loved the song, it was one of those that never failed to give him a vicious earworm. He'd be hearing it in his head for at least the next three days.

Hey, now. Hey, now . . . Iko Iko unday . . . See! It was already starting.

Oh man, someone shoot me.

As he looked around for an empty table, his gaze was caught by something pink and creamy. When he focused on the girl's face, his stomach plummeted south. With soft brown hair and great big eyes, it was the most beautiful girl in the world.

Nekoda.

And when she recognized him, the prettiest smile he'd ever seen lit her entire face and did things to him he barely understood. His body was hot and cold all at once. His throat turned dry, and a part of him wanted to turn around and run for cover.

Yeah, that would be the smart thing to do.

When have you ever been smart?

Before he knew what he was doing, his feet took him to her table.

"Hi," she said, flashing him an adorable dimple.

How could one syllable sound like a heavenly choir? Yet that was the sweetest sound he'd ever heard. It even sent a shiver down his spine. "Hey."

Say something else. Quick.

Why was his mind completely blank? It wasn't like he'd never spoken to her before. Heck, she'd even kissed him last night.

Yeah, and he could still taste her lips.

That was the problem, he realized. It was so awkward to see her after they'd kissed. Had he screwed it up? Had it been okay for her?

Ah gah, I'm pathetic. I don't even know how to talk to a girl.

At this rate, he'd never get a girlfriend.

She glanced around nervously. "You want to sit down?" She stretched the words out like maybe she was as uncomfortable as he was.

Oh no. Don't tell me she's going to give me the let's be friends *speech.* He hated that SOB.

"Uh, yeah." His hands shaking, he pulled the vinyl chair back and took a seat. "Sorry I'm a space cadet today. My mom got me up way too early this morning, and I'm not fully awake after last night. Then Bubba had me helping clean his store. I could really go for a nap." *You're yammering too much, and don't talk about beds or she might think you're inviting her to something that might offend her, or get you slapped.* "How are you feeling?" Yeah, that was a safe topic.

For both of them.

"Glad to be alive."

The waitress came up to take their order. Nick started to tell her to bring him water when he remembered that for once he actually had cash from Kyrian and Mr. Poitiers. Thank God. He could even cover Kody's tab. "Two orders of beignets and a chocolate milk for me." He looked at Nekoda. "What would you like to drink?"

"The milk sounds good. I'll have that, too."

The waitress headed off.

"Have you heard anything about what happened at school?" he asked her. School was usually another safe topic.

"Not yet. What about you?"

"Nothing, other than we have a new coach."

She looked as shocked as he'd been. "Really?"

"Yeah, scary, right? I think they replaced the coach before they finished mopping the blood up in the hallway." Nick cringed as soon as he heard those words come out of his mouth. *Don't talk about blood with a girl. Are you stupid?*

Luckily, she changed the subject for him. "How's your arm feeling?"

"Better. No pain at all today."

"Good."

Then it was awkward again. But the one thing he was grateful for was the fact that she was still a girl. Plain and simple. Not a shape-shifter, vampire slayer, or a demon. Just another human being having a bite with him. It was good to be around normal again.

"So do you like New Orleans?" he asked her. "Is it different from where you lived before?"

"*Very* different. But I like it. Except for the heat. I can't believe it's still this warm so late in October."

"Yeah, well, there's an old saying here. If you don't like the weather, wait a minute. We can swing from hot to cold faster than a turbo wash with a tankless system."

Nekoda felt her guard slipping as she laughed at his humor. *It's his demon glamour. Don't fall for it.* But it was hard. Nick Gautier was charming and sweet. Adorable.

Gorgeous with eyes so blue, it should be a sin and thick brown hair that begged to be touched. At fourteen, the promise of the man he'd grow into was already there. The chiseled features and sharp intelligence. And even though he was lean, his muscle tone was perfect and showed that in time, his body would be well defined.

The best part was, he had no idea just how handsome he was.

Timid and unsure, yet he could tap some of the most destructive forces ever unleashed. Once he was grown, he would have the potential to become evil in its purest, coldest form. She must never lose sight of that.

Still, his smile was infectious. His kindness touching.

When she went to pay for her food, he stopped her and took care of the bill. He wouldn't even let her tip the waitress.

Then, he excused himself and took his change so that he could drop it in the trombone case for the street musicians. He didn't keep a single cent of it.

She arched a brow at that as he rejoined her and took a seat. "I thought you were really poor."

He blushed profusely. "I am, but I've got a new job that pays well, and I believe in sharing my good fortune whenever I have some. Lucas helps his daughter at school, so . . . I figured he needs it more than I do."

"That's really sweet of you."

"I have moments of that, but don't tell anyone. Let that be our secret."

She smiled at his sincerity. He was so different from the Malachai she'd once battled. How could this generous boy have come from the most evil of all powers? It was inconceivable, and yet there he sat. . . .

Caring. Joking. Precious.

But for the fact she knew better, she'd swear they had identified the wrong person. And yet, somehow this boy in front of her would grow into a demon who would one day end the world.

A demon she'd have to kill.

If she had any brains, she'd do it right now, before those powers grew stronger. But she had protocols to follow. There was still a chance that he could be saved.

A bargain made . . .

She had to honor that bargain, even though it went against every part of her being. Like him, she'd been born a soldier. Her sole duty to protect the natural order and to put down any and all enemies.

Including charming teenage boys.

The wealth of a soul is measured by how much it can feel . . . its poverty by how little.

Right now, in this time and place, Nick's soul was rich and pure. If they could keep it this way, he wouldn't be lost. A tool they could use and a power they could harness . . .

That was the landscape they were painting, and failure wasn't an option.

Nick had the sudden feeling that Kody was dissecting him like some mutant lab experiment. "Did I sprout a new head?"

She blinked. "What?"

"You look like you're trying to figure me out. I probably shouldn't say anything, but it's making me really uncomfortable."

"I'm sorry. I didn't mean anything by it. I was just . . . Never mind. Some things a woman has to keep to herself."

"Hey, good quality people! What are you doing out and about in the daylight?"

Nick grinned at the high-pitched, singsongy voice that belonged to Simi. Another newbie he'd met last night. She'd shown up to help them all out, and boy had she ever. "Hi, Simi. Want to join us?"

Her hair was jet black with red streaks running through it. Today she had it pulled up in pigtails that were held with spiked bands that matched the spiked collar around her neck. A good six feet tall, she also wore stacked boots that added another four to five inches to her height. Her short skirt was a purple plaid that matched her purple fishnet top and black tank.

She plopped down in the chair next to Kody and opened her coffin-shaped purse. Nick exchanged a frown with Kody as Simi pulled out a lobster bib and tied it around her neck. Next came a small bottle of hot sauce.

Their waitress came up with a big smile on her face. "Hi, Simi. Your usual?"

"Absolutely, Tracy. Keep 'em coming till the Simi pops."

The waitress laughed. "Girl, I don't know where you put it. I swear you have hollow legs."

"Ooo, the Simi wishes. Then she could eat even more. Yum!"

Laughing, the waitress headed back to kitchen.

"How often you eat here?" Nick asked.

Simi pulled out several napkins from the silver dispenser and put them in her lap. "Whenever we're in town and Akri lets me."

Akri. She kept mentioning that name last night, too, but Nick had no idea who it was, even though Simi acted like he should. "Who's Akri?"

She huffed in irritation. "The Simi's daddy. Silly partial human, don't you know nothing?"

Nick opened his mouth to respond, but the moment he did, he saw . . .

He wasn't sure. It was rapid-fire images. Him and Simi. Only it wasn't him. It was . . . Another time and place.

No, it was here. No . . . he saw her as a demon with wings and horns. His head spun as he tried to sort through the kaleidoscope that left him feeling sick to his stomach.

"Nick?" Kody asked in a concerned tone. "Are you all right?"

Simi answered for him. "He's fine. Just freaking out 'cause the Simi's a demon and he didn't know until now. He'll be all right in a few." She held his glass of milk out to him. "This'll help."

Nick blinked as he tried to calm down. "Am I dreaming?"

Kody hadn't reacted to Simi's news at all. In fact, she acted as if she hadn't heard it. Maybe she hadn't. Maybe Simi was like Grim, and he and Tracy were the only ones who could see and hear her.

Still, the images tore through his head, making it hard to focus on anything. He could barely catch his breath.

I have to get away from here.

His head pounding, he looked at Kody. "I need to . . . I got to leave. I'll catch you later, okay?"

"You sure you don't need me to help you?" Kody asked.

"No. I mean yeah, I'm sure." He got up and stumbled away from them. He didn't know where to go, so he headed toward the only safe place he could think of.

His mom.

Kody arched a brow as she watched Nick hurry away from them. "Was that you or me who spooked him?"

"Pretty sure it was me." Simi grinned. "The Simi has that effect or is it *affect* on people? Affect. Effect. What is this difference between those two words and really, does it matter? Some people get so testy when you misuse a word. But I likes doing it. Language should be fun and so long as people know what you mean, what difference does it make? Really. Really. Really."

Kody shook her head at the Charonte. Simi belonged to an ancient race of demons who'd been created to protect the Atlantean gods. Now, she was assigned watch duty to only one of them.

Acheron Parthenopaeus.

While she knew of the ancient god, she'd never met him. For many reasons. One being the fact that Acheron didn't want anyone to know about his godhood. It was a well-kept secret, and she could respect that. The only reason she knew of his identity was that they had a mutual friend. One who, like Nick, could see the truth no matter how hard someone or something tried to hide it. The waitress returned with ten plates of beignets and a large milk for Simi.

"Ooo, the Simi's favorite person is always the one who brings her food. Thank you, Tracy."

"You're welcome, Simi."

Simi pulled out a handful of cash and handed it over. "You keep the change and have fun with it."

By Tracy's expression, it was obvious Simi had seriously overtipped her. "You sure about that?"

"Absolutely." Simi drenched the beignets with her hot sauce.

"Thank you." Tracy went to wait on another table.

Nekoda cringed as Simi took a bite. And on that note . . . "It was nice seeing you again, Simi. But I think I need to be going."

Simi wiped at the powder on her face. "Okay, but Nekoda-Akra needs to know something important."

"That is?"

"They something evil done come to town and set up shot . . . no, shop. That's the word the Simi needs."

"What kind of evil?"

Simi licked her lips before she answered. "Akri not sure. Can you not feel it?"

Nekoda snorted. "In this town? There's all kinds of spirits here, and quite a few of them are hostile."

"True, which is why the Simi likes to come here. I eat the evil, and akri all happy. There's no 'no, Simi' if it's something that preys on people. The Simi can eat all that she wants to."

Yeah, the Simi was a unique being.

"Do you think this evil is Nick?"

Simi shook her head. "No. The evil is stalking him."

CHAPTER 7

Nick paused outside the Mediterranean Greek Café on Decatur to catch his breath. At least the images had finally stopped shifting through his head and he had some clarity of thought.

Not much, but better than it'd been when he'd left the Café Du Monde. At least now the people around him looked normal.

Man, how had the hippies in the sixties ever survived drug binges? What idiot would do this to himself intentionally? It was bad enough when it happened by accident. Who would want to live like this if they could stop it?

Nick rubbed his eyes and took a deep, fortifying breath.

All of a sudden, he heard a bell sound as the door to the restaurant opened and out came a beautiful dream.

For a second, he thought he was still hallucinating as Casey Woods, one of the cheerleaders from his school, stopped in front of him. Up until Nekoda had joined their class, Casey had been the only woman for him. Her long dark hair was always brushed until it shone, and her curves were killer in street clothes, but in her cheerleader uniform they were the stuff of legends. He'd spent more days than he could count trying to imagine how great life would be with her as a girlfriend. Unlike the Neanderthals she went with, he'd actually treat her right and dote on her.

Unfortunately, she hadn't even noticed he was alive. An impressive feat, since he'd sat right beside and in front of her in several classes over the years. But hey, Casey was Casey, and a girl that popular couldn't be bothered to notice the poor, awkward scholarship student who'd invaded their ranks. For that matter, almost no one in his school really saw him as anything other than a target to be kicked and bullied. He was used to that.

Dressed in a lacy blue top and a pair of jeans, she smiled as she caught sight of him. "Hey, Nick. You okay?"

Oh yeah, he had to be a coma or something. The last time Casey had been this close to him, she'd argued with her best friend that she had no idea who he was.

"Uh, all good."

She frowned at him. "You don't look good. You look kind of green. Are you going to hurl?"

"I hope not." 'Cause that was all he'd need for this day to be even better. Barf all over their homecoming queen. Yeah, that'd just make it for him and get him relegated to loser status until the day they graduated.

To his complete shock, she reached out and touched his forehead. "You don't have a fever." She held her bottle of water out toward him. "Here, sip some of this, and see if it helps."

Stunned, he straightened. "Are *you* all right?"

"Of course. Why would you ask that?"

'Cause she had never been this nice to him, ever. Honestly, it was scary. Was the apocalypse coming?

Was this Death in disguise screwing with him? Now that would make sense. There had to be some horrifyingly foul reason why Ms. Hottie-Snotty was talking to him like he mattered.

"You and I don't normally hang out."

She smiled. "I know. My bad. But now that you're hanging with Tad, it's okay."

Ah, that explained it. Tad Addams was one of the cool, rich kids. The older brother of Nick's friend, Brynna, he'd taken him to school with Casey the other day.

Man, she was shallow. Most people didn't admit that about themselves. He had to give her credit that at least she was honest.

He shrugged the water away. "I'm fine." He indicated his arm in the sling. "Pain got to me for a minute. But I'm all good now."

"Oh, okay." She pulled the water back and cradled it against her breasts—second thought, he should have taken it. "By the way, have you heard the latest gossip?"

"That we have a new coach?"

She blinked at him with a vacuous expression. "We have a new coach?"

Obviously not the gossip she'd heard. "Uh, yeah. Caleb told me about him."

"Oh, I hadn't heard that. Good. I know Stone and Rick were worried about us making it to State this year with the team down and the coach arrested."

Stone . . .

It took all Nick's willpower not to curl his lip at the mention of that pig. No, dog. He'd just learned last night that Stone was a shape-shifting werewolf who was a pig in both incarnations.

Not wanting to think about Stone and his running crew of imbeciles, Nick turned Casey back to their original discussion. "What did you hear?"

"Oh, there's been a rash of thefts at school. Tanya went in to get her homework this morning from the office, and she overheard the secretaries talking about it. A bunch of lockers were broken into, and some things were taken out of classrooms."

"No kidding?"

"She said it was a bad scene. Hope you had nothing in your locker worth stealing."

He snorted. Yeah, right. He didn't own anything of value. "Just books. They're free to take as many of those as they want."

"I hear you. Oh, and she said we have a new principal they're bringing in from Baton Rouge. His name is—get this—Richard Head." She burst out laughing.

Nick winced as he saw the detention train a-coming. Dick Head. Ah man, that was so wrong to have a name like that and to go into education on a high school level. Twisted, twisted, twisted. "And I'll bet he has no sense of humor about it."

"You know it. But then again, you can call him Dick Head all you want and say you were only using his name."

"True. Man, his parents must have hated his guts."

"Makes you wonder, doesn't it?"

It did, indeed. "Well, I guess I better get going. I need to check in with my mom at work."

Casey frowned. "Can't you call her?"

"It's her first day on this job, and I don't want to get her into trouble." If he got her fired again in less than twenty-four hours of losing her last job, she would absolutely kill him. Better to go poke his head in the door to see what she was up to, then head over to Kyrian's to work. "I'll catch you later." He started toward Ursuline.

"You mind if I walk with you?"

Nick's eyes widened as a total state of befuddled *huh* possessed him. Was he in the Twilight Zone? "You want to walk with me?"

She smiled a smile that warmed him completely. "Do you mind?"

"Uh, no."

"Cool." Then she did the most peculiar and amazing thing of all—she stepped forward and wrapped her arm around his good one so that they could walk arm in arm. "So, Brynna told me you have a job. Aren't you young to be working?"

Am I in some alternative universe? Was his evil doppelgänger going to shoot out of the alley and attack them like some character in a video game?

All right, Grim. What's going on?

Grim didn't answer. No one did.

Casey stared up at him expectantly with a pair of goo-goo eyes that made his insides quiver.

C'mon, Nick. Answer her question. "I've had a job since I was twelve."

"Really?" Her eyes brightened. "That's so impressive."

For the first time in his life, he actually felt proud. "Well, I'm the man of the house and I have to take care of my mom. I like buying her nice things, and I don't want to spend her money on her—that just seems wrong to me."

"You know, it's so rare to find a boy who thinks that way. Last Christmas, Stone gave me his sister's earrings their mother had given her that she didn't want. I was so angry when I found out, I didn't speak to him for two whole hours."

"Wow, two whole hours. You really punished him."

She screwed her face up at him. "Are you mocking me?"

"I would never mock the homecoming queen, especially not when she's holding on to me. Why are you doing that, by the way?"

She rubbed her hand up and down his biceps in a way that made him really uncomfortable. "You have nice arms. Manly."

Yeah, right. He had arms like the Flying Spaghetti Monster. Hardly manly. More like thin and stringy.

She started stroking his biceps.

Nick jumped away from her. "Um, Casey. I'm kind of seeing someone." Though they weren't technically going together, he had feelings for Nekoda, and he didn't want her to think he was two-timing her even though he wasn't single-timing her either. Okay, that didn't make sense.

Still . . .

Casey put her hands on her hips. "Since when do you have a girlfriend?"

"Don't you have a boyfriend?"

"Not at the moment." There was no missing the invitation in her tone or the one in her eyes.

It was so tempting. . . . But the one thing he knew about her and Stone was that they were constantly breaking up and getting back together. Last thing he needed was to give Stone another reason to harass him.

"Look, I really need to go."

Before he could break clear, Casey pulled his phone

out of his pocket with something that suspiciously felt like a grope. That and the hot look on her face sent a shiver over him. She put her phone number in and then added it to his speed dial.

"Call me sometime." This time when she slid the phone back in, there was no missing her grope. Rising up on her tiptoes, she nipped his chin with her teeth and tongue. "But don't wait too long, Nick." Her breath went straight into his ear, making his entire body burn.

Stunned, scared, and intrigued, he couldn't move as she sashayed down the street. She cast a look at him over her shoulder and bit her lip in the most provocative way he'd ever seen.

Oh yeah, the world was definitely going to end. There had to be a countdown clock somewhere. 'Cause stuff like this didn't happen to Nick Gautier. It was more believable that his classmates were turning into zombies out to kill him than it was for Casey Woods to come on to him.

Why?

Yesterday he'd been completely invisible to her. Today it was like someone had decloaked him in the middle of enemy territory.

Unsure of what to make of it all, Nick headed to Sanctuary. Home of the weirdest of weird.

"Is there no normality left anywhere?"

Relax, kid.

Nick let out a relieved breath as he heard that familiar voice in his head. "Ambrose, bro. Where have you been?"

Busy. Why? Have you missed me?

Not really. "I just had one of the hottest girls in school come on to me."

Casey Woods?

"Yeah. How'd you know?"

Relax. You'll end up taking her to your junior prom.

Nick arched a brow at that land mine Ambrose had shoved him into. "How do you know that?" he asked again.

I know a lot of things about you, Nick. Past, present, and future. Casey isn't one of the people you need to fear. She'll be a good girlfriend in high school and an even better friend later on.

And that, too, made him drop his jaw. "She's going to be my girlfriend?"

Ambrose laughed in his head. *Getting women won't*

be your problem. Keeping them is another. And whatever you do, make sure you don't ever touch Simi. Don't even hold her hand. Think of her and Tabitha Devereaux like sisters.

"Why?"

Just do what I say! This time he got the demon tone from Ambrose. That deep, guttural growl that actually made him jump. After a second, he heard Ambrose sigh. *Sorry, Nick. But there are things you have to trust me on. Things I can't explain. Believe me when I say I am truly the only person in your life, besides your mother and Kyrian, who truly has your back. When everyone else turns on you and seeks to bring you down, I'm the only one who will never betray you. You have to believe that.*

"You say that, and yet where have you been all my life?"

I've always been with you. From the moment you were born. There's never been a time in your life when I wasn't there beside you. Just like now. I see everything you see. Hear what you hear and feel what you feel.

"How?"

I'll teach you that power in time. For now, trust me.

One day you'll understand why I've been hidden all these years and why I had to wait for certain things to happen before I made my presence known.

His mom always said that trust was something you earned. And it wasn't something you gave easy. Too often, it was a tool your enemies used to hurt you with. *Give them nothing, baby. Not until you have no choice. The world is harsh and it is cold. People can be good and decent, but most of them are only out for themselves and they'll hurt anyone they can.*

Sad thing was, he knew his mom didn't say things like that lightly. Criticism wasn't in her nature, so whenever she did it, he knew to pay attention.

Go live your life, Nick, Ambrose said, intruding into his thoughts. *Enjoy your day and stop worrying so much. Check on your mom and go to work.*

He felt Ambrose leave him.

Nick looked up at the perfect blue sky above. It was a beautiful day. "And I am certifiably insane. I'm seeing demons in my friends, shape-shifters, and hearing voices from lunatic uncles." How had this nut farm become his?

Sighing, he turned the corner and crossed the street to Sanctuary. This time, he saw the difference in the bouncers. While this one looked just like Rémi, he had his hair down around his shoulders and an easy smile that somehow managed to be both friendly and intimidating all at once. As Aimee had told him about earlier, this one had a cool double bow and arrow tattoo on his biceps.

"You must be Dev."

His grin widened. "You must be Pain in the Nick."

"Huh?" A wave of apprehensive nervousness went through him.

"Don't wet your pets. Just a figure of speech. Your mom's been talking about you all day, boy. You are her favorite topic."

"Well, I try hard not to be her favorite hemorrhoid."

Dev laughed. "She said you were sharp and entertaining. I can see she's right. Go on in and make yourself at home."

Their friendliness amazed him. Mostly because he had a feeling they weren't like that with everyone. How could they be? They had one heck of a secret they kept from the public.

Nick wandered inside. It was a lot busier now. Wren was still busing tables, but the bartenders had been changed out. They were two more Dev clones, which should make one of them Cherif and the other Quinn. But the coolest thing was that the band was onstage doing a sound check.

Mesmerized, Nick wandered over to watch them. So this was the Howlers. He'd never seen a live band perform before. It was actually kind of neat.

"Hey, Colt, your mic's not on," the lead singer said to the guitarist.

"Done on purpose, Angel. I don't need to be singing backup, anyway. We don't want to clear the house."

The drummer laughed as he adjusted the wing nut on his snare.

They were so cool. Aside from the fact that they were all shape-shifters, they were dressed in clothes his mom would throw away. Torn jeans and ragged shirts. And when they played, it was magic.

Oh yeah, he wanted to be in a band.

"Hey, baby."

He turned at the sound of his mom's voice. "Hey, Ma. How's it going?"

She was beaming and her face was bright. "It's been a great day. How about you?"

"Generic." Not entirely true, but she didn't need to know about his weirdness. Otherwise, she'd ban him from leaving the house until he was ninety.

She ruffled his hair. "I have about an hour before I get off work."

"Oh, okay. I need to get to Kyrian's, anyway. I'll catch a streetcar over."

"I'll drive you."

Nick jumped at the sound of Acheron's deep, scary voice right behind him. If that wasn't terrifying enough, Acheron stood an even six feet eight. Swathed in Goth black from the top of his long hair to the tips of his biker boots, he had an aura of *I'll kill you for breathing* that was more intimidating than Grim's. "Dude! Put a bell on. You don't walk up on a brother like that and scare the crap out of him."

"Sorry. Didn't realize you scared like a little girl."

Nick stiffened in indignation. "Ain't no little girl here, honcho. Maybe *you*. Definitely not me."

Shaking his head, Ash laughed.

His mom looked at the two of them skeptically.

"Be careful with my baby, Ash. He's all I got, so drive like you're hauling eggs."

"Yes, ma'am." Ash indicated the door with his head. "You coming?"

"Depends. You going to drive at Warp Speed One or Ten?" 'Cause the last time Nick was in Ash's Porsche, the ancient immortal had done things a car shouldn't be able to do.

"I'll keep it under ninety."

"Then I'll try not to claw the interior." Nick waved at his mom as he followed Ash out the rear side door to the lot in back, where his black Porsche made an awesome sight.

One day, he needed to get him one of those. Of course, that was after he managed to get his license. For now, though, he was content to ride in Ash's.

"Do I have to open the door for you again?" Ash asked as he pressed the button to unlock it.

Nick gave him a droll stare. "Nah, I think I can manage." He'd been afraid of tarnishing it before. Now he was getting a little used to it.

As soon as he was in and buckled tight, he looked over at Acheron. "Kyrian said you have fangs. Do you?"

Ash tilted his head down, but since he was still wearing those black opaque sunglasses that never left his face, Nick couldn't see his eyes. "Is it important?"

"Maybe."

Ash opened his mouth, and sure enough, there they were.

"Wow. You *are* good at hiding them."

"You have *no* idea." He tore out of the lot and gunned the engine.

"So have *you* ever drunk blood?"

Ash downshifted to get around a cab. "What did the two of you talk about?"

"Kyrian said he doesn't drink blood. Made me wonder if you do."

Ash ignored the question as he slowed down. Frowning, Nick looked to see what had caught the immortal Atlantean's attention. To the right, down a side alley, the police had gathered and cordoned off a section of the street. Unfortunately, such sights tended to be common in New Orleans.

"Looks like a burglary."

"No, Nick. That's a murder scene."

"How can you tell?"

"Psychic powers, remember?"

Oh yeah. How could he forget?

Acheron pulled to the corner and parked his car. "You stay put. I want to check this out."

You know, for an immortal being with eleven thousand years of living, Acheron could be mighty stupid. Like Nick was going to wait in the car while there was something to see . . .

He did at least give Ash time to get out of sight before he opened the car door and headed over to the scene. There were a bunch of tourists and locals loitering as well as several journalists and camera people. Nick sidled along the edge of them until he could see the outline of where the body lay, covered by a black tarp. The sight of blood on the street was disconcerting. Man, it looked brutal, and it made him wonder what had happened.

"How many does this make?" one of the officers asked another.

"Second one in twenty-four hours."

"Did they notify the parents?"

"Not yet. No one wants to have to go knock on the door and tell someone their fourteen-year-old son won't be coming for dinner. Damn. I hate it when it's a kid. Friggin' senseless. I got a son the same age. Makes me want to go home and hug him, then lock him in his room until he's grown."

Those words slammed hard into Nick. The vic had been his age.

And no sooner had that thought gone through his head than he felt his pendulum heat up to a burning level.

The book, too.

Hissing from the pain of it, Nick snatched the book out of his back pocket and flipped it open. "What Lassie? You going to tell Timmy about the well?"

On the page where he'd dropped his blood the night before, the words rearranged themselves.

Look and you will see,
That which was can never be.
When they seek a boy your age,
Run, you flippin moron, run!

CHAPTER 8

So much for rhyming, but at the moment, Nick wasn't going to argue with the book. If it told him to run, run he'd do. He started for the car, then stopped.

Safest place would be with Acheron. With his epic Jedi powers, Ash would be able to put down anyone or anything that came after him. And lucky for him, Ash was so tall, he was easy to spot even in this crowd.

Nick headed straight for him as fast as he could without drawing the attention of the police—his past experiences had shown him that even if innocent, it was never good to grab their attention. Especially not when you were related to someone on death row for multiple homicides and there was a body on the ground nearby.

Bad move.

Ash did a double take as he joined him. "I would ask what it is you think you're doing, but . . . you are a teenager. I should have known better than to leave you in the car unattended. Next time, I'll seal you in there . . . probably with bricks. Maybe even mortar."

Nick ignored his dry tone. "Just so long as you make sure nothing can get *inside* to kill me, I'm good with that."

Ash frowned. "What are you talking about?"

"The kid dead on the ground. Fourteen, Ash. Fourteen. *I'm* fourteen."

"Yeah . . ."

"Ash, I'm *fourteen*."

"Got it. You're fourteen. I'm so proud you can count that high. It's a testament to the modern American educational system. But I should probably point out that you're not the only one. I'm told you go to a school with a whole class of—get this—kids who are fourteen."

Nick rolled his eyes at the sarcasm. No wonder

his mom wanted to hurt him for it. He finally understood. "Yeah, but they're not dead. Someone's killing fourteen-year-old boys, which I happen to be one. The cops said so. This is the second one in a day who's been murdered."

"Yeah, well, given the lippiness of the average teenager, I can understand the urge."

"You're not funny."

"And you need to calm down. The only person you need to fear killing you when I'm around is me."

A chill went down his spine at words that seemed oddly prophetic. Was this the precog sensation Grim had told him about earlier?

Not to mention the small fact that Ambrose's warning echoed in his head.

Don't trust Ash. . . . He's not what he seems.

Ash put one hand on each of his shoulders. "Nick, take a deep breath and look around. You're safe here. There are police everywhere. It's all good."

Not what his book had said. He started to tell Ash about that, but something inside told him to keep it quiet.

For once, he decided to listen to his instincts.

"Why are they killing teenage boys?"

Ash gestured to the bloody graffiti that the killer or killers had left on the street. It was a circle around the body with strange symbols he'd never seen before. "Whoever killed him was hunting a demon. My guess is they thought the boy on the street was possessed, although I don't know why they'd kill him."

"Who are *they*?"

"I'm not sure. I was trying to get a fix on it when you came running up and broke my concentration. It's not normal for me to be blind to things like this, but that being said, these kind of demons aren't my specialty."

Nick was confused by that. "What do you mean?"

"I'm a Dark-Hunter, Nick. Not a demonologist. There are thousands of species of demons in a variety of belief systems, and while I may be fluent in all languages and customs, some—not many, but some—of the world's demons are alien to me because they don't come out and play often. Some are so terrifying that their own people don't speak of them or have forgotten them. As a result, I don't stay on top of it. Now wishing I had."

That made sense. Nick glanced over at the weird design on the street. "What about those symbols? What are they?"

"A language that was dead before *I* was born."

Whoa. Given Ash's geriatrics, if that predated him . . . that was scary. "How can that be?"

"Contrary to popular misbelief, I wasn't born with the dinosaurs, Nick. As old as I am, I know many beings who make me look like an infant. Whoever did this might be one of them, or it's something or someone who's had recent contact with them." He looked back at the symbols. "I honestly haven't seen that writing since I passed ruins in Atlantis when I was about your age."

"You can remember that far back?"

An angry tic started in Ash's jaw. "With a clarity I wish to the gods I could burn out of my mind." There was a lot of hidden pain in Ash's tone. Kyrian had told him that Ash didn't like talking about his past. From his tone of voice, Nick would guess that Ash hadn't had a very happy childhood.

Then again, it had to be gruesome for Ash to have died so brutally at age twenty-one that he'd sold his soul to the goddess Artemis for vengeance.

"So what do we do?" Nick asked.

"Give me a few more minutes, then I'll take you to Kyrian's."

"Ash!"

Nick looked around Ash to see a young African-American guy rushing over to them.

Ash turned to face him. "Hey, Tate. You investigating?"

He nodded. "I was out with my dad when the call came in." He gestured to the medical examiner, who was talking to the police. Then his gaze went to Nick.

"This is Nick Gautier. He's working for Kyrian and knows about our darker side."

"Ah . . ." He smiled at Nick. "Tate Bennett. Nice to meet you." He seemed friendly enough as he held his hand out.

Nick shook it. "You, too."

Tate leaned in to speak in a low tone with Ash. "It's a demon thing, isn't it?"

"Yeah. But I don't think a demon killed him. I'm pretty sure the killer was human and so was the kid."

Tate appeared confused. "How do you mean?"

Ash gestured toward the circle. "That's a containment and destruction spell. The kind meant to trap and weaken a demon so that you can kill it easily."

Tate's eyes widened. "The kid was possessed?"

"I don't think so. It's a weird vibe. I'm really not sure what went on. All I know is it ain't right."

Tate's frown deepened. "How can you not know what happened?"

Ash lowered his tone even more. "That's what I'm trying to say. Whatever human did this has me blocked and with those symbols. . . . I don't know. But I'm thinking the kid was in the wrong place at the wrong time. In spite of the fact that the kid is dead, I don't think he was the target. I think the killer was after something else. What about you? You have anything?"

"Only the vic's description: Caucasian. Male. Fourteen years old. We think he was killed this morning around eight. No ID at all, but he did have—"

"Hey, I know those shoes."

Tate and Ash turned to him as Nick pointed at the body they were now moving. As they'd lifted the kid, the tarp had been pulled back from his feet.

"What?" Ash asked.

Nick inclined his head to the lime green Converse they were zipping the body bag around, which were decorated with a Magic Marker. "That's Barry Thornton. He sits behind me in study hall."

Tate stepped toward him. "Are you sure?"

"Yeah. Those shoes are distinctive. No one else in high school draws Pokémon on their clothes." Not to mention the green was pretty neon, and most of the kids he knew preferred more sedate colors.

Tate considered that for a second before he spoke. "Has he been messing with the occult?"

Nick gave Tate an agitated stare. "Let's go back to the Pokémon on his shoes, shall we? Dead giveaway. He wouldn't even play D&D, 'cause he thought it was Satanic. He didn't believe in anything paranormal." Which was ironic when you thought about how many preternatural beings went to their high school.

"He was the captain of the chess club and an A-plus student."

Tate met Ash's gaze. "Why would anyone think he's a demon?"

Ash shrugged. "The world is insane, and you're asking me for the reasoning of a psycho? I'm not a profiler."

"But you are omniscient," Tate reminded him.

"It, like my immortality, has its limitations. I can't see everything, unfortunately." Ash sighed. "Nick said this was the second boy found?"

"Yeah. There was a kid named Alistair Sloan found last night."

They both looked over at Nick.

"Why y'all looking at me for? I don't know him at all."

Ash snorted. "You seem to know everyone else in town."

"Well, I do get around." Nick grinned.

Ash shook his head before he returned his attention to Tate. "This entire event isn't adding up."

Tate agreed. "Could be a zealot on a killing spree. Sometimes the weird crap is human. I know it doesn't happen often in this town. But . . . every now and again, we do find humans being insane."

Ash appeared less than convinced. "Maybe."

Tate gestured over his shoulder. "I better get back to it. Let me know if you uncover something."

"You, too."

As soon as Tate was gone, Ash turned back to Nick. "Do me a favor."

"Don't lick your seat belt?"

Ash's expression was total confusion. "Huh? Where did that randomness come from?"

"When I was a kid, I did that once in my aunt Mennie's new car. Now every time I get in her car and she's driving, she says do me a favor, and that's what always follows after it. Sorry. Habit."

"Okay. If your bizarre flashbacks are over, can I have your attention for a second?"

Nick straightened up. "Absolutely."

"All right. Keep your eyes open, and don't go *anywhere* alone until we figure out what's happening and why someone is killing fourteen-year-old boys."

"You got it."

Ash started toward the body, then seemed to think better of it. "Let's get you to Kyrian's."

"Fine with me." He liked the idea of being safe and alive.

Ash waved to Tate to let him know they were leaving before he led Nick back to the gleaming black Porsche. Nick got in and buckled his seat belt while Ash started the car.

They didn't speak at all while Ash took him the rest of the way to the Garden District, where row after row of antebellum homes paid tribute to and housed some of the wealthiest people in New Orleans.

Man, the size of Kyrian's place never failed to impress him. It was one heck of a house. In the classical Greek revival style, it kind of reminded Nick of a wedding cake, what with the wraparound porches, the ornate flourishes, and white color. Ash opened the gate, then parked in front of the marble steps that led up to the front door.

Nick got out and headed up the stairs. When he

started to ring the bell, Ash materialized beside him and pushed the door open.

He arched a brow at that. "Were you raised in a barn? You don't just walk into someone's house."

Ash laughed. "I have an open invitation to enter whenever I'm here."

"Yeah, but what if he's naked or something?"

Ash led him into the foyer. "I've known Kyrian for over two thousand years, and I can honestly say that I have never once caught him naked in his living room." The door closed behind them without Ash or Nick touching it—something that always unnerved Nick when Ash did it. "Besides, Rosa's still here. I know he's not walking around bare-assed with her on duty."

"Oh yeah." There was that.

As if she'd heard them come in, Rosa entered the hall from the direction of the kitchen. "Ah, Acheron, good to see you again."

"*Hola*, Rosa. Is Kyrian upstairs still?"

"*Sí.*"

While Ash headed up, Nick went toward Rosa with a hopeful look on his face. "Do I smell something . . . sweet?"

She laughed. "You live on your stomach, mi'jo. Go, there are cookies waiting for you."

Nick gave her a Roman salute. "Rosa, I am your eternal servant. So long as you feed me cookies, you may ask and I will do without any complaint."

"Good. I have a list of your chores on the counter beside the plate."

Ah, man . . . Nick bit back a whine. This was his job, and he wouldn't complain. At least not to Rosa, maker of great food.

Kyrian was another matter. He was subject to the full whiny teenager moodiness.

Nick headed into the kitchen and grabbed a cookie before he glanced over his list. Chewing the cookie, he scratched at his chin.

1. Replace upstairs hall bathroom lightbulb.
2. Get online and research Ferragamo shoes, then e-mail someone named Kell to see if he could convert Ferragamos into weapons.
3. Order a replacement coat for the one that was torn. (See closet for coat.) Make sure it matches exactly.

4. Wash cars.

5. Take out trash for Rosa.

6. Most important, don't bitch.

Hmmm . . .

"Rosa?"

She arched a brow as she came into the kitchen. *"Sí?"*

"How many cars does Kyrian own?"

She paused to consider it. "I believe there are six of them, but I don't know for sure. I don't go into the garage."

Six. Kyrian wanted him to wash six? Was he out of his friggin' mind? No way. That was too much. It'd take him all night.

Grumbling under his breath, Nick headed for the garage to see just how big these things were. In spite of what Kyrian thought, he wasn't a slave. He had . . .

His thoughts scattered as he opened the door.

Y ou're sure they're not Daimon attacks?" Kyrian asked Acheron as he shrugged on his coat.

"Oh yeah. What I really hate is that one of the kids was killed on our watch. I don't want that to happen again. So keep your eyes open tonight for predators other than Daimons."

"Definitely. Speaking of demon spawn . . . where's Nick?"

Ash shrugged. "He came in with me, and that was the last I paid attention to him."

"Yeah, and I was fully expecting him to object to his list of assignments." Kyrian paused to listen with his psychic hearing. He furrowed his brow as he heard nothing. "It's too quiet. I better go make sure he's not harassing Rosa. My luck, she's put a choke hold on him and I'll have to explain the bruising to his overly protective, paranoid mother."

Acheron laughed. "Don't worry, General. I'll bail you out before dawn."

"Thanks." Leaving Acheron, Kyrian headed straight downstairs and searched for his pain, who never ceased to irritate him.

There was no sign of him.

Not even in Nick's office. Where could he be?

Kyrian grimaced as he entered the kitchen. "Where's Nick?" he asked Rosa, who was putting away dishes.

She wiped her hands on a white dishcloth before she answered. "He went out to the garage, and I've not seen him since."

Strange. There was no sound of running water or any sign of the kid out there that he could hear.

A surge of panic seized him. Had the preternatural killer found the kid? Could Nick be lying dead out there, right now?

He rushed to the door and yanked it open, then froze at the last thing he expected to find.

Nick sat on the stairs, completely comatose. He stared straight ahead as if he'd been frozen in place.

"Nick? You all right?"

He didn't respond.

Kyrian moved around him until he stood in front of him. He snapped his fingers in front of Nick's face. "Kid?"

Nick blinked before he met Kyrian's gaze. "I'm not worthy," he said in a breathless tone.

Baffled by his comment, Kyrian stared at him. "What?"

Nick gestured toward his cars. "Dude, that's a Ferrari, Lamborghini, Bugatti, Alfa Romeo, Aston Martin, and Bentley. And I'm not talking the cheap models. Those are the top of the top of the top of the line, fully loaded. I swear, that's real gold trim in the Bugatti. There's more money in metal in here than my brain can even tabulate. Oh my God! I shouldn't even be breathing the same air."

Kyrian laughed at his awed tone. "It's all right, Nick. I need you to clean them."

"Are you out of your ever-loving mind? What if I scratch them?"

"You won't."

"Nah, I might. Those aren't cars, Kyrian. Those are works of art. I'm talking serious modes of transportation."

"I know, and I drive them all the time."

"No, no, no, no, no. I can't touch something so fine. I can't."

Kyrian cuffed him on the shoulder. "Yes, you can. They don't bite, and they need to be washed."

Nick let out a sound of appreciation. "I ought to be paying you for this."

Kyrian snorted. "Then I'll dock your pay." He held his hand out to help Nick stand. "C'mon."

Nick allowed him to pull him to his feet, but he was still intimidated by the cars around him. He'd never even thought to see one in real life, never mind touch it. These were sweet. "How much money you make, anyway?"

"Obviously a lot."

"Dude, make me a Dark-Hunter."

Something cold and painful flickered through Kyrian's eyes. "Don't even joke about that, Nick. You don't ever want to become what I am. It all looks great from the outside, but two thousand years gets hard. All my family is long gone, and while I have my Dark-Hunter brethren and Acheron, it's not the same. I'd give everything I have and then some if I could just see my parents one more time. Tell my dad that I'm sorry for things I said to him. Never, ever leave your mother after a fight. Whatever you do, don't let the last words you say to her be hurtful."

"You fought with your father?"

He nodded. "Acheron has a saying, and it's so true. There are some things sorry can't fix. Life is all about regrets. Don't let those regrets be that you've hurt someone who really loves you. Keep those to a minimum. It's bad enough when you have to carry them through a single lifetime. When you have to carry them through thousands, it's brutal."

He'd never thought of it that way. Still, he'd give anything to have an eternal life with this kind of wealth. Heck, he'd settle for having it for ten minutes.

"Don't worry about getting to all the cars tonight. You can do the Lamborghini and then save the others for tomorrow. Just make sure you get the rest of the list done."

"Will do."

Kyrian inclined his head to him before he went back inside.

Nick walked down the three steps to get a closer look at the Bugatti. Yeah . . . that was a car. "I would hug you, but I don't want to get my skin oils on your paint."

But as Nick stared into the tinted window, he didn't see the inside of the car. He saw something that looked more like a movie playing on it. Mesmerized, he stepped closer so that he could see it more clearly.

It was a battle in Kyrian's house. He saw his boss with a woman who looked a lot like an older version of Tabitha Devereaux, only she had dark auburn hair and was dressed in a nightgown. There were fanged blond Daimons attacking them on the stairs. Kyrian was trying to keep them away from the woman who stood behind him on the landing with a sword.

There was another Dark-Hunter there. One he didn't recognize. He wasn't even sure how he knew it was a Dark-Hunter, and yet . . .

The stranger was beheaded by the Daimons.

He flinched at the horror and closed his eyes. When he opened them again, the scene had changed.

This time, he saw something far worse. . . .

He was the kid on the street who was lying dead while a hooded man absorbed some kind of energy that was spewing out his chest like a laser light show. But it was Nick's eyes that haunted him most. They were solid black, like something out of a horror movie, and in his open hand, resting against his palm, was the diamond necklace that Nekoda always wore. . . .

Your destiny is shaped by choice, never by chance. Beware the decisions you make, no matter how small, for they will be your salvation . . .

Or your death.

CHAPTER 9

Nick lay low for several days as those visions haunted him. With Grim's help, he was trying to hone his ability to see if he could get anything more or see more clearly. But it wasn't easy. Much like with the perspicacity, it came and went on its own timetable, not his.

Bloody inconsiderate powers.

Grim kept promising that he'd be able to control them with practice.

He was much more optimistic than Nick was. Of course, he wasn't the one hallucinating and spazzing.

For now, it was just another aggravation in a life that was already irritating. Puberty was bad enough with his body doing things he didn't want it to do at inconvenient times. Now his mind was doing it, too. One minute he'd be fine; in the next he'd see someone "normal" shift into something not, or he'd have some psychedelic flash of an event to come.

It was getting so bad, his mom was starting with the drug inquisition again every time he had one around her. At this rate, she'd be after him with a specimen jar to pee in.

The only good news was that they hadn't found any more kids slain by whatever had killed the other two.

And Nick wasn't dead.

Yet.

But that came into question as he walked into his schoolyard to find Stone and his crew of crotch-sniffing sycophants waiting for him.

Great. Just what he needed. Another suspension. Any time Stone neared him, he went to the principal's office, and it never went well for him. It was a given, like the golden shower that inevitably followed the lifting of a dog's leg.

Sure enough, right as he neared the bottom step that led up to the door of the redbrick building, Stone, who was a huge brute of a knuckle-dragging Cro-Mag, stepped forward to block his path.

Stone crossed his beefy arms and looked down his nose at Nick. Something that really set his ire off.

"Not in the mood." *Jackweed.* Nick refrained from the insult that really wanted to spill out and tried to brush past him. Always best to avoid a fight.

Too late. The rest of his merd (herd of morons), surrounded Nick. He felt his blood pressure rising even more as they did that *we're invading your personal space 'cause we're dickheads* maneuver. Nick ground his teeth, trying to hold his temper back.

Something that wasn't helped when Stone shoved him.

"Someone's been stealing our stuff out of the lockers, Gautier. Makes me think of only one person I know who'd be that desperate." He raked a sneer over Nick's tacky blue Hawaiian shirt that his mother made him wear and faded jeans. Both of which had been bought from Goodwill for the staggering price of a dollar each.

Nick snorted at Stone's insult. "I don't know. Word around the girls' locker room is that all of you are so hard up, you were cruising the senior center, trying to find a prom date."

Stone bellowed in rage. He started forward, only to have Caleb come out of nowhere to shove him back.

Dang, the demon could move. No wonder he was the star of the football team.

Then again, Caleb had an unfair advantage. Superhuman strength and centuries of soldier training.

Caleb sneered at Stone. "It's too early in the day to have to wash blood out of my clothes, Blakemore. But I am willing to smell Tide if that's what it takes to get you to act human." A hysterical comment, given the fact that Stone was a werewolf.

"What's going on here?"

Nick stepped back as a huge bear of a man moved forward to break everyone apart.

He sneered at both of the combatants. "Stone? Caleb? Don't you dare start fighting. I'll make you run laps until you drop if you do. Last thing we need is for a player to get suspended. We're already about to have to forfeit as it is. Right now, I can't afford to lose even a single man. You hear me?"

Caleb held his hands up in surrender. "I wasn't looking for trouble, but I'm not about to run either. You push me and I will push back."

The coach shook his head. "Blakemore, get your girls and leave. Now."

Curling his lip, Stone took off with his zoo crew of thugs following after him.

The coach narrowed his eyes on Nick. "Who are *you?*" *Scum-sucking dog.* He didn't say those words, but his tone implied it.

Forcing himself not to say or do anything to get himself added to detention, he spoke carefully. "Nick Gautier."

Recognition lit the coach's deep blue eyes. He actually appeared impressed. "You were first-string running back last year. What happened?"

Nick shrugged. "Stone's mouth happened. It needed to be closed, and I was a little too obliging to shut it."

The coach scratched his chin. "Your file says you were kicked off the team for your attitude."

"File's wrong. I was kicked off the team for *Stone's* attitude. Mine was just fine. Still is, to be honest."

The man made a sound that might be a laugh. Or a growl. "You interested in playing again?"

Nick gestured to his arm that was in the sling. "Can't. I'm still recovering. Doc doesn't want me to do anything to stress it." An excuse he was milking for everything it was worth. One that worked with his mother, but not so much on Kyrian, who was a pitiless taskmaster. Every time he said something, Kyrian always shot back with, "Boy, I've gutted men who whined less than you. Now, move it."

And apparently, the coach was in the latter category, too. "Yeah, but I can add you to the roster. Even if you don't play. You are a legitimate player. C'mon, Gautier. I need just three more jerseys, and we're all set for the play-offs. Do it for the school, or if not that, do it for Malphas. He's worked hard this year. You gonna deprive him of a championship game because of a minor injury?"

Minor injury? He'd been shot and almost beaten to death by people he'd thought were his friends.

He looked at Caleb.

Go ahead and say yes. It'll make it easier for me to keep an eye on you if you're at practice with me.

He hated when Caleb and Ambrose played in his head. But Caleb was right. Since it was his fault Caleb was on the team in the first place, the least he could do was rejoin. Not to mention, he did look good in the black and gold jersey, and it kept him out of the hideous shirts his mother insisted he wear. At least on game days.

"All right. I'll do it."

"Great." The coach grinned. "I'll bring a jersey to you and see you after school today."

Nick opened his mouth to tell him he was supposed to work, but the coach was gone before he could do more than gape. He met Caleb's gaze. "Kyrian's going to kill me."

"Nah, he won't. I'm sure he'll understand."

Nick wished he had that kind of confidence. In anything. But he didn't. Life and jerks had basically kicked it out of him about the time he was two . . . maybe three. Sighing, he started up the stairs with Caleb one step behind him. As they entered the building, it seemed like everyone was chattering about items that had been stolen while the school was closed.

There were times when being poor was a blessing.
Since he didn't have anything to steal . . .

Even so, he remembered once a few years ago when
his mom had splurged and bought them two five-
dollar lawn chairs at Walmart. Dang if someone
hadn't stolen them off the back porch of their run-
down condo. His mom had cried for a week, and if he
could lay hands on the thief, they'd spend eternity
limping. What kind of human being would steal plas-
tic lawn chairs from someone who was so obviously
poor? Surely there was a special corner of hell waiting
with their name engraved on a plaque.

"Hey, Nick."

He froze at his locker as Nekoda came up to him.
"Hi, Kody. How you doing?"

She gave him that smile that never failed to heat
his body up to an equatorial level. "Better now that I
get to see you. I tried to call last night, but you didn't
answer. Did you get my message?"

Nick scowled. "My phone didn't ring." Pulling it
out, he checked the log. "See." He held it out for her
inspection.

"Weird. I rang it three times."

That was odd. Then again . . . "There might be something with our condo." Other than the fact that it lived under a perpetual dismal cloud and was infested with roaches the size of his fist. It was probably over a hellmouth, too, that didn't allow for any kind of reception other than two cans joined by a lengthy string. "Sorry I missed it. Did you need anything?"

"Just wanted to talk to you."

He didn't know why, but those words made his face heat up. Even though he kept having nightmares about her, there was something that drew him to her. She was irresistible, and the taste of her kiss was perpetually branded on his lips. He'd give anything to have another one.

"Nick! I just heard!"

Before he could identify who was speaking, Casey threw herself into his arm and slammed him against the lockers.

"You're on the football team again! I'm so happy for you. Now you can be my escort at homecoming. Won't that be great?"

He felt like a mouse caught between two cats as he saw the look of anger on Nekoda's face.

Casey paid her no attention. "When do you get your jersey? You'll be so hot in it."

Help me. His voice sounded like a fly in his head.

Without a word, Nekoda spun around and headed down the hallway.

"Kody!" He tried to follow after her, but Casey cut him off.

"You don't want to talk to her, Nick. She's a loser."

Yeah, right. She was also the only person from his school who'd visited him when he'd been in the hospital. Yeah, okay, so she volunteered there, but she had made it a point to come to his room every day and cheer him up. *That* she hadn't had to do.

He tried to get around Casey. She was like a Velcro spider. Everywhere he moved, she was there, clinging to him. He didn't know how to escape her without hurting her.

Frustrated, he gave her a vicious glare. "What is up with you?"

"Nothing. I only want to spend time with you, Nick."

"Since when?"

"You're working for Kyrian Hunter now. You're one of us."

He wasn't so sure he wanted to be one of them. Because of the way they'd treated him, he'd learned a long time ago not to want to be part of the in-crowd. He didn't like the way they operated. If being one of them meant being cruel to someone else, he'd rather be a social outcast.

"Look, I'm not some teen movie. I'm not going to get so caught up with being popular that I forget my friends. You can't undo years of ignoring me with one act of kindness. Now, excuse me." He finally pushed past her to go after Kody.

But it was too late. There was no sign of her anywhere.

Fantastic. He felt like an even bigger heel. *Gah, I'm such an idiot. . . .*

"Nick?" Casey took his hand, shocking him completely that she'd dare touch him, the unwashed. "I'm sorry if I treated you wrong in the past or hurt your feelings. Like anyone else, I can be self-absorbed at times and not see what's in front of my face. Maybe my mom's right, and I need to look up from my phone once in a while." She peered at him from underneath her lashes in what had to be the hottest expression he'd ever seen on a living girl's face. "You're right. I didn't see you then. My bad. But I see you now. Can you not forgive me for being stupid?"

Those unexpected words touched a part of him that was foreign and strange. Then he remembered what Ambrose had said. Casey would be a good girl-friend to him while he was in high school.

And yet he wanted Kody for that role. She was the one who'd been kind when he needed it. She was the one he really enjoyed talking to.

Fourteen years, and I can't get the time of day from a single female. Now I'm torn between two of them. . . .

The most popular girl he'd been pining for since he was a kid and another one who'd only just entered his world and sent it reeling.

Life wasn't right. And he had no idea what he should do. Listen to Ambrose, or listen to his gut. . . .

"C'mon," Casey said, tugging at his arm. "I'll walk you to class."

G rim paused as he felt a slight breeze kiss his cold skin. It was a presence he'd known since before the dawn of time. Vicious and callous, she was his best friend.

And his worst enemy.

Together they'd wreaked more destruction than an F5 tornado on a week-long bender.

That was just on their good days. On their bad ones . . . Well, scientists claimed an F6 was impossible. With their combined powers, it was not only possible, but even that category was petulant compared to the damage he and Wynter Laguerre could do.

"Laguerre . . . what brings you here?"

Lithe, sexy, and vibrant, she came into his private domain like she owned it. With an abundance of dark brown curls that fell to her waist, she was exquisitely formed. As always, her lips were a bright blood red that was matched by her pants and blazer. The moment she flashed herself to his side, the fire in his black marble hearth flared, shooting embers across the ebony wood floor.

She had that effect on most things.

"I wanted you to know that I'm facilitating things."

Those words laced him with foreboding. Whenever Laguerre facilitated something, it was never good. Not for him and especially not for her target. "How do you mean?"

She screwed her face up. "There's too much good in Nick Gautier. No matter how much abuse we heap on him, he won't turn. Therefore we need to do something to purge it from him."

"You can't kill his mother." They all knew that was the only surefire way to unleash the darkest parts of Gautier's powers and soul. If Cherise Gautier died, he'd be beyond redemption and easy to turn. But . . .

"She's off-limits to us." Whoever killed her was guaranteed a brutal demise, and not even he, Death itself, was immune.

Wynter ran her long red fingernail down his jawbone. "Yes, but there are other ways to turn him and make sure he sides with us in this battle."

Not one that he'd been able to identify. Nick's fortitude was duly impressive. The more he was around the kid, the more he doubted their ability to corrupt him, even with the help of the primal source. "He has to finish his training before he's any good to us."

"Perhaps, but if he has a reason to turn, he might embrace those powers even more and use them where we tell him to."

Grim wasn't so sure. "He's still naïve. He actually believes in happy endings."

She shrugged nonchalantly. "Then we'll have to kick those delusions right out of him."

If anyone could do that, War was the one. Killing people's aspirations was her specialty.

"What do you have in mind?"

With an evil smile, she moved away from him to warm her hands by the fire. "I already have my person in place. Someone Nick trusts who isn't who he thinks."

"How do you mean?"

She laughed. "I conjured an old accomplice of ours who has agreed to help us with our quest. One who is now corporeal in the human realm."

That explained the dead teenagers who'd been un-covered by the police. Sacrifices made to get their man into the thick of things.

"And our friend has promised that Nick's life will be turned inside out. Before everything is said and done, his true friends will be killed and he will be ours." She turned to face him with another evil smile. "Then we will control the world once more, and not even the old powers will be able to control us."

Grim returned her smile. That was definitely some-thing he could sink his teeth into.

CHAPTER 10

Nick sat in English, bored out of his mind. Why was this even a subject? Really? He spoke English, rather fluently most days, first thing in the morning or really late at night notwithstanding. It, like everything else they forced him to suffer through in school, was such an epic waste of his time. Completely irrelevant. Would it honestly matter in a hundred years whether or not he'd read *Moby Dick*?

Was he ever going to have a job application where they made him diagram a sentence or pick out a gerund?

Stop your bitching, Nick. You should try being an immortal demon who's lived since the dawn of time having to sit through this crap when English is not *my native tongue, and if you think you're fluent in it, buddy, I actu-ally know what a gerund is.*

Nick looked askance at Caleb, who sat beside him on the other row, doing the wiggy mind meld with him. *Yeah, but these handful of years are just a blip in your massively long life. They're a significant percentage of mine.*

Caleb scoffed in his head. *Look, there you go using some of the stuff you've learned. Math. What a concept? Maybe it's not a waste after all.*

Nick snorted.

"Look who's come out of his coma. Did you have something to say to the class?"

Blinking, Nick focused on his teacher.

Which tactic to use? Better go with dumb. If nothing else, that one usually kept him out of deten-tion. "Um, what?"

Mrs. Richardson came forward to eye him like the bitter troll she was. She hated teaching, and everyone knew it. Her favorite part of her job was embarrassing or belittling her students every time she forced them to open their mouths. "Are we boring you, Mr. Gautier?"

Man, it was impressive how she made his name

sound like an insult. He'd like to master those evil human tricks.

But first, he had to get out of the frying pan and hopefully bypass the fire. "Not bored. I sneezed. Sorry."

"That was a pathetic excuse for a sneeze."

I swear she should argue before the Supreme Court. "I was trying not to disturb the class with it."

She narrowed her gaze even more, as if she knew he was lying, but not so positive that she called him on it. "Then perhaps you'd like to give us *your* view of Ahab's need for vengeance?"

I'd really rather not. But he knew he had to, since the chances of her letting him off the hook now ranked up there with him spontaneously combusting into flames in his seat, so he answered honestly. "It was stupid."

She arched a brow at him. "Stupid how? Like the way you and your friends spend all your time playing video games and feeding into a useless consumer-driven society? Or stupid like those of you who think you can doze off and text in my class and still pass?"

Stupid like you were when you believed the saleswoman who told you that *dress looked good on you?* It was hard to bite that comment back, but he knew better than to let it spew out. Only she was allowed to be venomous in the classroom. Anyone else would be suspended.

Clearing his throat, Nick scratched his neck, uncomfortable at the fact that everyone was now staring at him. A handful were snickering. Two more sneering and one girl rolled her eyes as if he were mentally defective. He hated being the center of attention. Why did teachers have to do this? It was like they purposefully singled out the kids who least wanted to participate or they waited until they knew it was the wrong time to send a guy to the board. Couldn't they let him fly under the radar? At least for a day or two?

No, let's humiliate Nick even more. 'Cause face it, life just didn't suck enough.

Nick braced himself for her ridicule before he defended his position. "Well . . . he lets it ruin his life. He gets so obsessed with going after the one thing that hurt him that he loses sight of everything else. He becomes isolated from everyone and everything.

Paranoid. He feels like he can't trust anyone around him ever. In the end, he loses everything, even his life. And for what? Total stupidity, if you ask me."

"So you're saying that if you were Ahab, you'd let it go and move on with your life? Even if it was the person you loved most on this earth who was killed and you were left with a lingering deformity from it?"

"Absolutely. Crap happens to everyone. Put on your big-boy pants and deal. You got to let it go and move on."

She tapped her cheek with her pencil as if considering his take on the book. "Interesting idea. Naïve and immature, but interesting." She looked to Caleb. "What about you, Mr. Malphas? Do you have anything to add to Mr. Gautier's ill-conceived opinion? What did you take out of the book, provided you actually read it instead of watching the movie like Ms. Harris did?"

Tina slinked down low in her desk. Richardson was never going to let the poor girl live that one down.

Caleb leaned back and folded his arms over his chest, cocky in a way only someone who'd probably read every book ever written could be. "I see it as a parallel for *Oedipus Rex*."

"Intriguing. Do continue."

Caleb yawned before he answered. "Even though someone can see the course they're on and know their fate, they can't change or stop it. Prophecy is prophecy. Things happen that we can't control. It's when you try to prevent it that life really gets screwed up."

"Explain."

"Well, Ahab is told repeatedly by a variety of people that if he doesn't stop his obsessive quest, he'll die. Like Starbuck says, ''Tis an ill voyage! ill begun, ill continued; let me square the yards, while we may, old man, and make a fair wind of it homewards, to go on a better voyage than this.'" Caleb looked at Nick. "Ahab doesn't listen and dies because he's stupid."

Nick laughed.

Until his teacher glared at him.

Cringing, he sobered instantly.

"Nice summation, Mr. Malphas." She headed for the board. "It's essay time, class. Hope all of you are up to date on your reading. If not, I will soon know and you will regret it, and don't even try siccing your parents on me. If I get one phone call about unfair treatment, I'll automatically deduct thirty-five points off your final grade. And ten points off everyone else's, just for good measure."

Ignoring her, Nick wanted to know why Caleb had so obviously directed those last words to him. He might be a lot of things in life, but he'd never been an idiot. Especially not where his life was concerned. Obsession was not his thing. He believed in rolling with the punches. . . .

Oh, wait. Did Caleb know about his wanting to go after Alan for shooting him?

Yeah, okay, so that wasn't so easy to let go. But the turd had shot him. *Shot* him. Would have killed him, too, without a second thought, had Kyrian not stopped him, and Alan would have beaten up two innocent older people. Someone needed to stop that animal. Going after Alan wasn't obsession. That was a public service.

Suddenly, the intercom turned on, making several kids, including Nick, jump in their seats. "Mrs.

Richardson? Could you send Nick Gautier to the office?"

Nick's stomach hit the floor. Such a summons was never good, at least not where he was concerned.

What did I do now?

Actually that wasn't the question. *What are they blaming me for now?* He was the one person who could never get away with anything without getting caught. And he was always the one they held up as an example to everyone else. Or worse, he was totally innocent in the matter and blamed anyway and still held up as an example.

She curled her lip at him as she spoke to the intercom. "He's on his way."

Nick packed his bag up, just in case a suspension was looming, then stood. Someone threw a wadded-up piece of paper at him while Richardson wrote the assignment on the board with her back to them. Of course she missed *that*.

Had Nick done it, she'd have turned and caught him the moment it left his hand.

Ignoring the insult, which he was pretty sure had come from one of Stone's minions, and the fact that it completely ticked him off, he slung the backpack over his shoulder and made the Bataan Death March toward the office. Gah, could it be any farther? Could he dread it any worse?

Can I have one day at school where I'm not forced to the office? Just one? Really, is that asking too much?

His gut completely knotted, he pushed open the door and walked to the long light wood counter. The secretary, who was around his mother's age, but nowhere near as attractive, gave him a smug lip curl. "Mr. Head wants to see you."

Of course. Why else would he be here? Not like he was making a delivery.

Nick went for the door behind the counter that was slightly ajar and knocked on the fogged glass that gleamed with the new principal's name on it.

RICHARD HEAD.
PRINCIPAL

"Come in."

Nick pushed the door open wider so that he could enter the Chamber of Doom. It was even dark and gloomy inside. For some reason, the fluorescent lights in this room cast a grayish wash that hung over everything like a ghoulish pall.

"Close it behind you."

Yeah, that tone said his butt was in for it. Nick obeyed, then went to take a seat in front of the dark wood desk.

Strange, all traces of Peters had been removed, and Head's personal items were all in place as if he'd been principal here for years. It was kind of creepy when you thought about it. You got eaten by a co-worker one day at work, and the next the world went on as if you'd never existed. No one even talked about Peters anymore.

He was completely erased. A shiver went down Nick's spine. Even though Peters had been a jerk, it was sobering to realize how little the world cared once you were gone.

Meanwhile, here they were. . . .

A middle-aged man with a bald head, the new principal looked even more stern than Peters had. Did they send them to a special training camp to give them all that pompous, condescending twist to their mouths?

He glared at Nick over the rim of his brown glasses. "Do you know why you're here?"

You needed somebody to kick, and I drew the lucky straw? He kept that belief to himself. "No, sir."

"Think, Gautier. Think."

I am the most unfortunate human ever born, and you guys like to screw with my head? Biting back that sarcasm was much easier said than done. "Sorry, sir. Not a clue."

Head set a handheld Nintendo down on his desk. "Look familiar?"

Duh. What was he supposed to answer? Of course it did. Most of his classmates had one. They were common and unless decorated by the owner, ubiquitous.

Head's smug glower intensified. "Cat got your tongue, boy?"

No, confusion had his tongue. He still had absolutely no idea what was going on. But before he could speak, a knock sounded on the door.

The new coach pushed it open. "Am I interrupting?"

"Yes." Head's tone was even colder than his grimace.

The coach ignored it. "Gautier. Glad you're here. I

was just about to track you down." He came in and handed Nick his jersey.

Nick would be excited, but under the circumstances, he was going to wait to celebrate.

"You might want to hold off on doing that," Head said in a dire tone.

The coach scowled. "Why?"

"I'm about to send this little punk to jail, and the last thing we need is another person in lockup wearing one of our school jerseys."

Nick choked. Jail? For what? Breathing?

"What did he do?" the coach asked.

Yeah, what did I do?

"Stealing. This—" He held up the Nintendo. "—was found in his locker. It belongs to—"

"Kyl Poitiers. He loaned it to Nick in gym class."

"What?"

Nick was as stunned as the principal, who mirrored the word that was screaming in his mind. No one had loaned him that, and he'd definitely not stolen it. But he knew better than to speak up until he understood what was going on. *Anything can and will be used against you.*

The coach gestured to Nick. "I saw Kyl give it to him."

Head still refused to believe it. "You're mistaken. The serial number's on my list of stolen objects, and it belongs to Bryce Parkington."

"And again, I know what I saw in class. If it's stolen, Poitiers is framing Nick. But that's a stretch. Are you sure the number's correct?"

"Of course I'm sure. The number is right here." Head compared the two numbers, then cursed under his breath. "Well, that's odd. I swear the numbers matched earlier."

The coach shrugged. "It's an honest mistake. Happens to the best of us. Besides, those numbers are so small on the devices, it's easy to misread them." He gestured to Nick. "C'mon, Gautier. I'll walk you back to class."

Head continued to sputter as he went back and forth with the serial numbers, trying to make them match.

"Wait," he said as they reached the door. He held the system out toward Nick. "You might as well take it back with you, since it's not one of the stolen items."

Then his tone went sharp again. "And don't let me catch you playing it in class or the hallway, or I'll confiscate it."

"Yes, sir." Nick grabbed the handheld and made a quick getaway. He still had no idea what was going on, but he wasn't about to open his mouth and get himself into trouble now that he was clear. Especially since he was innocent of any wrongdoing.

As soon as they were outside the office and in the hallway away from anyone who might overhear them, the coach stopped him. "Bet you're wondering what's going on, aren't you?"

"Lot of confused. Definitely."

The coach took the Nintendo from Nick's hand and toyed with it. "I did some digging into your school file. It's actually quite impressive."

Nick had a bad feeling he wasn't talking about his grades or test scores. "How so?"

"You scored the highest for the entrance exam of any kid ever tested. You're the only one who's ever made a hundred on it and got all three of the bonus questions correct, too. Did you know that?"

All right. For once he was wrong. A wave of pride filled him. That was saying something, since this was one of the best schools in the country, never mind the state of Louisiana, and harder than even Ben Franklin High to get into. "No." They'd told him he'd done really well and given him a full scholarship, but no one had ever told him that he'd scored perfect on it. Wow. No wonder his mom got so bent whenever she thought he was slacking off.

"But that wasn't what I found the most fascinating. It's your other record I want to talk to you about."

His stomach shrank. *Here it comes. . . .*

Loser. Dork. Your family history blows. You have no hope for a future, so we might as well throw you out now, right into the gutter that spawned you. He'd heard it all more times than he could count and from more people than he could name. Peters in particular had taken a sadistic pleasure in letting him know that he had no future whatsoever.

"Last year alone," the coach continued, "you were in thirty-five fights. Thirty-five. Kid, that has to be a record. When you take out the days you were absent, it's like one every third day you're in school. The fact that you're still a student here, even with your exemplary test scores and grades, is the most amazing thing I've ever heard of. I've taught at a lot of schools over the years and never have I seen anyone who was a worse troublemaker. Truly impressive."

That annihilated every bit of pride Nick'd temporarily had. He knew it looked bad, but it wasn't entirely his fault. He didn't care when they insulted him, which was pretty much hourly, it was when they went after his mom that it was on like *Donkey Kong*. Unfortunately, Stone knew that, and so they relentlessly called his mom names and said horrifying things about her and her character. In spite of a few mistakes that everyone made, his mom was a saint, and he'd bust anyone who said differently—which apparently happened every third day he was in school.

Sighing, Nick held the jersey out. "Guess you want this back."

The coach refused to take it. "No. I have another proposition for a boy with your unique . . . skills."

Nick didn't need his pendulum or his book to see

where this was going. His gut said he wouldn't like it, and when the coach spoke, he confirmed that suspicion. Loudly.

"I have a group of boys who do favors for me. I'd like for you to join our elite group."

Oh yeah, right. No thank you. There were some groups he wanted no part of, and this sounded like one that needed to be at the top of his *never* list. "Dude, I don't do nothing perverse. In fact—"

"Nothing like that, Nick." He held the Nintendo up. "We *procure* things."

No flippin' way . . . The coach was part of *that*?

It wasn't possible. Why would he do such a thing?

Then again, the thefts hadn't started until the coach had come on board. Given that, it freakishly made sense. A supplemental income for an underpaid staffer. All the teachers he knew complained about their pay, and most looked for other ways to augment their income.

This was over the top, however.

"You steal," Nick accused.

The coach screwed his face up. "That's such an ugly

word. We merely procure and borrow. After all, people never return what they borrow anyway, and the snobby rich kids here have so much, they don't even appreciate it. Mummy and Daddy will replace their stuff without a second thought, and file claims with their insurance. It's what it's for, right? Think of it like Robin Hood. You're alleviating the rich of wealth they don't deserve and are giving it to those in need. Us."

Nick shook his head at the manure the coach was spreading. Semantics couldn't couch it. This was theft, pure and simple. There was no justifying it. Taking was taking, and it was wrong. His mother had raised him better than that. "Forget it. I'm not a thief." He started to leave, but the coach stopped him.

"You will help us, Gautier. If you don't, I'll make sure the next item found in your locker carries a much longer jail sentence than this." He wiggled the Nintendo in Nick's face. "And with Principal Dick just itching to call the cops and have a scapegoat to placate the angry parent phone calls demanding he catch his thief, no one will mourn *your* sacrifice."

Nick felt his panic rise. He knew it was the truth.

The people at this school wouldn't bat an eyelash to see him go and would think it was his just desserts to be brought down as a criminal. No one would ever believe he, the poorest kid in school, hadn't been desperate enough to do it. "You wouldn't dare."

"Try me. Everyone here already thinks you're a liar and a thief. Ninety percent of the students and a hundred percent of the faculty are convinced you cheated to get in. Given that, do you really think they'd believe you over me? After all, seeing is believing."

Nick wanted to deny it, but he knew the truth. Many of his classmates hated him. And those who did would love to see him tossed out on his rump. To have him go to jail would be the bonus round.

That would kill his mother.

Don't ever go to jail, Nicky. Whatever you do, don't be like your father. I've worked too hard and sacrificed too much to see you come to that end. She said that to him so much that it kept a constant earworm going in his head.

"Why would you do this to me?"

The coach gave a cruel smirk. "Because you have the skills I need. I have a list of items and a very short time to gather them. If I fail, you won't like what happens to you. That I promise. But if you help . . . I will reward you greatly."

Why would he need Nick's help to steal? "What? You got a gambling problem or something?"

"You're a smart kid. This is one debt I have to pay and one I will do anything to meet. You help me and I'll help you."

And if he didn't, the jerk would send him to juvie. He shuddered at the very thought.

Then an idea hit him. "What if I borrowed the money you need? You could pay back your loan sharks or bookie or whoever, and everyone would be happy."

The coach shook his head. "My items are very specific. Money won't do either of us any good, and it won't pay my debt. Or keep you out of jail."

"Look, I don't want to be a thief."

"Fine. As I said, *borrow* them. I don't care how you get what I need so long as all the items are in my possession and they are the exact, and I do mean *exact*, items on my list from the people I tell you to take them from. You understand? There can be no substitutions whatsoever."

Nick nodded. If he could borrow them, that wouldn't be so bad. Except he knew the coach wouldn't return them. . . .

Man, how did he get into these things?

The coach handed him a folded-up piece of paper. "You have six days, Gautier. After that, I'm going to make Mr. Head very happy where you're concerned."

Fabulous.

Nick watched as the coach left. His heart pounding, he unfolded the paper and read it. Stunned, he felt his jaw go slack over what the coach wanted him to take from his classmates. But one item in particular leapt out at him.

The coach wanted him to steal Nekoda's solitaire diamond necklace.

No way. I won't do it. He had no intention of hurting Kody. Not in any way or form. He wouldn't do it.

The coach could roast, for all he cared.

And he held that resolve tight until his sixth

period, when the police came and arrested Dave Smithfield out of their classroom.

Dave cried like a baby while they handcuffed him and read him his rights. "I don't do drugs. I swear it! Someone planted that in my locker. I'm telling the truth. Why won't you believe me? I didn't do it. I didn't!"

They refused to listen as they hauled him out of the school while Nick and the rest watched on in horror.

Until he met Coach Devus's satisfied smirk and warning gaze. Then he knew the truth.

The coach had planted it in Dave's locker and he'd probably called the cops, too.

And later that night, after football practice, while Nick watched the news at Kyrian's house, he learned just how sick his new coach really was.

The woman commentator's face was sad as she read from the teleprompter. "A tragedy tonight coming from juvenile lockup. A fourteen-year-old student at St. Richards High School, David James Smithfield, who was arrested earlier today after drugs were discovered in his locker at school, was found dead in his cell an hour ago. Authorities are awaiting the autopsy results, but at this point, they believe it to be a suicide. . . ."

Yeah, right. Nick had a really bad feeling about that as he pulled the pendulum from his pocket. Dave wasn't the kind of person who'd kill himself. Not even after being arrested. He'd known the guy for years. Always happy-go-lucky, Dave had never been involved in anything immoral or illegal. And as small as their school was, Nick would know if he had.

His heart pounding, Nick opened his book on the desk and flipped to the pendulum page.

Holding the chain the way Grim had taught him, he concentrated on his question. "Was the coach responsible for Dave's death?"

Without hesitation, it swung over *yes*. Forcefully. Then it started moving in a strange pattern he couldn't identify. Unable to decipher it, he turned to a blank page and made sure that neither Rosa nor Kyrian saw him use it.

"All right, book. Tell me what's going on." He used the pendulum to prick his finger before he let three drops of blood fall.

It made bright splashes against the white before it began twisting and moving like an exotic snake. Nick watched as the words wrote themselves on his pages.

Easy come, easy go.
The future is sometimes hard to know.
But if you don't follow through . . .
Your life you will soon bid adieu.

His stomach drew so tight, it could form a diamond. "Follow through what? What the coach wants or with my convictions?"

The page turned completely bright, blood red, then exploded. Literally. The words rearranged into more fluid script.

Through the fog light will shine.
Then the answer will be thine.

What the crap did that mean? Why did he even use this worthless thing?

Nick growled. "You stupid, flippin' book. You're not going to answer me, are you?"

You have the answer you have sought.

No matter what you do, you will be distraught.

Life is never easy, no matter what they say.

And every decision you must carefully weigh.

In the end, the consequences are yours and yours alone
*   to face.*

So think it through and be wary of the race.

What race?

Now he had a migraine from trying to decipher all that. But one thing kept chasing through his mind. One thing he had to have answered. "Did the coach kill Dave?"

That answer already came your way.

Asking again, the outcome won't sway.

But, yes, the coach is not what he seems.

And you are at the heart of all his schemes.

That Nick understood all too well. He would become one of the coach's tools. The very thought sickened him. He didn't want to do this. "Is there any way to avoid stealing for him?"

Ask your heart what it wants.
And never fear other's taunts.

The problem was, he didn't fear anyone's taunts. He'd been spoon-fed those since his birth. What he feared was his coach sending him to prison for most of his adult life.

Or worse, killing him like he'd done Dave.

With that thought came the memory of the vision he'd seen. The one of him lying dead while clutching Kody's necklace.

The same necklace the coach wanted him to steal . . .

And Grim thought his precog was broken.

CHAPTER 11

Nick knew he needed leverage against the coach. The coach had said it himself earlier that he'd taught at a lot of schools. If he'd made a habit of stealing, then it stood to reason that he wouldn't be able to stay in one place long without people catching on. Or one of his students getting caught and ratting on him. That would explain why he was so willing to pick up and move in the middle of the year.

While Nick waited on Kyrian to come downstairs and approve the order for a new coat, he did an online search that turned up nothing. Mostly because he wasn't all that well versed in searching for people. He needed someone with a lot more computer experience.

Picking up his phone, he called Bubba.

"You've reached 1-800-Ca'-Bubba. Sorry I'm not available to take your call. I'm either tied up tending someone else's computer nightmare or am out ridding the world of its zombie predators. Either way, leave a message, and as soon as I kill whatever pains me, I'll get right back to you. Thank you for calling, and have a positive day."

Nick shook his head as he laughed. At least once a week, Bubba changed out his message. How the man kept a thriving business given his lunacy was beyond Nick's comprehension. That being said, Bubba was extremely entertaining.

After hanging up, he dialed Mark.

"Fingerman here . . . Hah, you're talking to my voice and not me. Unfortunately, I'm off with Bubba and not a woman 'cause I'm dumb. No telling what I'm into, but if this is my parents, I assure you I'm not doing anything illegal or immoral, and I ain't disturbing no farm animals. However, please reserve bail money 'cause you know the stuff Bubba gets me into, and I might be needing it soon. Everyone else, leave a message and as soon as I get back to an area where I have reception again, I'll return your call. Even if I have to do it from the great beyond. Thanks."

Farm animals? Now Nick knew Mark meant cow-tipping, which had been a pastime of Mark's from high school (one that had stopped abruptly when a cow fell on him and broke his leg in three places), but the way he had that phrased . . .

Yeah, Mark needed a VM editor.

Nick sighed as he considered his other options.

Wait . . . He knew another geek.

Madaug St. James. If anyone could give Bubba a run for his money when it came to computers, Madaug was it. His classmate had been born with a keyboard in one hand and a modem chip in his brain.

Besides, Madaug owed him for saving his hide from the zombies the moron had created and then unleashed on all of them.

He scrolled through his contacts until he got to the right number and called him.

"Hello?"

Nick let out a breath in relief that he'd finally reached a living person. "Madaug?"

"Yeah?"

"Nick Gautier. Um, I have a bit of a problem that I need some help with."

"Homework?"

"Kind of."

"What's 'kind of' homework?"

"You know the new coach?"

Madaug growled. "The troglodyte who let Stone defile my gym shorts and then wrote me up because I wouldn't wear them afterwards? Yeah, I know him, may he choke to death on a jockstrap not his."

Okay, obviously Madaug had issues left over from PE.

"What do you need me to do? And does it involve any kind of vengeance on him?"

Nick nodded even though Madaug couldn't see it over the phone. "If what I'm thinking is true, that's an affirmative. I was wondering if you could do a background check on him and find out where he's taught in the past and what his record at those schools was."

"That sounds tedious. Why do you want me to do that?"

"'Cause I think he's hiding something."

"Like what?" Madaug asked.

"I'm not sure. Suffice it to say that I think he has some skeletons in his closet that might be interesting and useful to us both."

Madaug paused as if considering it. After a minute, he agreed to be Nick's accomplice. "Fine. But it'll cost you."

"Cost me what?" Nick was aghast. "Dude, you owe me. Big-time. So log off *Doom* and help a brother out."

Madaug sputtered. "How did you know what I was doing?"

Simple. It was all he ever did. If you ever asked him how his day went, his response was always his *Doom* progress report such as how many creatures he'd killed and how many zones he'd opened. "An educated guess."

"All right. I'll get started and call you if I find something interesting."

"Thanks, M. Appreciate it."

"Any time." Madaug hung up.

Nick set his phone aside as he heard footsteps

approaching his office. He'd just switched back to the online shopping cart when Kyrian came in. "Hey, boss. I have your coat ready. I just need a method of payment."

"Top drawer on your right."

Nick opened it, expecting to see one of Kyrian's credit cards. Instead, it was one with Nick's name on it.

Totally stunned, he couldn't breathe as he stared at the NICHOLAS A. GAUTIER on the Visa card. Wow, it was the coolest thing he'd ever seen.

Kyrian walked over and closed Nick's mouth with his forefinger. "It has a thousand-dollar limit on it, and it's for business purchases only. If you prove yourself responsible, I'll get you one of your own in a few months with a higher limit. Deal?"

"Yes, sir." Thrilled beyond belief, Nick entered the number into the fields and finished buying the coat for Kyrian. "I also spoke with Kell, and he said that he'd have no problem putting blades into the Ferragamos if that's what you want."

"Fantastic. When the shoes come in, make sure they get sent to him."

"You got it." Nick paused to watch as Kyrian pulled the curtain back to look outside at the dark yard—something that was highly unusual for him. Not to mention, he was surrounded by an air of melancholy. "Is something wrong, boss?"

Kyrian hesitated before he answered. "Not sure. I have a . . . I don't know. Bad feeling, I guess."

His words caused Nick to have one, too. "About me?"

He shook his head. "Ash would quote the song, there's a bad moon on the rise. I have a feeling it's summoning something that should be left alone." He met Nick's gaze. "Why don't you let me take you home tonight?"

Yeah okay, Kyrian's strange behavior was starting to freak him out a little. "Sure." Another fear went through him. "Did they find another kid murdered?"

"No. It's not that. I'd feel better making sure you and your mom are safe. Get your stuff, and I'll take you now."

He wouldn't argue that. Nothing better than heading home early. He shoved his books back into his pack, then slung it over his shoulder. "Did Rosa leave already?"

"About an hour ago. Did you get dinner?"

"Oh yeah. Never had turkey tetrazzini before. It was really good."

"You want to take some home for your mom?"

Kyrian's generosity never failed to surprise him. The man was always thinking of other people. *Good thing I didn't stake him when I discovered his fangs.* "Can I?"

"Absolutely."

Nick headed to the kitchen with Kyrian right behind him. As he was pulling out the container and contemplating his employer's unorthodox existence, a thought struck him. "How do you keep your anonymity in this day and age? Don't people get suspicious over the fact that you don't age?"

"Ironically, it's easier now than in the past. People today don't want to believe in the paranormal. Back when, you had a serious problem with Bubba and the mob and their pitchforks."

Nick laughed. "I know you don't mean Bubba Burdette, but the image in my head . . . Highly entertaining."

Kyrian smiled before he continued his explanation. "That's why Dark-Hunters have human Squires." Which was what Nick would become once he was old enough to be sworn into the council. They were humans who made it their life's task to protect their immortal bosses and the world that mankind as a whole wasn't ready to accept. "With you guys coming and going during the daylight hours, it cuts down on people being curious. Our property is also listed under the Squire's name."

"Ah, I get it. So no one knows you exist."

"Exactly. Rule number one. Be a part of the world, but not in it."

Nick frowned. "Rule number one?"

"When we're created and Acheron comes to train us, we're all given a Dark-Hunter handbook. It has a list of rules we have to abide by, and that's the first one Acheron teaches us."

Dark-Hunters with a handbook. Who knew? But then it made sense that they'd have a code of conduct to abide by.

Which made Nick wonder about Kyrian's past and his experiences. "Has the world changed all that much?"

Kyrian shrugged. "The toys are infinitely better. But people haven't changed at all. Same concerns, same hang-ups. Different clothes. Different century."

He made it sound so simple, but Nick had a feeling it was anything but. There was no telling all the changes and marvels Kyrian had lived through. The discovery of electricity, flying, television . . . toilet paper.

"It must be amazing to live so long."

"Sometimes." Kyrian put the container back in the fridge while Nick fastened the lid on his mom's dish.

"Did you ever have a wife and kids?" Nick asked.

Kyrian hesitated as if the question bothered him. "Had the wife. Wanted the kids."

Part of Nick told him to keep quiet, but he wanted to understand Kyrian's strange reaction. "You miss her?"

His eyes darkened angrily. "No offense, I don't want to talk about her."

That told Nick much about Kyrian and his relationship with his wife. It made him wonder if she was the one who'd betrayed him and made him become a Dark-Hunter. Man, that had to suck to have your wife betray you, bad enough you'd trade your own soul for vengeance. "Sorry. I won't mention her ever again."

Kyrian's features softened. "Be careful whom you give your heart to, Nick. Make sure when you hand yours off, you get hers in return."

"Yeah, but how do you know?" Obviously Kyrian had been tricked. How could Nick avoid it when someone as smart and savvy as Kyrian had been taken?

Kyrian sighed. "That's the trick. People deceive and they lie. The more you have, the more they scheme to take and the more often they try. The world's an ugly place, and apparently many people think it's easier and better to take from others than it is to earn it themselves."

Nick frowned at the bitterness in Kyrian's voice. "Then why do you fight to protect us?"

Kyrian gave an odd half smile. "Because every time I think that it's not worth it—that the people in it deserve the misery of their lives—I come across someone who makes me rethink that."

"Like who?"

He ruffled Nick's hair as they left the kitchen and

went to Kyrian's Lamborghini. "A smart-mouth Cajun who worships the ground his mother walks on. One who was willing to lay down his life to protect two strangers from his best friends, even though he needed the money to eat. A woman who's willing to debase herself to feed her son. Another who faced down a drug cartel in order to protect her family and her small town. That kind of love reminds me of the human I once was. People like you, your mom, and Rosa deserve someone to watch your backs."

Nick thought about that as a warm feeling rushed through him. No one had ever said anything kinder to him, especially not someone so respectable and decent. Kyrian was the type of man he wanted to be.

"What were you when you were human?" he asked.

"An ancient Greek general."

"Really?" For some reason, that surprised him.

Kyrian inclined his head as he pulled out of the driveway and headed toward Nick's condo.

"Did you win any big battles?"

"Oh yeah. I was the scourge of Rome. Me and my friend and mentor Julian Augustus held them back and fought them off like machines. During our human lives, we were regaled as Greek heroes, and our stories were told for centuries after we'd died."

That was truly impressive. "Did you die in battle?"

Kyrian let out a bitter laugh. "Hardly. There was no man alive who could defeat me. None."

Suddenly Nick understood, as he remembered the one thing he had learned from his convict father. "It's never the enemy without who brings you down. It's always the enemy within."

He nodded. "Guard your back, Nick. It's the one you don't see coming. The one you trust whose betrayal is most lethal. They know your weakness and they know how to hit the lowest. It's when your back is turned and your guard is down that they move in for the kill."

His dad had told him the same thing. "Sorry."

Kyrian shrugged before he made a right turn. "Don't be. Everyone suffers at least one bad betrayal in their lifetime. It's what unites us. The trick is not to let it destroy your trust in others when it happens. Don't let them take that from you, too."

Nick nodded. "You think you'll ever get married again?"

"No. Dark-Hunters aren't allowed to date or have girlfriends. Marriage is absolutely off the table."

"What about kids?"

"I'm dead, Nick. No ability to procreate."

Nick cringed and cupped his boys in horror. "So you can't—?"

"I didn't say *that*," Kyrian snapped as if completely offended. "We can sleep with someone. We just can't impregnate them."

Ah, okay. That made sense. "Can you get any diseases?"

"No."

Nick fell silent as he contemplated what it would be like to be impervious to illness. He watched the traffic speed past them as Kyrian turned into his neighborhood. Dilapidated and junked up with broken-down cars and browned-out lawns, it was a stark contrast to Kyrian's immaculate stomping grounds.

Sighing, Nick saw the stark, weathered duplex he and his mom called home.

Kyrian parked out front. "See you tomorrow."

"Yeah. Stay safe."

"Always. Call me if you need anything."

Nick nodded as he opened the door and got out. He didn't move until Kyrian had gone, then he turned around and headed up the broken sidewalk that led to his house.

Menyara came out of her side to greet him. Tiny and beautiful, she'd been the midwife who brought him into this world. For reasons she never really went into, she'd taken his mom in when his mom had been pregnant with him. Aunt Mennie had been with him the whole of his life, and she was the only family he and his mom had. Dressed in a flowing white skirt and light blue top, she had her Sisterlocks pulled back from her face with a white scarf.

"Hi, Aunt Mennie."

She hugged him as he drew near her. "Where you been, boo?"

"At work. Mom home?"

She nodded. "I was heading over to see if she wanted to watch TV tonight."

Since they didn't have a set of their own, Mennie often let them watch it at her place. She also shared her phone with them.

Nick opened the door to their tiny condo, which was basically two rooms. His mom's small bedroom and then the "big" room that had a kitchen area in it. On the far wall was his room, which consisted of blue blankets strung up on a wire. His mom and Mennie had made it for him once he hit puberty so that he could have some degree of privacy.

His mom sat on their one and only barstool at the breakfast counter, reading the paper. She looked up and smiled at their entrance.

Nick dropped his backpack by the door before he crossed the small area to hug her. "What are you doing?"

Mennie closed the door, then moved to join them.

"I was looking to see if there might be an apartment for rent in the Quarter."

He didn't know who was the most stunned by his mom's unexpected words. Him or Menyara. "Really?"

Mennie arched a brow, but she didn't say anything.

"Nothing against you, Menyara," his mom said quickly. "You know how much I love you and how grateful I am for everything you've done."

"But you want to be closer to work," Mennie's Creole accent was thicker than normal.

His mom nodded. "And Nick's school. He's always having to run for the streetcar. I'd like for him not to have to start the day off in such a panic."

"The devil is sitting on icicles, isn't he?" Nick asked.

She laughed. "No, sweetie. It's just . . . you wouldn't believe what people tip at Sanctuary. Oh my God, I had no idea. Between my salary and tips, I'm making four times the money I used to."

Nick gave her a hopeful grin.

She screwed her face up at him. "All right. Both you *and* Bubba are forgiven for getting me fired."

"Really?"

"Absolutely. In fact, I was thinking of taking you and Mennie out to eat tonight to celebrate."

That sounded great, but there was one little problem. "I'm stuffed. Rosa made this turkey tetrazzini that is unbelievably tasty. I brought some home for you, too.

There's even enough for Mennie." He returned to his backpack to dig it out.

No sooner had he put his jersey on the floor than his mother sucked her breath in sharply.

Nick froze at the sound that usually heralded him getting into trouble. "Something wrong?"

"What are you doing with that?" She pointed at his shirt.

He glanced down at it and wondered why its presence had warranted her reaction. "The coach wants me back on the team."

His mom appeared skeptical. "Are you serious?"

"Yeah. They're short a few guys for the team, so . . ."

"You don't seem happy about it," Menyara said. That was the only drawback to Mennie. She had the gift of second sight and knew all kinds of things about him that he didn't say.

He gave them both a fake smile. The last thing he needed was for them to find out what the coach wanted from him. God help him if Mennie figured that out. "I'm happy."

"Nicky. I'm your mom. Don't lie to me. What's wrong?"

His coach was a psycho, that was what was wrong, but he couldn't tell her that. If he did, she'd go marching into the office and cause such a stink that he'd be framed for sure. When it came to him, his mom tended to lose all sanity. "Nothing. I promise."

She gave him a look that said she wasn't convinced. Luckily, Mennie distracted her while he pulled out the leftovers and took the container to the kitchen.

As soon as they were done eating, Mennie and his mom headed over to Mennie's to watch TV while he stayed in on the pretext of doing homework.

Not an entire lie. He was working on something that involved school.

Once he was sure he wouldn't be disturbed, he called Madaug again.

"What?" Man, Madaug didn't even bother to disguise his irritation at being interrupted.

"Have you found anything?" Nick asked.

"No."

"Nothing?"

"You're missing my point, Nick. I haven't uncovered anything at all. This guy's a complete ghost. There's no background on him that can be found. Not a school in this country has a Coach Devus, and with a name that unusual, he should be pretty easy to find. Right?"

Nick sat there, trying to digest it. Madaug was right. They shouldn't have any trouble finding information on a guy with a name like that. "Are you serious?"

"Yeah. The only Coach Devus I can find was one who coached at Georgia Tech in—get this—1890."

"1890?" Nick gaped. "Like over a hundred years ago, 1890?"

"Yeah. He was the lead coach in the first rivalry game between UGA and Tech for the Governor's Cup. Tech trounced the Dawgs 28 to 6. And get this . . . the next day, the entire team, including the coach, was killed in a fire that started in the building where they were celebrating their victory."

"That sucks." It was something that would happen to him. Crappy Gautier luck was the stuff of legends.

"Don't it, though? Anyway, that was the only De-vus I can find."

That didn't make any sense at all. "He told me he's been coaching for years. He has to have a coaching history somewhere."

"Can't find a trace of it, and believe me, I've looked. I even hacked the school records. His résumé isn't online. Without that, I'm stuck. I don't know where else to look. I've hit more walls at this point than a blind mouse in a test maze with shifting walls."

Only Madaug, whose parents were both scientists, would come up with that for an example.

Nick sighed as disgust filled him. He dreaded what was to come, but he knew it meant only one thing.

He'd have to search the coach's office and see if he could find something about his past. Crap. Crap. Crap. *How do I always get into these things?*

Whatever he'd done in his previous life that war-ranted the misery of this one, he hoped he'd enjoyed every minute of it.

C'mon, Nick. Think. There has to be another way.

Unfortunately, there wasn't. This was it. He'd have to go in and pray he didn't get caught.

"All right," Nick said. "I'll get more information for you tomorrow. Thanks for looking it up for me."

"*De nada.* And be careful. I don't know why, but he creeps me out."

Given the fact that Nick was pretty sure the coach had killed his classmate, Devus didn't exactly fill him with warmth and sunshine. "Good night, M."

"Bye."

Nick hung up, then called Caleb, who answered on the second ring.

"You dying?" Was that a note of hope in Caleb's tone?

Or was he being paranoid?

"No," Nick answered, praying for paranoia but pretty sure Caleb was hoping he was on the brink of death.

Caleb let out a deep breath. "Then why are you calling me?"

"I was wondering if you knew anything about Devus."

"Other than he's our new coach?"

"Yeah, Caleb. Something a little more than that."

"Not really. Why?"

Nick hesitated, then decided this was the one crea-ture he could trust with the truth. "He threatened me earlier."

Caleb materialized right in front of him with his phone still in his hand. "What do you mean, he threatened you?" he said in his demon's tone.

Now that was service. Completely shocked by the sudden appearance, Nick looked from the phone in his hand to Caleb, then back again. Yeah, okay, so he knew Caleb had demon powers and such, but dang . . .

Impressive.

He hung up the phone, since he obviously didn't need it any longer to talk to Caleb. "He told me that if I didn't steal some things for him, he'd have me put in jail."

Caleb snorted. "And you believed something that stupid?"

Offended to his core, Nick glared at him. "Stupid or not, I'm pretty sure he's the one who framed Dave and then had him killed while he was in lockup to-night."

Caleb rolled his eyes, which set off his temper. "Nick,

really? Your paranoia should be in a record hall of fame somewhere."

"I'm not paranoid," he growled. "Use your powers and see. I'm telling you the truth."

Caleb gave him a look of irritation before he closed his eyes and concentrated.

Feeling cocky, Nick folded his arms over his chest and tapped his foot. Now the truth would come out and he'd be vindicated and one vicious demon would owe him a massive apology.

One Caleb was going to serve with a huge slice of humble pie.

After a few minutes, Caleb opened his eyes. "I'm not getting anything."

Dread went through Nick. He had a feeling this wasn't good, and he was about to have to put the humble pie back in the oven. "What do you mean?" he asked apprehensively.

Caleb's cold stare went right through him. "The coach is human. I know that much, but . . ."

Hope came back as he mentally put an oven mitt on the pie again. "But what?" Nick asked.

Caleb shrugged. "It's like he's a wraith."

"A ghost?"

"Not exactly. Wraiths are apparitions who appear in the form of someone who's living."

Nick was trying to understand. "Like an after image?"

"Closer analogy. But unlike an after image, a wraith usually appears right before someone dies . . . to the person who's marked for death."

Now that wasn't something Nick wanted to hear. "You just made my flesh crawl."

"Mine, too." Caleb hesitated before he spoke again. "I've been around a lot of wraiths, and he doesn't feel like that either, though. It's a strange sensation. Like human wrapped in evil."

"Oh, great. Our coach is a pig-in-the-blanket for Satan."

Caleb let out a sound of frustration. "You know there's no dealing with you when you're in this mood. Let me do some digging and get back to you."

"I'll be here . . . unless the coach kills me."

Caleb appeared less than amused by his attempt at

humor. "Don't let him in the door, and if he shows up, call me."

"As long as the fingers work."

With one eye fluttering with his annoyance, Caleb vanished in a cloud of red smoke.

Alone and worried, Nick considered everything going on. None of it boded well for him. In fact, he felt the flames licking his hindquarters. He had to get the coach off his back. That was the first order.

Wanting more answers, he thought about consulting his book again, but the last thing he needed was another migraine.

No, this was something he could figure out on his own. He was sure of it. Sitting down on the pallet that made up his bed, he pulled out the coach's theft list and looked over the items again.

Underneath Kody's necklace was Stone's class ring. Yeah . . . like that would work. He could just see it now in his mind. Him walking up to Stone and smiling. *Hi, Stone. Would you mind handing me over your ring that's made out of 24 karat real gold?* One that had a real diamond in it? *Just pretend I'm your girl and give it to me.*

The werewolf would disembowel him.

But because that was on the list, he knew Stone wasn't one of the coach's "chosen group." The question was, who else had been recruited, and why had they been chosen. Did Devus know about his criminal past? Nick hated that part of himself. Desperation had motivated him to do some things he wasn't proud of, such as watch out for cops while his "friends" had shoplifted. At the time, it had seemed harmless—a victimless crime—and he made a lot of money that had helped his mom with bills. He'd convinced himself that it wasn't hurting a real person, just some innocuous mondo corporation that didn't care about people like him. He'd told himself the mondo corps preyed on people like him and laughed while they did it. That had been his justification.

On his last visit to see his dad in Angola, his mind had been changed while listening to some of the other inmates trying to excuse their crimes. Last thing he wanted was to be one of them, sitting in jail, blaming the world for his wrong decisions. Nothing was worth his freedom and self-respect, especially not money, and certainly not hurting someone else. If he could give back some of what Alan had stolen, he would. Unfortunately, he'd used the money to buy food.

But one day . . .

He would pay back everyone they'd ever taken a nickel from.

There's no way the coach knows about that. Because the guilt was so harsh over it, Nick rarely thought about it, and he'd never once, ever told a single soul outside of Tyree and Alan, who'd been there for it. Since they didn't go to school, the coach couldn't have talked to them.

He doesn't know.

Yet somehow, he'd singled Nick out of the herd for this awful plan of his. Looking back at the list, he cringed. The coach wanted something from almost everyone in his first two periods.

What an odd assortment, though. Watches, rings, necklaces, and two hairbrushes. Why hairbrushes? How could the coach get any money from that?

His phone rang, startling him. Trying to calm himself, he answered it.

It was Caleb. "Where's Menyara?"

"Next door with my mom, why?"

"Do me a favor and go stay with them."

"Any particular reason?"

"Yeah. I just crossed paths with a Fringe Guard."

Nick frowned at a term he didn't understand. "A what?"

"Fringe Guard," Caleb repeated. "They're bounty hunters who go after other preternatural beings. In this case, he's seeking a demon who's hiding in the body of a kid."

"What's that got to do with me? I have a demon hanging near me"—Caleb—"but not one in me."

Aggravation was thick in his tone. "He was searching for a fourteen-year-old boy, Nick. I think we now know who killed those other teenagers that you and Ash saw."

A tremor of fear went down his spine. Had the demon been in them, or had he merely tried to get inside them? "But I'm not possessed."

Caleb cursed. "Would you stop arguing with me, Nick, and just do it? These aren't the kind of creatures you want to meet on your own, and where there's one, there's usually more, and they're not known for their mercy or humanity. So do what I said and don't be alone. The last thing I want is for you to be interrogated by one."

"Why?"

"Nick, I swear . . . stop acting like a three-year-old at bedtime and haul ass next door or I'm coming over there and dragging you myself, and you won't enjoy the experience."

"All right. Calm down. Put your horns in. I'm headed over." He hung up the phone. Unlike Caleb, he wasn't sure Mennie was strong enough to fight something like that. While she was a voodoo priestess with some rather impressive skills, he didn't want to put her in harm's way. However, she did have a lot of protection symbols in her home. Least he could do was make use of them.

Tucking his arm back into the sling, he got up and went for the door.

He walked outside, then shut and locked the door. Wrinkling his nose, he curled his lip. *Ew!* What was that godawful smell? It was rotten eggs mixed with fertilizer and a dash of vomit. Gah, it smelled like Stone had another accident in Chem class. He pressed his hand to his nose and started for Mennie's.

But the moment he did, a shadow fell over him and he was grabbed from behind.

CHAPTER 12

Cursing, Nick spun around, ready to brawl. Then he froze in place and blinked twice just to make sure he wasn't hallucinating.

He wasn't.

Tall, shaggy haired, and swathed in flannel and jeans, Mark, who was again drenched in the smell of duck urine, stood on the stoop like a hyena with a broken laugh track. "Boy, you should have seen the look on your face. I ain't seen you that floppy rabbit scared since you were trying to get into the store before the zombies ate your brains. Oh my God. If I'd had a camera on you, I'd have made a fortune."

Incensed over the needless scare the idiot had

given him, Nick glared at him. "You dickhead! You're not funny."

"You're right about that. Funny is *you,* boy." He continued laughing until Nick was ready to kick him where it would leave a lasting impression. It was a good thing he owed Mark, or he would definitely give into that urge.

Nick growled low in his throat. "What are you doing here anyway, besides stinking up my porch and skinning a decade off my life?"

Mark wiped at his eyes. "*Lo siento* about the u-rine, *mi amigo,* but better safe than sorry when in the swamp. That's my motto." He finally stopped grinning and got down to business. "I saw that you'd called, and I was trying to call you back, but my battery went dead. So I went to car charge it. Unfortunately, I'd used the car charger to tie my glove box closed, which frayed it, and when I plugged it in to use it, it started a small electrical fire in the Jeep, which ignited a stack of papers and burned out the whole passenger seat before I could douse it with enough Coke to put it out—that stuff's not as good at putting out fires as you'd think . . . Well, anyway, here I am. What did you need?"

Only Mark or Bubba could set their car on fire with a battery charger. Nick would laugh at it if it wasn't so (*a*) typical of their luck and (*b*) pathetic.

"Um yeah, about that . . ." Nick scratched at his arm that was in the sling. "I took care of it already."

Mark actually pouted. "You telling me I burned up my Jeep for no good reason? Dude, that sucks. At least tell me there was a zombie at your door or something trying to kill you."

"No. Sorry."

Mark muttered under his breath.

But as Nick stared at Mark's Jeep, which had burn marks on the passenger-side window, a weird thought occurred to him. This might be the one person, aside from Caleb, who could really help him in this.

At least he was the one person insane enough to try. Everyone else would try to talk sense into him.

Mark was also the one person, aside from Mennie and Caleb, he knew could keep him safe from any preternatural attack. In fact, Mark lived to fight off anything he perceived as not human.

"You wouldn't want to do a little recon with me, would you?"

That perked Mark up. "What kind of recon?"

"Well . . . it's what I was calling you about. I have a teacher at school who is a strange enigma."

One of Mark's eyebrows shot north. "How so? Like zombie enigma or normal enigma?"

"I don't think he's a zombie." However, he wouldn't rule anything out at this point. Psycho was the best bet. Still, this was New Orleans and he was learning real fast about a whole crop of residents that he'd never suspected existed before. So the coach could be some kind of zombie he knew nothing about.

And to think, six months ago, he'd thought Mark and Bubba were the most bizarre residents in Louisiana.

How soon everything changes.

Now, they should be so lucky.

Nick brought his attention back to the discussion at hand. "He told me he's taught at a bunch of schools, but Madaug can't find anything on him. And I mean *nothing*. Not a single school where he's taught or anything else. It's like he never existed until my school hired him."

"Neo-Luddite." Mark nodded in approval. "I like that. Could just mean the man has a brain. I'm telling you, Nick, we're all going to get hooked into a massive server one day and become nothing but bytes in a data stream. Even our primal, individualistic essence will be reduced to simple binary code. Could have already happened and all we are now are play actors in a Rod Serling episode on permanent syndication. In fact—"

Nick snapped his fingers in front of Mark's face. "Can you come back to reality with me for a second? I kind of need you here on earth for a few minutes more."

"Sure. Not that I like it here, since I'm still waiting for my mother ship to return. But . . . what do you need?"

Nick took a deep breath for patience. Keeping Bubba and Mark focused on task at times was like dealing with a herd of ADD cats at a mouse farm. "Well, the new coach is . . ." He didn't want to tell Mark about the blackmail or theft ring. While he trusted Mark implicitly, he didn't trust him not to go up to the coach's door, kick it in, then drag him out into the yard and beat the snot out of him for threatening people. Mark didn't like abusers or bullies of any kind and considered beating one of them down a valuable public service. "Something's not right about him. I can feel it." That was something Mark could understand and agree to. "I was wondering if you'd mind swinging by his house to see what it looks like. That might give me some clue about who"—and what—"he is. After all, I know how much you like to profile people."

That sparked Mark up a lot more. "You know where he lives?"

Nick nodded. "I do." It was one of the few things the coach had told him after practice. The creep wanted Nick to bring the loot to his house so that the coach wouldn't be caught with it on campus.

But if Nick was caught, that was fine. *Burn the kid, burn the kid.*

"A'ight, then," Mark agreed. "I'm through zombie hunting tonight, and since my woman liberated me"—by burning everything Mark owned and making him leave, but that was another story—"I'll do it. Get in." He stepped down from the porch.

Nick stopped him from leaving just yet. "Let me tell my mom where I'm going." 'Cause if he didn't, she'd set his fields on fire once he came back.

He stepped over and opened the door to Menyara's condo.

Mennie and his mom were already settled on the couch, under a thick red and white blanket with all the lights off while they snacked on potato chips and dip.

His mom looked up expectantly.

"Hey, Ma? Can I have a few minutes to run an errand with Mark?"

She narrowed her gaze at him. "Crazy Mark?"

Mark stuck his head in the door to grin at her. "I heard that, Cherise."

His mom's face flamed. She was actually closer to Mark's age than Nick was. Not to mention, Mark had once worked the door at the club where his mom used to dance, which was how Nick first met him.

Lowering her potato chip back into the sack, she

cleared her throat and gave him a bashful look. "Didn't realize you were right there. Sorry, boo."

Mark laughed good-naturedly. "Sa'ight. I've been called a lot worse. At least you didn't insult my parentage while you were at it. But don't worry. I'm not doing anything too weird tonight."

"Please don't."

Mark exchanged an amused glance with Nick. "Don't worry, cher. I'll guard him with my life."

"Good," she warned, "'cause that's what I'll be taking from you if you let even one hair on his head get harmed. I'm dead serious, Mark. There is no corner of hell you can find where I will not hunt you down, drag you out, and torture you until you bleed out at my feet. That boy is my life, and I don't want him coming back here in pieces. So don't you pull none of your crap with him around. I mean it."

"Yes, ma'am."

As Nick started to leave, his mom aimed one warning pointy finger at him. "Don't be gone long. You have school tomorrow."

He repeated Mark's last words. "Yes, ma'am." Then he closed the door.

Whoa, for a tiny, little pocket woman, she could be scarier than a rampaging bear on steroids. Even Mark appeared shaken by her threats.

Heading down the steps, her insane rant reminded him of Caleb's stern warning. "Hey, Mark? Do you know what a Fringe Guard is?"

"Duh. What you think I am? Stupid? Who doesn't know what those are?"

Nick gave him a sullen grimace. *For the record, I be the idiot.* Thanks to Caleb, though, he didn't have to own that. "You ever fought one?"

Mark scratched at the whiskers on his cheek. "Not personally. Don't think I'd want to, from what I've heard about them. Got friends who have, though. Why?"

"A friend of mine told me he ran across one tonight and that I should be careful."

Mark gave him a stare so piercing, it felt like it went all the way through him. "He told you to hide, didn't he?"

"How'd you know?"

"I can read your body language, Nick. You're scared all of a sudden. What else did your friend say?"

"That I should stay in protected areas."

Mark closed the distance between them and pulled something out from under his shirt. It took Nick a second to realize it was a silver necklace with a symbol similar to the one on his grimoire.

"Wear this. Unless the devil himself comes after you, that'll protect you."

Nick screwed his face up as he caught a whiff of the duck urine, which almost caused him to gag. "You sure?"

Mark stood up straight. "I'm still breathing, aren't I?"

"I think so. But with that stench all over you, it's hard to tell. God knows, I'm trying real hard not to breathe at the moment. And I could understand if you had to stop because of it."

Mark scratched his eyebrow with his middle finger. "Then trust me, short stack. I've put that thing through the wringer. Ain't nothing going to get past it to hurt you. I've staked my life on that many a day."

Nick didn't quite share Mark's faith. Okay, so maybe the necklace was a placebo, but for some reason, it made him feel a lot better to have it. And when Mark put it around his neck, he swore he felt a small spark.

Now they've got me doing it. . . .

If this kept up, he'd be taking swamp duty with Mark and Bubba, waiting in the boat while they searched for the undead. *Please tell me I'll have better things to do as an adult.*

Without another complaint, he followed Mark to the Jeep. "When did you get this?"

Mark let him in on the driver's side so that he could climb into the undamaged backseat. Nick tried to ignore the stench of burned vinyl and paper.

Well, at least it overrode the stench of duck urine.

Mark got in and slammed the door shut. "It's always been my backup vehicle. It's what my dad bought for my sixteenth birthday. She's not much to look at. Still, I'd run her up against just about anything. She's as reliable as they come and faster than you'd ever give her credit for."

The NOS tank strapped between the front seats probably had a lot to do with that. Good thing *that* hadn't caught fire. Otherwise, they'd still be scraping pieces of Mark off the sidewalk.

Mark rolled down the windows before he took off with Nick buckled in the center of the backseat so that he could lean forward to give him directions.

It didn't take long to head over to Frenchmen, where his coach had a rental house. A ubiquitous shotgun like hundreds of others in New Orleans, the house had a fresh coat of white paint. The green plantation shutters were left open so that he and Mark could easily see straight inside to where Devus sat watching the same show his mom and Menyara had been tuned into. What was it with older people and news shows? They were glued to it, and while Nick could watch it, it wasn't his favorite genre.

Sighing in frustration, he realized this had been a futile exercise. There was nothing here he could use.

Nothing.

Just another row house with an unremarkable Toyota in the driveway.

Mark shuddered. "Man oh man, don't he look like someone who would play strip poker to lose? Why can't that ever be some fine piece of womanhood like

Angelina Jolie? Nah, it's always got to be the one man you'd least like to see naked."

"Ange-who?"

Mark scowled at him. "Oh, c'mon. You know. Acid Burn from *Hackers*."

Nick snorted. That was Mark's favorite movie of all time, and for some reason that made no sense to anyone other than Mark, references to it were forever finding its way into Mark's conversations.

Meanwhile, Mark continued to rant. "If you're going to sit in your living room in your underwear, the least you could do is cover the windows. Old dude . . . really? I don't think I can drive you home, Nick. I'm snowblind from the miles and miles of exposed white flesh."

Nick laughed.

Suddenly, Mark went silent and cocked his head as he stared at the porch. "That's weird."

Nick leaned forward, trying to see what had caught his friend's attention. "What?"

"I'm having déjà vu."

Most people would disregard that, but with Mark . . .

This could be serious.

"What's going on?"

Mark shook his head. "I don't know. It's . . . I know your coach. He's familiar to me for some reason, but I can't think why."

"Have you gone to one of the schools he's taught at?" Nick asked hopefully. If he had, then that might give them some well-needed intel on the beast.

Mark considered it. "Maybe. What does he teach and coach?"

"History and football."

"Nah." He stretched that one word out. "I don't think I've ever had him for history, and I know he was never one of my coaches. Their faces are forever burned into my memory."

That information caught Nick off guard. There was something Mark had never mentioned before. "You played ball?"

Mark stiffened as if the question offended him. "Uh, yeah. I was first-string quarterback all the way to college. Went to school on a full-blown scholarship, too, I'll have you know. I'd have gone pro had I not blown out my knee my sophomore year."

Nick was surprised and impressed. "I never knew you played ball."

"Uh, yeah. Hello? I was born to it. Where you think I get all my good evasive zombie moves from? My uncle was even one of the coaches who worked under Bear Bryant."

Whoa, that was seriously impressive. . . . "Really?"

He nodded. "My real dad was a coach, too."

This was the first time Mark had ever talked about his father other than to say he was gone. Bubba had told him that Mark's dad had died of cancer when Mark was seven. His mother had remarried two years later, and Mark had felt so betrayed by both his parents that he didn't speak about his father to this day. Bubba said the pain was just too raw for him still.

Mark continued to stare at the coach on the couch. "He is *so* familiar. I can see his face clear as a bell. I just can't remember where. But it's somewhere odd. Somewhere I spent a lot of time. If I could just re-member . . ."

"Maybe you played a team where he was the coach?"

"Could be." Mark grunted. "What's his name?"

"Devus."

"His first name?"

"Coach."

Mark gave him an expression of pain. "I can see your education isn't wasted."

"Hey, now . . . I'm offended. I never thought to ask what his name was. Really didn't care." Who would? Since Nick wasn't allowed to use faculty first names, why waste the brain space to store it? It might kick out something he really needed, like the ability to play *Donkey Kong*. Now *that* would be tragic.

Mark didn't say anything. He merely let out sounds of deep annoyance.

While he bellyached, Nick returned his gaze to the coach and tried to use his powers to see if he could pick up anything.

Nothing was there. It was as empty as the dark street. Which made sense to him, since he didn't think the coach was all that deep a well anyway.

"Can you pick up anything off his house itself?" he asked Mark.

"Not really. There's nothing much here. It's all as generic as his white Toyota."

"Great. Better get me home, then. I don't want my mom to kill either of us."

Without another word, Mark turned the Jeep back on and headed down the street.

A fter a fretful night of dreams where he was forced to steal against his will, Nick woke up completely exhausted. It felt like he hadn't slept at all. Groggy and with a headache that wouldn't quit, he dressed and made his way to school.

For once, he arrived early. Which was good, since he wanted to look around Devus's office and not get caught. This time of morning, the coach was on bus duty. He should have a good fifteen minutes alone to poke around.

At least that was his thought until he found the coach's door locked.

Dang it all . . . He looked up at the ceiling in frustration. "Was one break really too much to ask?"

That being said, Nick wasn't without a few skills. One of them being the ability to pick a lock fairly quickly. It'd been a gift from one of his dad's "room-mates" who'd thought it would be funny to teach a six-year-old how to enter.

Even though he should have, it was a skill Nick had never allowed to atrophy.

Just in case.

Five minutes later, he was inside the office. Making sure to stay away from the cameras and to keep the lights off, he went through the desk drawers first.

Nothing.

Just the typical stuff you'd expect to find in a coach's desk. Grade book. Whistle. Pens. Pencils. Paper clips. Agenda. Hall passes. Play books. Schedules. Rosters. Player lineup.

And then it struck him. Something that had toyed at the edges of his mind last night at the coach's house, but here in the office, it was epically clear.

There was nothing personal in the entire office. Not a photo, a trophy, certificate.

Not even an Altoid.

Nothing.

Hired at the same time as Devus, Principal Dick

had completely taken over Peters's office and made it his own. This one looked like the coach could quit and walk straight out the door without packing up a single item.

Literally.

His house last night had been the same way. Sterile and impersonal. Ubiquitous. Unremarkable. Just like the coach himself. Everything was forgettable.

Now it all made sense.

Wow . . . Devus must owe some serious change that kept him running constantly. What kind of mondo gambling debt had he accrued? It must be steep for him to live in this kind of fear all the time. A fear that wouldn't even allow him his choice of car since he drove one that wouldn't stand out on the road. Everything about him was a study in vanishing.

No wonder we can't find any trace of him.

He must be staying off grid to avoid loan sharks or collection thugs. Nick almost felt sorry for the man. Had Devus not been the ruthless killer who was blackmailing him, he would have. As it was, Nick wouldn't really mind handing him over to whoever was after him.

Shaking his head, he slid the drawer shut.

"What are you doing here, Gautier?"

He jumped out of his skin at the deep baritone of the coach's voice coming from behind him.

Ah, crap. I'm dead.

CHAPTER 13

Trying to act as normal as possible, Nick turned around even though he was shaking so hard, he wondered if the coach could hear his knees knocking and his heart racing.

C'mon, Nick. Think. Don't blow this.

But in his mind, all he heard was the sound of a police siren coming for him to take him away. Meanwhile, an image of him hanging dead in an isolated jail cell danced in his head. *Ah, gah, don't let that be my psychic powers kicking in now.* Not when he really didn't want them.

His panic rose higher.

Nick forced it down and decided on the simplest tactic.

A bald-faced lie. "Waiting for you, Coach."

Devus's gaze narrowed dangerously. "How did you get in here?"

Okay, time to seriously jack it up a couple of notches. Save your butt while you can. He swallowed hard before he answered. "Door was open."

Granted he'd unlocked it first, but it was true. It had been open when he'd entered. Minus one important detail.

Normally such a lie would bother him. However, new rules were applied when dealing with a homicidal lunatic.

Devus closed the distance between them to stand toe to toe with Nick so that he could intimidate him. He shoved one shoulder into Nick's and glared down his nose. "You're lying, boy. I *always* lock it."

That wasn't a smart tactic to use on a backwoods Cajun whose father was a career felon currently sitting on death row. One who was used to standing up to the worst sort of people and not backing down, no matter what.

Not even if they were holding a loaded gun on him.

As his mama so often said, Gautiers don't run. Sometimes you want to. Sometimes you ought to. But Gautiers don't run.

Ever.

Nick rose up on his tiptoes to level the difference in their heights and stiffened as his anger overrode every shred of fear . . . and probably his sanity, too. "I opened it without any problem at all."

Actually that *was* the truth.

And that made Devus furious. "Why were you in here, boy? What were you looking for?"

Since he couldn't admit the truth, Nick blurted out the only lie he could think of. "I lost the list you gave me yesterday. And I need to get another one."

Devus's entire face turned bright red. He reminded Nick of a pressure cooker about to blow its gasket. "How could you have lost the list? How is that possible?"

Nick shrugged with a nonchalance he didn't feel. "Mom says I'd lose my head if it wasn't attached to my shoulders. Guess she's right, huh?"

Devus grabbed him by the front of his hideous

yellow Hawaiian shirt and held him in two tight fists. "Listen to me, you little punk. Time is running out, and if you think I'll spare you, think again. I need you to get started immediately today. If I don't have five of those items in my hand by three, I swear I'll see you jailed by four. You hear me? And you *know* what happens to boys who get sent to jail from this school. . . ."

A cold chill and premonition danced down the length of his spine at the look in Devus's eyes and the twist of his features. If he'd had any doubt before about Dave's suicide, that ended it.

The coach was psycho.

And he'd killed Dave.

I'm so dead. How could he get out of this?

A knock sounded on the door an instant before Casey walked in. "Coach Devus?"

The coach literally flung him into the desk before he stepped between Nick and Casey. "What?" he snarled down at her.

Grimacing, Nick straightened to watch the confrontation.

To Casey's credit, she didn't back down or flinch at

his irate tone. Dressed in a pair of tight jeans and her red cheerleading camp T-shirt, she was exceptionally cute today. She blinked in that vacuous way Nick was beginning to suspect was staged, and smiled. "Miss Dale wanted me to ask you for Friday night's schedule to make sure she knows what time to have us meet the buses. You can't do the play-offs without the cheerleaders, you know? We're a vital part of team motivation, and we've been working hard on new cheers for the game." She winked at Nick. "It's guaranteed to lift the players' morales."

Nick didn't dare comment on that.

The coach growled before he went to his desk and opened the drawer Nick had searched last. *Did I put everything back?* If something was out of place, the coach didn't notice—thanks to Casey's interference. Devus snatched a sheet of paper out, then slammed the drawer shut. "I already gave this to her."

Casey shrugged. "She said she misplaced it."

The coach cut his glare toward Nick. "There's a lot of that going around lately."

Ignoring the dig, Casey pranced to the desk to take

the paper from his hand. "Thank you, Coach Devus." Then she faced Nick. "Do you mind helping me for minute? I need someone who's tall or at least taller than me." She smiled back at Devus. "You don't mind my borrowing him, do you, Coach?"

His snarl deepened as he snatched a piece of paper from his clipboard. Folding it up, he held it out to Nick. "You better remember what you're doing, boy. You hear me?"

Nick nodded and then before he could stop it, the suicidal part of his personality blurted out. "That was three by five, right?"

His nostrils flared. "Five. By. Three. You better remember it."

"Got it." Nick tucked the paper into his back pocket as he silently cursed the coach.

"Thank you, Coach Devus," Casey said, holding the door open for Nick, who felt ill over the entire encounter.

How was he ever going to get out of this?

Casey led him toward the gym. But instead of heading into it, she pulled him toward the alcove where the vending machines were kept so that they would have a little privacy as the students started arriving for school.

"Are you okay?" The concern in her voice mystified him. If he didn't know better, he might think that she actually had feelings for him, but that was impossible.

"Yeah, why?"

He saw the panic in her eyes as she looked back toward Devus's office. "I thought he was going to hurt you, Nick. What did you do to him?"

Like he was dumb enough to answer . . . Well, there were times he was that stupid.

Today wasn't one of them.

"It was nothing."

"Nick," she chided, "that wasn't nothing. That was pure, ugly rage, and you're lucky he didn't rebreak your arm."

He wasn't recovering from a break. He'd been shot, but he didn't want to get into that with her, so he tried to move past her. Before he could make it, she had her hand in his pocket. The next thing he knew, she'd pulled the paper out and was reading it.

His stomach shrank as he tried to take it back. "Give me that."

She moved like a three-year-old avoiding her parent's attempt to take away a toy. "What is this?"

Irritated and annoyed, he stopped chasing her. There was no need if she kept prancing out of reach. All it was doing was making him angrier. "It's mine. Now, give it back."

She arched a brow at him.

"C'mon, it's nothing."

"Nothing?" she asked doubtfully. "It has a lot of . . . significant things on it. Stone's class ring? Have you any idea how much his parents paid for that? The ring rep actually called his father at home just to make sure it wasn't a mistake and that they meant to order something that cost that much."

Nick hissed at her. "Don't talk about this out loud. Okay?"

She walked up to him and lowered her voice. "Nick, tell me what's going on, or I'll go to the principal with this. I swear I will."

That was all he needed. He could see this scenario clear as day.

NICK: Uh, yeah, Mr. Dick, that's my steal list from the coach that he gave me. If I don't do it, he'll kill me. (Sounded nuts to the one who knew it wasn't. Imagine what it would sound like to someone who hated him.)

COACH: Gautier's a lying piece of trash. You know how they are. Come into the world as worthless thieves.

PRINCIPAL: Yes, they're all scheming scumbags out to steal anything not nailed down.

COACH: Here, let me call the police for you.

PRINCIPAL: Very well. I'll just sit here and look down my nose at him while you do that.

Yeah, it'd be some variation of that play. But no matter the exact scene, the ending would always be the same.

Him dead in jail.

No thank you.

"Casey . . ." He tried again to make her see reason. "This is between me and the coach. Leave it alone and let me have that paper back."

She sucked her breath in audibly between her teeth

as she pulled the sheet away from him. "I'm not real good at that. Especially not when I see something that looks like a shopping list, and don't think for one minute *I* don't know all about those."

Of course she would. Shopping was what she lived for.

I'm so screwed. "Please, I'm begging you to forget you saw that."

"Why?"

He had no choice but to be at least a little honest with her. "Because if you don't, I'll be in a *lot* of trouble."

And dead by morning. He shuddered at the mere thought.

She glared up at him as if debating whether or not to believe him. "Something tells me you're already in a lot of trouble. The coach has you stealing for him, too, doesn't he?"

Nick's jaw went slack at the last words he'd expected to come out of her mouth. "What?"

She gave him a cocky toss of her head. "I'm not as stupid as people think, you know? But when everyone thinks you are, you'd be amazed at what they'll talk about around you."

"Such as who's stealing for him?"

She nodded. "I overheard them talking about it a few days ago."

His heart sped up at the thought of having someone who could corroborate his story with the principal. If he could get a couple of the school pets to back him, he stood a chance of bringing the coach to justice. "Who?"

"Dave and Barry."

His stomach sank. Not good. Not good at all. "Barry Thornton?"

She nodded.

Both dead. Oh yeah, all of this was making sense now. The coach used who he could, then killed them off to keep them from telling on him. No wonder Ash had said the attack on Barry hadn't seemed right.

It wasn't.

Nothing more than human cruelty by a coward who was trying to cover his tracks. What a dog . . .

"You know anyone else?" he asked, hoping to salvage a little of his plan.

"No, just them." Dang her for dashing his hopes again.

Suddenly, her eyes widened. "You don't think he had any part in their deaths, do you?"

Absolutely, but he wasn't about to start slandering a school official when he had nothing to prove his suspicions. "Why do you say that?"

"Well, they stole for him and now they're both dead. What other conclusion can I draw?"

That Nick was screwed and probably soon to follow them to the grave himself.

He wanted to whimper as he realized just how inevitable that was. He *was* going to die a poor, pedestrian virgin. . . .

Why, Lord? Why?

She pulled him into the room, farther away from the student crowd that was quickly growing as people came in the back door of the school. "Okay, listen. I have a thought. How about I help you?"

His brain automatically snapped to his previous thought. *Nah, I ain't that lucky.* She had no idea why he feared dying so young. He must be misconstruing her intentions. "Help me do what?"

"Take what you need."

Oh, yeah right . . . "Are you out of your mind?" he snapped at her. "You can't do that, Casey."

"Of course I can. I don't want to see you killed. It's not right."

He couldn't agree more. However, he didn't want her to die for doing a good deed either. No need in both of them haunting the gym. "Maybe we can go to the principal. I know he won't believe me, but with you there, he—"

"I have no proof. Why would he listen to me?"

Nick shrugged. "You come from a good family. Why would *you* lie?"

"I don't know. The coach could tell him we're sleeping together or some other lie. You know how adults are. They never believe kids our age, and they're always expecting us to be on drugs or in trouble. Anytime something happens, they immediately blame it on the video games we play, cartoons we watch, music we listen to, or some occult thing that's as ludicrous as blaming D&D and RPG."

She was right. Most adults did do that, but he knew Kyrian and Ash would believe him.

And his mom might. . . .

Bubba and Mark would definitely, but since they also believed in Bigfoot, little green men, and the tooth fairy, no one would ever believe them. In fact, having them on board could be a liability.

Still, there was nothing any of them could do without proof. It all came back to that one word. The only way to bring the coach down would be to catch him in the act and to show the principal and everyone else just what a demented nut job he was.

"We've got to find other students he's blackmailed."

Casey scowled. "How?"

"I have no idea. But you know everyone at this school. Can't you find out something? How did you find out about Barry and Dave?"

"Same way I did you. On accident. They were talking, and I was walking by."

That wasn't helpful. They didn't have time for her to "accidentally" discover all the students Devus was harassing. She'd have to walk the hallway like a brainless automaton, which they'd then write up and put in detention.

The clock was ticking like the tell-tale heart, and

he had to steal items and get them to the coach before school let out, or literally his head would be on the chopping block. He could already feel the guillotine falling.

In the end, as much as he hated it, he had to agree with Casey's stupid idea. He couldn't do this alone and survive it.

I'm going to burn for this. . . .

"All right, Casey. We're not stealing anything, okay? We're borrowing it, and I will make sure to give it all back once we're done. You got it?"

"If you say so." She glanced over the list and selected her items. "I can grab Shannon's hairbrush and Stone's ring without a problem."

Not that he doubted her, but . . . "Really?"

She nodded. "Me and Stone are supposed to be dating. I smile at the oaf, and he'll let me have it back. For all the money his parents paid, he couldn't care less. To him it's only something that sits in a box or marks me as his property. I hate that whole territorial thing he does. I'm lucky he's not marking me in a more personal way."

Ew. There was a thought he didn't even want to

contemplate. *Where is the mental eye bleach when you need it?*

Not close enough. Obviously. "What else?"

"I can borrow Shannon's brush without a problem, too."

Good. That just left Nick to pick up his side of the partnership. "I can ask Mason if he'll loan me his notes from history." His handwriting was one of the things the coach needed for some reason. Made no sense to Nick, but far be it from him to try to educate a man with a college degree.

"What else?" she asked.

Nick glanced back and saw another easy target to procure. "Michael's always leaving one of his scarves in the cafeteria. I'm betting I can nab one of his out of lost and found."

Why a scarf? No clue. Maybe it was the big hulking man's security blanket, and he needed it for game days.

For that matter, maybe the coach was just strange.

Casey pointed down the list to another item. "I can get Kody's necklace."

Nick drew back at her offer. That was the one thing he had no intention of taking. "Absolutely not."

"No?"

"No," he repeated sternly.

She actually stomped her foot like a kid. "Why? You want to steal it?"

No, but he didn't want her to become a criminal either. How awkward would it be to take a date to the prom with a police escort? There were some things a guy didn't want to experience, and that was near the top of his list.

"We're not stealing, Casey. We're borrowing."

"Fine. I'll 'borrow'"—she made mocking air quotes around the word with her fingers—"her necklace."

And before Nick could protest that declaration, she was gone.

Come back, you little . . .

But there was nothing he could do. She'd left him in the dust.

Disgusted, he wished he could call her back without starting a scene. Unfortunately, there were too many students in the building now for him to use his powers.

And more were filing in through the doors.

Fine. He'd deal with Casey later. Right now, he had a scarf to find and some handwriting to borrow.

Ms. Grider kept her beady little eyes on him as he dug through the large box of unclaimed items the school kept in the checkout office. "Are you sure that's your scarf? I don't recall you ever having one before. Seems to me you don't have any coats either. All I remember you in are ragged jeans, hideous tourist shirts they sell cheap at the Goodwill, and worn-out shoes."

Nick cringed at the L&F Nazi's unrivaled memory. At 904 years old, her memory should be going by now, or so one would think. But apparently the only things she'd lost were her personality and human decency. "Well, Ms. Grider, if you remembered everything that belonged to everyone in the school, it seems we wouldn't really need a lost and found, would we?"

She glared at him. "That better be yours. I'm making a note of what it looks like and who's taking it."

Of course you are.

"If someone comes looking for it, I'm going to tell them exactly who took it."

With a fake smile, Nick shoved the scarf into his backpack and headed out the door. *The things I do for you, Mom.* If it were up to him, he'd drop out of this school and go to one where he wasn't a pariah. One where he was normal and these people were the freaks. But his mom wanted him to have the best education possible.

So here he was.

In hell for three and a half more years.

Again, *thanks Mom.*

As he headed toward his locker to switch out books, something moved fast to his right. Always on the lookout for Stone or his buds to ambush him, Nick jumped left and . . .

Nothing.

Frowning in confusion, he scanned the wall and saw no trace of whatever he'd glimpsed. Weird. A slow circle turn in the middle of the hall didn't uncover anything either as the sea of students moved around him.

But as he looked, everything slowed down like some

replay footage. The pendulum in his pocket heated up at the same time he felt Mark's necklace vibrate.

His ears buzzed, and some noxious smell filled his head.

"That better not be you again, Mark." He was in no mood for it.

No sooner had those words left his lips than the lights in the school went out. The screams of his classmates were deafening and thick . . . slowed down to match their current snail speed.

Out of nowhere, a bolt of lightning shot through his chest, picking him up from his feet and throwing him down the hallway.

CHAPTER 14

Nick couldn't breathe. It felt like his lungs had collapsed. He hit the wall above their lockers so hard, he wasn't sure how he didn't break through the concrete and crush every bone in his body. With nothing to catch him, he fell from the top of the wall, straight to the floor.

Dazed and tasting blood, he lay in a heap until something seized him by the shirt and shoved him against the wall. It pinned him there in an invisible fist that left him dangling.

"Are you the one?" The thick, monster voice wasn't speaking English, and yet he understood it somehow. "Are you?"

The one for what?

To bleed on his shoes? Check.

To dent the wall? Check.

To kick his demon butt . . .

Highly unlikely.

Nick clapped his hands over the creature's claw, trying to pry it away from his body. It was useless and rated right up there with stepping on Clark Kent's glasses. "Let me go!"

It pulled him closer to its nasty-smelling, bulbous body so that it could examine him. Then it slid him against something wet and slimy. What was that?

A nose?

Oh yeah, the thing was definitely sniffing him.

"Uh, gah! Get off me! What are you?"

"It's something ugly. Nick, get down."

He barely had time to duck in the thing's grasp before Caleb in full demon gear attacked it. The moment he did, the creature lost all interest in Nick as it turned to face Caleb.

Nick shot across the floor, to an area of relative safety so that he could figure out what was going on.

Walking backwards like a total badass, Caleb circled it, making it turn around to keep him in his line of sight. Dressed in gold battle armor that covered all but his glowing, evil snake eyes, Caleb made quite an impressive sight. Especially with the wingspan he had on his back. Two sheathed swords were crossed over his shoulders, but by his movements, Nick could tell Caleb could have those drawn and in the beast faster than anyone could say Liu Kang. Yeah, okay, so he looked more like Kano. But . . .

Liu Kang sounded cooler.

"Malphas . . ." The creature slurred his name into an insult. "I heard the Malachai had a lapdog. Who would have ever dreamed it was *you*?"

Caleb flinched. "Now, that just hurts me in my tender place, Bricis. Really? Was it necessary to add that insult?"

Ignoring him, Bricis jerked his chin toward Nick. "Is he the one?"

Caleb hit his breastplate twice to draw the creature's attention back to him. "Right now, I'm the only one you need to concern yourself with."

Bricis went for Caleb's throat. Caleb caught his hand, then kicked him into the wall. Holding on to its arm, Caleb twisted it and drove its head into the wall, then the lockers. Growling, it twisted out of his hold and backhanded him hard.

The two went at each other like Jet Li and Jackie Chan in a historical death match, slashing, punching, lunging, and dodging. It was a beautiful, macabre dance to a tune only they could hear. Nick was awed by their skills.

Man, to have a little bit of *that* . . .

At least that was his thought until Caleb stabbed Bricis, slicing open its arm. The moment that stanky blood fell to the ground, it manifested into demonic helpers who went for Caleb.

Not good.

He wasn't about to let his friend go down for protecting him. *Time to get your hands dirty.*

Yeah, right. What was he thinking? This wasn't like facing down a human coach. *You're about to get your butt kicked back to the Dark Ages. Maybe even the Stone Age. Them things got teeth like piranha.* And they were chewing on Caleb.

Man or a mouse, Nick?

Squeak.

As if. Cowardice wasn't in him. With a deep breath to brace himself for the additional pain he was about to be in, Nick ran at them. He caught the first one with fist to the gut.

It laughed like he'd tickled it.

Ah, snap. This was going to hurt, real bad.

But when it lunged at him, something miraculous happened. The same force that had taken control of him when he'd fought off the Mortents came back with a vengeance.

"No, Nick! Stop!" Caleb shouted.

Easier said than done. Whatever the power was, it radiated through him, raising his hair on end and washing him in a soft warm blanket of light. It was as if a part of him craved it and suckled on it the same way a baby craved his bottle. He needed this . . . whatever *this* was.

Caleb spoke in a language he couldn't decipher. Suddenly a cloak appeared in his hands.

One second, Nick was hovering in the hall, beating off the sprout demons; the next, he'd been shoved into a locker. "Hey!" he shouted at Caleb. "I'm not Madaug! Why did you do this?"

Outside, he heard Caleb continue fighting Bricis and his blood minions.

"Where did he go, Malphas?" Bricis asked, as if he couldn't hear Nick calling out to them.

Caleb drew his swords and twisted them around his body in a beautiful and flawless display of power and skill. "He's no concern of yours. He's not what you think."

Bricis snorted a denial. "You wouldn't defend him unless he was."

"You don't know me. At all."

Bricis laughed as it and its offshoots pummeled Caleb with everything they had.

Nick struggled to get out of the cloak and rejoin the fight, but the harder he fought to escape, the tighter it wrapped itself around him. When he tried to call out to Caleb again, the cloak covered his mouth and stifled him.

What the—?

Angry and desperate, he had no choice except to eat this degradation while Caleb fought alone.

I have to do something. Wait. He knew.

"Ambrose!"

I know what you want, Nick, and I can't interfere.

Even though he knew it was futile, Nick continued to struggle. "What do you mean you can't interfere?"

There are rules, and if I intervene for Caleb, it would endanger you more. No offense, but you mean a lot more to me than he does.

"I don't care about me. Caleb's my friend. I don't want to see him hurt for trying to help me."

Ambrose snorted. *Caleb is not your friend. Never, ever make that mistake, or you will be sorry.*

Nick didn't buy that for a second. He knew better. "How do I know you're not the one lying to me?"

He could feel the presence of Ambrose's disgust with him. *Do we have to play this game again? I'm tired of it. No wonder Kyrian was always losing patience. Now I'm surprised he never killed you over it.*

That sent a shiver over him. "What do you mean?"

Patience, Nick. Patience. Caleb can hold his own. Believe me. He's fought much bigger and badder and meaner.

It didn't sound that way to him. It sounded like a bloodbath.

Nick leaned forward so that he could look out the metal slits. There was blood all over the hallway and on the walls. It poured out over Caleb's armor from numerous wounds.

Look, kid, I can't stay here. The longer I do, the more dangerous it becomes.

"Coward!" But it was too late. Ambrose was already gone. "Yeah, run. You're just like your brother, you worthless scum! Leave a friend to die for you. You sicken me!"

Still Ambrose didn't answer.

Fine. Not like he meant anything to Nick, anyway. His uncle was cut from the same wicked cloth as his father. They deserved each other.

All of a sudden, it was quiet again outside. Leaning forward, he had to squint to see what was happening.

A giant green blob sizzled against the far wall, smoldering against the light blue cinder blocks. Between Caleb's bleeding form and the blob, purple stains marred the tan tiled floor. Panting and clutching a bloodied sword, Caleb looked straight at him. He tucked his wings in as his armor melted into clothing. His scales flipped back over into human skin. The last things to change were those eerie serpentine eyes that glowed bright.

Caleb ran his hands through his hair before he closed the distance to the locker and opened it.

Nick fell out at his feet.

With a sound of disgust, Caleb stared down at him. "Was that really necessary?"

Nick tried to respond, but the cloth was still in his mouth.

"I know I'm going to regret this, but—" He snapped his fingers and Nick was released.

Nick came to his feet ready to choke him as he shoved the cloth away. "What do you think—?" He broke off as he realized Caleb was badly wounded. "Dude, you all right?"

"Need a minute to push the pain down before I free the others."

"Free—?" Again, Nick hesitated as he realized the students around him were moving so slowly now, you could barely detect it. They appeared caught in a time warp of some kind. "What's going on?"

"It's the same concept that will one day allow you to fly. You can manipulate time and move through its stream unseen. I slowed them so that we could battle and they wouldn't freak and be hurt by it."

Nick was aghast at what he described. They could really do that?

Wicked fun.

Except for the stain on the wall. He inclined his head to it. "What was that thing?"

Caleb leaned back against the wall. "Fringe Hunter. Nasty one, too."

"He wanted me?"

"No." Caleb wiped a hand across his damp forehead. "He was after another."

"That's not what he said. He kept asking if I was the one."

Caleb squinted at him. "That was something else that was aside from you. He wouldn't have gone after you at all had you not exposed yourself to him."

Excuse me? I do believe I kept it in my pants. "Meaning what?"

Caleb gestured toward the remains. "You cannot

use your powers unless you're around someone who can shield you. Dammit, Nick! You could have died. Do you not understand that? When I tell you something, you have got to listen. You idiot."

He remembered what Ambrose had said about Caleb's loyalty. "Why do you care?"

Caleb curled his lip into an expression that was purely demonic. "I don't. Really. You die and I walk free. To me, that would be a great day."

"Then why protect me?"

Caleb looked away from him as if the sight of Nick sickened him.

But Nick wanted answers, and he wasn't going to stop until he had some. "What aren't you telling me?"

"It's like a bad movie, Nick. You were born the most cursed and blessed of any creature. An abomination that should never have been created, and yet, here you are. Like an unprotected infant who has no understanding of the world that created it. No understanding of the power and destruction you're capable of. That you're destined to kill everyone who loves you. Everyone you love."

His heart pounded at what Caleb described.

No, it wasn't true. He refused to believe it. He would never kill the people he loved. It wasn't in him.

"You're lying to me," he accused Caleb.

"It's true. You're a plague, Nick. A pox on the—"

"Stop it, Malphas! Don't you dare."

Nick gaped at Kody's outraged tone. Astonished beyond belief, he turned to see her approaching them from the south hallway.

Why wasn't she frozen like the rest of their school? Instead, she was moving every bit as freely as they were.

Caleb sneered as she joined them. "I would suggest you leave us. This doesn't concern you."

She scoffed at his curt dismissal. "Of course it does. What are you trying to do?"

"He needs to know the truth. Not glossed over and prettied up. The pure, unvarnished truth of what he is and what he will do. If we were smart, we'd kill him now and do the world a favor."

She gestured at Caleb. "Do you hear yourself?"

"Like you wouldn't cut his throat if you were told

to do so? Go ahead, Nekoda. Tell him who *you* work for."

Panic darkened her eyes as she refused to meet his gaze.

This wasn't good. Just when he thought he could trust someone, they turned out to be . . .

What?

"Kody? Are you a demon, too?" Nick asked, desperate to know what he was dealing with now.

"No," Caleb said in a breathless tone. "She's something that makes us look kind."

Nick swallowed hard with that realization. There was something worse than a demon? That thought was highly sobering. "What are you, then?"

Caleb raked her with a smirk. "Humanity doesn't have a word for her. She's absolute agony."

Kody glared at him. "And what are you?"

"In a word? Damned."

Nick had heard enough. "And I'm gone." Before he could move, they both threw their hands out and froze him in place.

This feeling of being a fly trapped on flypaper was

getting really old. If they kept this up, he'd start charging them rent for the time of his they were eating alive with nonsense.

Kody shook her head. "This is not how I wanted him to find out about me. I was supposed to be incognito. Thanks for outing me, Malphas."

He gave her a fake bow. "My pleasure. Anything to ruin your day."

She cast a meaningful glare at his groin. "Yeah and I'm about to ruin your nights, lover boy. For eternity."

Caleb snorted. "What else is new? Not like I have free time, anyway."

"I don't understand where your head is," she said in a disgusted tone. "How can you be so cold after everything?"

"I'm tired, Nekoda. Unlike you, I don't get a break from my hellish existence. And I don't see why we're doing this ridiculous dance when we both know how this play ends. Prophecy is prophecy. Nothing ever changes it. Nothing."

She disagreed. "And human will is the strongest force ever created. There are those born to succeed and those who are determined to succeed. The former fall into it, and the latter pursue it at all costs. They won't be denied. Nothing daunts them."

Caleb rolled his eyes. "Do you really believe what you're spouting?"

"Yes."

"Look me in the eye and tell me that you've never once had a single doubt."

She screwed her face up. "Of course I have. Without doubt there can be no faith."

Shaking his head, Caleb stepped around her. "And I grow sick of your pithy little sayings. Really. Change your tune, hon."

Kody didn't try to stop Caleb from walking away from them.

"What's going on, Kody? Who are you? What are you doing here?"

She appeared heartsick. "Think of me as a guardian."

"For what?"

"I can't tell you that. It's forbidden."

Like everything else seemed to be these days. It

was really getting old to have no real answers. "Are you here to kill me?"

She shook her head. "I'm an observer who reports your progress to others."

"What?"

"It's true, Nick. Like Caleb, I'm here to watch over you, but for a whole other reason. We have to make sure that you stay human and that your feelings don't wither and die."

"Why?"

"Because when you stop caring about anyone or anything, Nick, you will become a pawn and a slave to some of the darkest powers ever created. When that happens, you will destroy the world."

CHAPTER 15

It wasn't every day you found out that you were destined to destroy the world. And as those words slammed into Nick, he felt as sluggish and lost as the people barely moving in the air around him. Like he was going in slow motion, attempting to catch up.

"What are you saying?" he asked Kody, trying to get a handle on this moment.

"It's true, Nick. It's why so many creatures are after you right now. If they can capture you while you're weak, they can harness your powers and use them for their own gain."

"I won't let them do that."

She inclined her head to him. "That's what we're

here to ensure. Caleb and I are your protectors. He for your body and I for your mind."

Huh? Other than the fact he was insane, there wasn't anything wrong with his mind. Why would it need its own protector. "That doesn't make sense."

"Of course it does. Think about it for a second. Your goodness and your free will are all that keep you from breaking and becoming apathetic. You have to hold on to that part of yourself always."

"And if I don't?"

"You know the answer."

He would kill everyone, and all the people around him would cease to exist. He shook his head. "I don't think I like this. I don't want this power. Take it away from me."

"I can't. No one can. And right now, you don't have the power either. You're just an embryo."

Maybe there was time. Maybe . . .

"Then I won't learn it." If he never embraced his powers, they couldn't be used by anyone, not even him. That should protect everyone.

Kody gave him no reprieve. "You have to. If you refuse, your hand will be forced one way or another, and everyone you love will pay the price. You have to become strong enough to protect yourself and those around you. It's the only hope any of you have. It's the only hope any of us have. Don't you understand, Nick?"

"No. I don't understand." He felt like the entire world was caving in on him. He had a principal dying to send him to jail. A coach out to kill him. A boss who was an immortal vampire slayer. His two best friends were certifiable, and a pseudo girlfriend who'd just told him he was the ultimate bomb that would end the world.

I'm not old enough to cope with this.

He was just a kid.

Unable to breathe, he met Kody's gaze. "I want to go back and be normal again. Forget all this. I want to spend mindless hours playing video games and—"

"Nick, you've never been irresponsible, and you know it."

It was true. But . . .

He could learn. He was willing to.

Stop it. Since the moment he'd been born, he'd had to take care of his mother. Watch out for her.

And . . .

The spell on his classmates broke. In the blink of an eye, everything went back to normal with a loud, angry rush. None of them the wiser for the battle that had been fought right in the middle of them while they scurried along, trying to make class before the next bell. None of them seeing the remains that had already faded to nothing more than his bad memory.

Except him.

Nick knew, and he'd never be normal again.

It's a lie. She's messing with you.

But deep down inside, he knew better. This wasn't a lie. It felt like the truth.

I won't do it. I won't.

You said that about stealing, and what are you doing?

Given the right stimulus, anyone was capable of anything. Bubba had hammered that thought into him repeatedly. Even Mother Teresa could be moved to violence if the right buttons were pushed.

Nick had never been too sure of that analogy, and yet . . .

"I need a break for minute."

Kody moved toward him. "You want me to stop—?"

"No!" he snapped, terrified of what she might do. "I don't want any kind of hocus-pocus or anything else. I just want to sit here for a minute and think."

The bell sounded.

He needed to get to class and start his day. He had a list of things to steal for his coach. . . .

That was laughable, given everything else going on. "Can I be killed?" he asked her, wondering exactly who and what he was.

"Oh yeah."

"What happens if I die?"

"Honestly, we're not completely sure. Other than your father's powers will continue to grow until—"

"Wh-wh-whoa-what? My father?"

She nodded. "Where do you think all of this came from? You were born to be your father's replacement. Once you are safe, he will have to surrender."

"Surrender or die?"

"If he doesn't yield his title willingly, he will be killed."

Well, that explained why the man hated him so badly. Why he couldn't stand to even look at him. Out of everything else he'd learned, that actually made him feel a little better. For the first time in his life, he understood his father.

And . . .

"The stuff my dad told the police about demons attacking him—"

"All true, and those forces will now be after you, too."

"Move, Gautier, you worthless hobo." Stone shoved him hard as he passed by.

Nick started after him, only to find Kody in the way. "That's the kind of reaction that will cause you to fail. It will lead your enemies to your door. Is Stone really worth that?"

No.

Maybe?

"What about my mom?"

"You already know the answer."

He was her protector, too. Always the man of the house. "If I died—"

"Your father would have another child. That one won't have your humanity. Your mother is what makes you special, Nick. Adarian's next woman wouldn't be her. His child wouldn't be you. All of us are a culmination of vital parts of our parents and their pasts. A vital part of the circumstances we were raised with. Everything that happens to us, good and bad, leaves a lasting impression in our souls. You take one part of that out, and you can completely rewrite something crucial about us. By and large, we're not shaped by the big things. It's the little, day-to-day moments that make us who we are. Who we're going to be."

His head was pounding from trying to digest all of this.

"I'm so overwhelmed."

"Most of us are, Nick. Even though we look calm and peaceful on the outside, most of us are barely hanging on by our fingernails. You know why Bubba watches *Oprah* every day?"

"He's insane?"

She shook her head slowly. "It was his wife's favorite show, and she died while watching it."

That news floored him every bit as much as the news of who he really was. "Bubba was married?"

"Bubba was a father."

He gaped. Bubba a dad? How was it possible he didn't know this? "Did she leave him?"

"Not willingly. She was home sick from work, tending the baby when someone broke into their house and killed them. Bubba came home from work to find them, and he had a nervous breakdown shortly there-after. He quit his high-tech, high-paying job and opened his store so that he could provide the world with the security and arms they needed to protect what they loved. It's why he prowls the night, looking for other predators out to take innocent lives. It's why he can't sleep and why he seems so obsessed. He is."

And that explained the free classes he taught at night on how to survive. The self-defense classes where he recruited as many women and kids as he could get. The reason why he kept everyone at a distance at times.

Everything made sense now.

Nick felt sick over what she described. "None of that was a small decision. It all looks pretty major from here."

"You're looking at the big picture that's made up of tiny little dots. Like that painting of a picnic on the beach. From a distance, it looks like a well-defined picture, but up close you can see all the tiny pinpricks that give the bigger illusion. Bubba's wife decided to leave work early and go straight home and not to the doctor. She decided to pick up their baby from the sitter and to wait to go to the grocery store for supplies. She'd asked Bubba to come home early, too, but he'd decided that he needed to work. Had just one of those tiny variables changed, his entire life would be completely different."

"Or would it?"

Kody arched a brow.

"If she'd left the baby with its sitter, she'd still be dead. How would that change anything?"

"With an infant to feed, Bubba wouldn't have dedicated himself to his store. He would have wrapped himself around the child, and that would be the focus of his world."

"How do you know that?"

"Look in your heart, and you know the answer."

He did, but he wasn't ready to accept it yet.

Kody leaned forward to whisper in his ear. "Had

you not gone to see your mother the night you were shot . . . had you headed home as you were supposed to after work, you wouldn't have met Kyrian. Your mother would still be—"

"I get it." Had he not stood up to Alan, Kyrian wouldn't have saved his life either. Kyrian would have thrown him in with the rest of the riffraff.

One little decision.

One life-altering event.

"How will we ever know when those important moments come?"

"That's why you have to learn your powers. You've heard the sayings, and they're absolutely true. Fore-warned is forearmed. Knowledge is power. By under-standing the nuances of the world around you and how to survive the temptations, you can rule anything. Even yourself."

"Master of my own destiny."

"Precisely."

"Master of your destiny, Mr. Gautier?" Mrs. Rich-ardson mocked as she neared them. "The only thing you're going to be master of is detention. You're late.

Both of you." She handed them write-ups. "Now, get to class before Cinderella turns both of those into suspensions."

Nick let out a frustrated breath. Beautiful.

Kody squeezed his hand. "You'll be fine, Nick. You have me and Caleb here. We're not leaving you."

"You still haven't told me what you are."

"I'm your friend. That's all that matters."

It's not the enemy from without who is the most lethal. He didn't know why that thought went through his head, but it did. Was it his subconscious trying to tell him something?

Or was it more paranoia?

Why was life so dang hard? Why did every decision have to be rough? Unable to cope anymore, he headed for his classroom while he tried to sort through some of this.

But in the end, he kept coming back to the same questions. Could something that had been conceived of darkness ever be used for good? What made someone evil?

Was it their birth or their life?

Did they control the direction of their fate or did something else?

A guy could lose his mind trying to sort all that out. He definitely felt like he was going crazy. And all the while, he was gathering up items for a cause he knew was wrong. *I'm making a bad decision.*

But what choice did he really have?

He couldn't go to jail, and he couldn't let the coach continue to prey on people. Someone had to stop him. For now, he'd play along, and somehow he'd find the evidence he needed to put a stop to the coach's corruption.

Then he'd find a way to stop his own.

At three o'clock, Nick was standing in Devus's office, feeling even worse than he had felt that morning. He didn't know why, but it was like he was selling out his brethren. Offering his classmates up for slaughter.

How stupid was that?

Yet he couldn't shake the sensation.

"What do you have, Gautier?"

"Bad case of indigestion, sir," he answered sarcastically. Something that didn't endear him to Coach Predator.

"Should I call the principal, then?"

"No." Nick emptied his pockets on the desk. He had the hairbrush, two writing samples from two students on his list, the scarf, and . . .

He hesitated with the class ring that Casey had given him after lunch—he'd told her to hold off on going after Kody's necklace. She had no idea what a challenge that little bit was going to give her, and he didn't want Kody to disembowel her in the hallway and make her another stain on the wall.

Nick looked down at the heavy ring in his hand that glinted in the dim light of the room. The bright stone in the center was as red as blood and surrounded by small diamonds that winked at him. Unlike the other items that he could write off his conscience, this one was definitely theft, and guilt tore at him. He felt like his dad, and he hated the coach most of all for giving him that sensation.

I won't be that man.

But right now. In this one moment . . .

He was.

Wincing, Nick held it out. So much for Devus not wanting him to hand stuff to him during school hours.

Devus grinned as he palmed it. "Good boy. You've bought yourself a reprieve. Now, get out there and finish the list, or I *will* finish you."

He took too much pleasure in causing pain. *Like my father.* The comparison really ate at him. Unfortunately, there was nothing he could do. In fifteen minutes, school would be out and he'd have to hustle to make it over to the St. Louis cemetery for his next lesson with Grim.

Nick turned to leave, but the coach stopped him. "Tell you what, Gautier. Why don't you skip practice today and make sure that I have four more items in the morning?"

"Or what?" The coach's tone had implied there was definitely an ultimatum in there.

"You're a smart kid. I think you know the answer."

I go to jail and die. "Can I ask a question?"

"What?"

"Why did you pick me for this?"

"You're a pathetic waste with nothing to lose. If you died tomorrow, no one would even know you were gone."

Nick ground his teeth. That wasn't true. His mother's life would be shattered. She'd never be the same. While the rest of the world would go on, she wouldn't. He knew that. And in that moment, he fully realized something.

How many lives one life touched. Not always with a major impact, but in little ways.

If he died, Liza would have to unload her deliveries alone. Yes, she could do it without him, but she always claimed to enjoy spending a few minutes chatting with him while he did it. She looked forward to his visits. Mennie wouldn't have anyone to take out her trash or clean the yard. Kyrian wouldn't have someone who busted his chops, and Acheron wouldn't have a human friend who knew all about his weirdness.

Not big things. It was the little things in life that really mattered.

He leaned forward over the desk. "There you're wrong, Coach."

The coach looked up with a smug sneer. "How so?"

Nick returned that sneer with a pompous smile he was sure set the coach's ire on fire. "I assure you if your garbage men stopped picking up your trash, you'd miss them real fast and want them back. No life, no matter what *you* think, is insignificant. Everyone has a purpose. Even you."

Devus sputtered while Nick turned around and left him to it. For the first time in his life, Nick felt like he was experiencing the real world for what it was. Like blinders had been ripped off his face and he saw the sunshine in all its natural glory.

Beautiful. Breathtaking.

And even though he wasn't certain about his future, for this one moment in time, he was thrilled to be alive.

As soon as the bell sounded, Nick grabbed his backpack and headed for the cemetery to meet Grim. Kody and Caleb had pretty much avoided him after their morning encounter with the Fringe Guard. Kody seemed sad about it.

Caleb's anger was so potent, it scared him.

There was something more going on with the demon than he was letting on. And since Nick couldn't fight him without dying, he decided to leave the demon be until he came to terms with whatever was eating at him.

It didn't take long to walk the handful of blocks up to the cemetery, which rested on the northwest side of the Quarter, one block outside of it between Conti Street and St. Louis on Basin. The white plaster walls that surrounded it spanned an entire block and shielded the massive city of the dead, where more than a hundred thousand former New Orleanians had been laid to rest. Some of the most notable people of the city were interred here.

Because New Orleans was so far below sea level that buried bodies had a nasty way of returning to the land of the living, the city had been forced to find another way to deal with the departed. Above ground tombs and mausoleums had been erected, which was what led to these areas being referred to as the cities of the dead. The grossest thing was that most of the tombs were shared spaces, usually with a single family, but sometimes with groups such as the massive Italian monument in the center. Once someone died, their remains were put on top of someone else who'd decomposed. It was why the city had a law that no tomb could be opened for a full year and a day—giving the bodies enough time to fully decay before the next one was added. He didn't know what they did with someone if they needed a tomb before that time elapsed, and he didn't want to know.

Some questions really didn't need answering, and that was definitely one of them.

Shoving that thought away, he headed through the black iron gate that was opened so that tourists and tour groups as well as loved ones could access the cemetery during the daylight hours.

Honestly, the cemetery was beautiful in a creepy kind of way. The elaborate tombs and statues went off in every direction, some dwarfing him. While most were white, others were brightly colored, and all manner of images and wrought iron decorations had been used to add flavor and beauty to the crypts.

"Boo."

Nick cursed as Grim appeared behind him and startled the crap out of him. "Don't do that!"

"Jumpy, are we?"

"We are in a cemetery, you know."

Grim laughed. "Of course I know. It's one of my favorite places."

"Yeah, well, not mine. I don't make it a habit of spending a lot of time here. I figure since one day I'll be a permanent resident, there's no need to rush and visit it while I'm not."

"I love the way you look at things, kid. Now follow me."

Nick did until he noticed that Grim didn't have a single shadow.

He had three.

"What the—?"

Grim paused to look at him over his shoulder. "What?"

Nick pointed to the shadows. "What's up with you?"

"You know my friends. Pain and Suffering were on

my nerves, so I relegated them to shadow status for the day." He continued forward.

Nick wasn't sure he liked that, but he knew better than to argue. Picking up the pace, he closed the distance between them. Grim didn't stop again until he reached the far back end, where one of the sarcophagi reminded Nick of a table. Images of death and angels were carved all over the intricate stonework.

"I think this will do for our next lesson." Grim skimmed his hand over the surface without touching it. A cloth appeared, shielding the blackened surface. "Much better." He held his hand out to Nick. "Have you been practicing?"

"For all the good it hasn't done me. Yeah." He handed the pendulum and book to Grim.

"Have you made friends with the pendulum?"

"Kind of one-sided if you ask me, but yeah. I think so."

Grim sighed irritably. "Fine. Today I wanted to show you how you can locate someone with your pendulum."

"Wouldn't calling them be easier?"

He passed a droll stare at him. "What if the phone doesn't work, Nick? Or you don't have their number. Better yet, what if you don't really know who you're hunting, but you still need to find them."

"Why would I waste time hunting for someone I don't know?"

Grim clenched his teeth. "Why would you waste time playing senseless video games for hours on end?"

"'Cause that's fun."

"And this can be lifesaving."

Yeah, okay, that might be better than mastering *Mario*.

Maybe.

As Grim opened the book to a blank page, a tourist came around the corner and gasped, then quickly retreated. A devilish grin lit his face. "Hold that thought."

Nick frowned as Death turned into a dark gray vapor and made a quick exit. A few seconds later, he heard a loud scream followed by the sound of running feet.

When Grim returned, he was beaming in satisfaction. "Aw, fear. How I love the fragrance."

"You are so sick, Grim."

"And one day, you will learn to take pleasure in the small things as well."

Yeah, but after what he'd learned about himself today, he hoped it wasn't from harming others. Even mildly.

"Now, where were we?"

"Finding lost things."

"Yes, yes." Grim returned, and a map of New Orleans appeared in the book.

"How do you get it to do that for you? Whenever I try something like that, it back-talks me."

"Much like a child, the book knows it can get away with back-talking you. I have no love or tolerance for it. If it annoys me, I will burn it without reservation."

Ah, intimidation did work. Who knew?

"Now," Grim said, drawing his attention back to the map. "Tell me someone you'd like to find."

Problem was, he knew where everyone lived who was important to him.

Everyone except Kody.

"Nekoda," he said to the pendulum. "Show me where Nekoda is."

Grim handed him the chain.

Nick hovered it over the map, and nothing happened. "This is a waste."

"No. Learning is never a waste. What you're doing right now is discovering how not to make a lightbulb."

"Huh?"

Grim shook his head. "I've said it before, and I'll say it again. Educate yourself, kid. All right, the pendulum isn't working. Sometimes you need an accelerant to help it."

"Like gasoline?"

"Yes, Nick. We're going to set the book and your pendulum on fire and then use them 'cause we're just that intelligent."

"Knock the sarcasm, okay? I've had a really bad day."

"You keep lipping off, and I can assure you it will get worse."

Nick cleared his throat as he reminded himself this wasn't someone he could be himself around. "Sorry. You were saying?"

"Do you have anything of Nekoda's?"

"Uh, yeah. I have her Nintendo she lent me and a pencil. Why?"

"Do you have one with you?"

"Both."

"Give me the Nintendo, since that is more uniquely hers. Whenever you're doing something like this, you want an item that means something to the person you seek. Such things can tell you a lot and aid you immensely."

Like his book and pendulum that Grim had told him to guard with his life . . .

Oh, no. A really bad feeling went through him.

Nick bit his lip as he balled the pendulum up in his hand. "You told me that things like that can be used to control someone, right?"

"Yes."

"Can it do anything else?"

Grim nodded. "Lots of things."

"Such as?"

Grim considered it a moment before he answered. "You can use it to bind them to a spell. Manipulate them. There are things you could do for good, such as help them with motivation or retrieve something else they've lost, but few entities do that. Usually it's reserved for hurting someone. Why?"

"Because I think I finally understand what Devus is up to."

"Who?"

"Never mind." It still didn't really make sense. Devus knew where everyone lived. All he had to do was access their student files.

Which meant Devus must be using the stolen items to control or manipulate them. But for what? The football team could be for the play-offs, but Kody and the ones not on the team . . .

Something wasn't right. He needed more information.

"Are you paying attention, Nick?"

"Absolutely. Undivided. Lead on."

Grim grimaced before he continued. "Okay, you can—"

"Can you use the item to test for something?"

"Stop interrupting me," Grim snarled. "Or I will skin you."

"Sorry . . . but can you?"

Grim let out a long-suffering sigh. "This is why I don't have children and why I've spent eternity avoiding them at all costs." He met Nick's gaze. "Yes. You could use the item to test for something personal about the owner."

"Like what?"

"Anything. Do they bake? Are they smart? Are they going to die for irritating me, et cetera."

"Yeah, I don't like that last one."

"I really don't care." Grim picked up the Nintendo.

Nick's phone started ringing.

Cursing, Grim glared at him.

"Sorry. I forgot to turn it to vibrate." Nick looked down at the number. It was Mark. "Um. I need to take this call. Is that okay?"

"Oh, by all means. Go ahead and hold up Death for that. It's such a smart move on your part." That sarcasm was thickest of all.

Nick knew it was stupid to taunt the being, but . . .

He answered the phone.

"Where are you?" Mark asked.

"St. Louis Number One. Why?"

"I just remembered where I saw your coach. And boy, you ain't gonna believe this one."

And boy, if you don't put that phone down, you're not going to live to draw another breath. . . .

CHAPTER 16

Ever irritated Death? Not recommended you try it even on the tiniest level.

Suffice it to say, the Grim Reaper was not long on patience, and if you really must press your luck with him, the best way to survive it was to be born of the ultimate evil and have him fear you screwing up unlocking your powers as much you feared screwing up unlocking your powers.

Only that could save your life.

Nick tried his best to pay attention, but his curiosity over Mark's discovery was killing him. While he was dying to know what they'd found, but he didn't want to die to know. If that made sense. And if he didn't pay attention and stop fidgeting, he still might become a stain on the pebbled walkway under his feet. . . .

This was the longest lesson of his life. Forget Richardson's class. Pendulum swinging was starting to bring tears of boredom to his eyes.

By the time they were through, he felt as though he'd been tortured on the rack. The most aggravating part was that Grim had refused to show him what he really wanted to know.

"We're working on my timetable, kid. Not yours. You follow me. I dance to no one's tune but my own." Really. Grim would make an awesomely annoying parent.

Ugh. But now that they were through, Nick was running full speed to the Triple B to catch up with Mark and Madaug.

By the time he reached the store, he was winded and exhausted. And his backpack had picked up an extra thirty, forty thousand pounds somewhere along the way. *At least it's not summertime.* That would have made his run excruciating.

Opening the door that was now fully repaired and in proper operating order, he headed for the counter.

Bubba came out of the back room to greet him. "Oh, it's you, Nick. I thought I might have a paying customer. Should have known."

"Thanks, Bubba. Love you, too."

He rolled his eyes before he wandered back toward the curtains. "Mark's in the office with Madaug. They said to send you in as soon as you arrived."

Nick paused as he watched Bubba close the tower shell on a computer, then move it to the pickup shelf for the owner to reclaim. He had to give Mark and Bubba credit as he glanced around the back area. They'd done an amazing job putting the store back together. There weren't hardly any signs that it'd ever been damaged, never mind burned, shot, and attacked with an ax.

Best not to remind Bubba of that, since Nick had been the one wielding it.

"Did they tell you why they wanted to see me?"

Bubba pulled down the next system waiting to be repaired and hooked it into the periphals, then started booting it up to run a diagnostic. "Nah, and I don't care. As long as you girls don't burn down my store, I'm happy in my ignorance."

Nick decided not to question that at all, given the damage they'd already wreaked, but as he neared the office door, he remembered what Kody had told him about his friend's past. Was any of that true at all?

Don't ask it, Nick. Don't.

But as was typical, his mouth took off without consulting his common sense or his brain. "Bubba? Can I ask you something?"

"Sure."

"Were you ever married?"

There was no mistaking the grief on his face over that normal question. The agony. The self-loathing. How awful that four simple words, one harmless question, could wring that much pain out of someone.

Bubba cleared his throat before he answered. "Yeah, I was. Long time ago."

Having inadvertently hurt him, Nick wanted to make Bubba feel better, but he didn't know how. He shouldn't have asked. He shouldn't have. And after seeing Bubba's reaction, he knew Kody had been telling him the truth. The man was eaten up with guilt. "I'm sorry, Bubba."

"For what?"

"You look real upset all of a sudden. I didn't mean to bring up an unhappy memory. Sorry."

Bubba swallowed hard as he turned to face him. "Nick . . . I hope one day you find you a woman who loves you like my Melissa loved me. Whatever you do, boy, don't turn your back on her. If she says she needs you for something, don't matter how stupid it sounds or what deadline you got, you go to her and you do it. Screw work or whatever else. In the end, the only things that matter are the people in your life. The ones who make your life worth living and whose smiles light up your world. Don't ever push them aside for fair-weather friends. Everything else is just cheap window dressing that you can replace. But once them people are gone . . ."

He winced. "You can't buy back time, Nick. Ever. It's the only thing in life you can't get more of, and it's the one thing that will mercilessly tear you up when it's gone. It takes pity on no soul and no heart. And all those fools who tell you it gets easier in time are lying dumb-asses. Losing someone you really love don't never get easier. You just go a few hours longer without breaking down. That's all . . . that's all."

Tears choked him at the pain he heard in Bubba's voice. It was rare for him to show that kind of emotion. Big Bubba Burdette was a growling bear of a man. Huge. Tough as nails. Never let anything bother him.

And loyal to the end.

Everyone deserved a friend like him.

Who would ever have thought that such a fearsome, larger-than-life beast could be haunted by something so human as the loss of his wife and child?

Without thinking, Nick went over and hugged him hard.

Bubba bristled. "Boy, what are you doing? Have you lost your ever-loving mind?"

Nick shook his head. "You looked like you could use a hug."

"Then call up Tyra Banks and send her over. That I'm always up for. Don't want no straggly teenager rubbing up against me. Jeez."

"Yeah, yeah. I hear you, you old grump."

Bubba scoffed. "Not that old. Not that wise. But still filled with enough venom to spank your butt if you don't leave me alone to my work. Now get on with you and get out of what little hair I got left."

Nick headed back to the office, but before he opened the door, Bubba stopped him.

"Hey, Nick? You're a good kid. Don't let anyone tell you different. I see how you come in here some days after school with your shoulders hanging down from the weight of the world and all its misery. But don't let them steal your day, boy. I know about your daddy and how you walk around with his ghost riding your back all the time. But those are his sins and his crimes, not yours." Bubba tapped his chest twice. "You got what counts right here. All you need and then some. More heart and more kindness than anyone I've ever met. Don't let anyone take it from you. You hear me?"

"Thanks, Bubba."

He inclined his head, then went back to work.

Feeling better than he had all day, Nick opened

the door to find Madaug and Mark spread out over Bubba's desk with what appeared to be hundreds of printed-out pages scattered everywhere. They were so intent on whatever they'd found that they didn't even hear him enter.

"Hey, guys. What's all this?"

Mark glanced up with his eyes so wide, they looked like saucers. "Hold on to your bootstraps, 'cause you're about to be blown out of your shoes."

"I take it you found something good?"

"Not just good," Madaug said. His blond curls were sticking out over his head like he'd been tugging at them—something he did unawares whenever he concentrated on a subject. "Incredible."

It was hard to take him seriously with his glasses askew and so smudged with fingerprints that it made Nick wonder how he didn't walk into walls. It strangely reminded Nick of his mother's favorite comedy, *My Cousin Vinny,* when Joe Pesci was interrogating the witness about what he'd seen through his scum-infested windows on his trailer.

Oblivious of that, Madaug dug under the stack of

papers in front of him. Wearing a gray sweatshirt that swallowed him whole—no doubt a hand-me-down from his older brother Eric's non-Goth days, Madaug smiled as he found what he'd been searching for. He shoved it in Nick's face.

Nick tilted his head back and took it from him so that he could hold it at a normal, viewable distance. He frowned. It was some old-timey football team, wearing antique clothes.

Dang, the players looked like old men and not college students. How hard did their ancestors live?

"What do you see?" Mark asked.

"Football."

"Yeah, and—?" he prompted.

Before Nick could answer, Madaug pointed at the man in the back on the far left-hand side. "Meet Coach Walter Devus."

Whoa. The guy was a dead ringer for the coach at their school. It must be his great-grandfather or something.

"I knew I'd seen him before." Mark tapped the sheet. "When I played at Tech, they had a wall of

honor for all the teams, and this one was hung by . . .
well someplace I spent a lot of time with a certain bi-
ology tutor. But that doesn't matter. I knew I'd seen
him, and I was right. The old toad was right there the
whole time, staring at me with those beady, greedy
eyes." He grinned at Madaug. "See what happens
when you bang your head getting out of the shower?
Total recall."

Nick laughed, then asked a random question that
occurred to him. "How old are you, anyway?"

Mark scowled at the sudden change in topic. "Huh?"

"I thought you were only like twenty-one or something. It just dawned on me that you weren't old enough
to do all of this."

"What? Is there some unwritten Gautier manual
on what a person can and can't do with their life? Really? My birthday's in November, so I was a year ahead
of my classmates, and graduated when I was seventeen.
Blew out my knee right before I turned nineteen and
doubled up on my classes to graduate by twenty. And
for the record, I'm almost twenty-three. That good
enough for you, or you want my whole résumé, too?"

"Sorry. Don't get so testy. I was just curious. I thought you told me you were younger."

"You want to see my license?"

Nick held his hands up in surrender. He could have sworn Mark had told him he was younger, but then, he could have been screwing with him. Mark was bad that way.

Madaug let out a low whistle to get their attention. "And this is a little more important than Mark's background." He shoved another piece of paper into Nick's face. "Remember I told you Devus coached the Tech team against Georgia?"

"Yeah, and the next day they were all killed." Nick was now holding the article that had been written about it.

"Exactly." Mark gave him a third piece of paper with another football team on it. The date on this photograph was a year later and . . .

Holy snikes . . .

It was Devus again. This time standing in front of the players. Nick stared in disbelief.

Surely there was some mistake.

He lined the pictures up side by side and compared them. While he did that, Madaug brought pages with the photos blown up larger so that he could see all the details in their faces.

Yeah, there was no denying it. They were all the same man. "How can this be?"

Mark rubbed his chin. "Apparently, that's his MO. Coach appears to lead a team to victory and a championship. Then the day after they win, all the players and the coach die." He handed Nick more pages. "Year, after year, after year."

Nick shook his head. "No, no, no. It's not possible. Why would he let them photograph him and keep records? For that matter, why keep his name the same? Wouldn't that be stupid?"

"He didn't keep his name all the time," Mark said. "If you look at the articles—and believe me, we have—he has a list of names he recycles. I think Walter Devus was his real name, but honestly we don't know. He's used a lot over the last century."

Well, that made more sense. If you wanted to hide, you couldn't always be you. "Okay, but why have your picture made?" Especially if you don't want people knowing you're immortal.

Nick had noticed that Kyrian didn't have one single photo of himself stashed anywhere at all. Not even a painting, bust. Nothing.

"I'm voting cocky arrogance." Madaug pulled out another paper where they'd charted all the schools Devus, if it was Devus, had taught at. "Think about it. Before now, pictures weren't all that clear, and they damaged easy. Once you left your little town, the chances of the next one having seen your photograph were pretty slim. It's only now that we have Photoshop and computers that we can clean the images up and compare them. More than that, we have online libraries, archives, and depositories where we can pull out the most obscure information imaginable. There's no hiding today, and once it goes online, it's there forever, just waiting for someone to stumble on it. So remember that the next time you take a picture of you mooning someone and want to post it somewhere."

Why did everyone have to keep bringing *that* up?

One little mistake . . .

Endless humiliation.

Mark brought his attention back to the subject at hand. "And once we'd figured out his MO, it was easy to start looking for a championship football team that won one night, then died the next day. Every year, like clockwork, there's always one team. The venue varies from college to high school all the way down to Little League. But it's always the same sequence of events."

That news sickened him most of all. Little League? "He kills kids?" As soon as he said that, he realized how stupid his statement was. Of course he killed kids. Dave was lying in a morgue right now because of him. "We have to stop this."

"We know," they said in unison.

Nick gestured to the papers around them. "We'll take this to the police and—"

"We can't."

He gaped at Mark. "What do you mean we can't? We've proved—"

"Nothing." Madaug handed him other articles. "During the gangster era, when the media was exploding and national coverage began to boom along

with newsreel footage that was shown in movie the-
aters across the country, Devus wised up and stopped
having his picture made. He also learned to kill off an
existing coach and then step in just long enough to
win the championship and supposedly die with his
team. No doubt to avoid any long-term relationships
or questions."

"Or media coverage," Mark added.

Maybe, but Nick kept coming back to one thing.
"Then how do you know it's him?"

Madaug gave him a *duh* stare. "Really? You asked
me that? What are the odds that every single year
across the country, one team and one team only has a
coach who dies under bizarre circumstances right as
they're heading to the play-offs? Then the school or rec
center is desperate for an experienced replacement. Out
of the blue, here comes Mr. Middle Age with roughly
the same description. He stays for four weeks . . . just
long enough for the championship games, and takes
his team to victory. And while drunk on their laurels,
wham!" He slapped his hands together. "They all die.
You really think that's just a coincidence?"

Well . . . no. "Not when you put it that way. But a cop will never believe this."

"You think?" Mark sighed. "No one would believe us. They'd all think we were high on something. So the question is, how do we stop him from killing again without going to the authorities?"

"Turn my zombies loose on him?"

Mark cut a murderous glower at Madaug. "I know you didn't go there, given what almost happened to your family."

"It was a joke, Mark. Believe me, I'm done trying to manipulate human brain patterns."

Ignoring them, Nick's thoughts raced as pieces slowly fell into place.

You can use personal items as a binding spell. Think of it like a heat-seeking missile. If you want something to happen to someone in particular, you take an item from them and you can use that as a focal point. It's the same principle that the pendulum works under.

Grim's words haunted him. Now he understood his list. The coach needed those specific items from all the football players.

But then what did he do with them after the game was over and the owners were killed? Since his home and office were so bare and he constantly moved, keeping them didn't seem feasible. Maybe he threw them out afterwards?

Didn't matter.

The most important thing was to break the cycle, especially since Nick was on the team and didn't want to die.

I thought you didn't want to live.

Well, that was true, but it didn't mean he wanted to die. He only wanted his life to calm down a little and go back to normal. Not flying off the tracks at warp speed toward Insanityville.

Madaug's phone rang. He picked it up and cringed. "Dang it. It's my little brother."

"Is that so bad?" Mark asked.

"Uh, yeah. Ian's voice is so high-pitched on the phone that I swear if we bottled it and put it in a grenade, we could make a fortune as arms dealers. It'd clear more rooms and cause more pain than a hydrogen bomb. I'm living for the day when that kid hits puberty and his voice drops down to a human level."

Nick was about to tell him he was overreacting when Madaug answered it and he heard for himself the truth of the matter.

Oh yeah. *That* could break glass. A screech demon had nothing on this kid. And it wasn't even in *his* ear. He was standing several feet away.

Even Mark was cringing.

"All right. All right," Madaug said to his younger brother. "Stop whining, you little brat. I'll be home later and fix it. I will, but if you don't stop nagging me about it, I'm going to erase Eric's hard drive and tell Dad you did it." Madaug hung up as Ian whined a very shrill no on the other end. He glared at Nick. "You're so lucky you're an only child."

"Not really. If I tell someone to stop touching me or blame something I broke on a sibling, it's a one-way ticket to a straitjacket."

"You know my twisted brother actually owns one of those? Eric spray-painted it black and hung it on his wall. Again, I say you are so lucky you're an only child.

Oh, to have the blessed quiet and not to be forced to endure endless hours of blaring Bauhaus out of Eric's dark hole, and 'Baby Rock' sung by Ian the Pirate, who walks around the house with a parakeet on his shoulder that he shoves in my face every night and tells me to pet or he'll make it peck out my eyes while I sleep."

Nick didn't mean to laugh, but he couldn't help it. And to think, his biggest complaint was his mom drying her bras on a string over the bathtub. He was sure he'd be in therapy for years dealing with that one.

Mark clapped his hands together to get their attention. "All right, guys. Focus. We have to come up with some way to stop Devus for good. Let's get our heads in the game and stop this psycho."

Walter Devus stood in front of his mirror, staring at a face that hadn't changed in more decades than he could count.

What'd happened?

But then he knew. Greed. Vanity. Pride. Take your

pick. They'd combined into a toxic mixture that had led him into making the worst mistake of his life.

And for what?

Andy Warhol's fifteen minutes of fame?

Only it wasn't supposed to be that short. It was supposed to have lasted a lifetime.

Be careful what you ask for. You just might get it.

Especially when dealing with things that were best left alone. If only he could go back in time, he'd have grabbed himself and stopped him.

But it was too late for that. The die was cast. The roll made. He would spend eternity in servitude, gathering souls for his master. Unknown. Uncelebrated. Obscure. The very things he'd wanted so desperately to avoid.

Funny how your fears always manifested and took over your life.

He'd been hopeless of ever discovering a way out of his slavery.

Until he came here. New Orleans. Land of Dark Magick and the birthplace of paranormal. He could feel the undercurrent of it that ran through the city like a living, breathing thing.

And here in its heart was the darkest of all.

The Malachai. If he could find the young one in time, his master would release him.

He would be free.

Walter savored that word. To be human once more. To be able to stay in one place and grow roots. Something that had been anathema to him as a young man.

Now it was paradise.

Holding that hope close, he continued to run his experiments on the items his "boys" had gathered. While the Fringe Guard looked for the escaped demon, he was after the Malachai they didn't know existed.

He was sure the Malachai was in his school masquerading as a student. It was a feeling he'd had from the moment he stepped inside the building.

But who?

He'd carefully searched files until he narrowed down the most likely suspects. So far, they'd all been wrong.

His timer went off, notifying him it was done.

His heart racing, he went to check on the latest batch. Biting his lip in trepidation, he pulled Stone's class ring out of the bowl.

Still intact. Still perfect.

Stone wasn't the Malachai. He'd been so sure of it, what with his cruelty and arrogance. But, no. He was wrong again.

Thoroughly agitated, he moved on to the next bowl. He wasn't expecting anything at all. Yanking the string, he froze.

It didn't come straight up.

Could it be?

Hope returned furiously as he pulled harder. He'd put in a piece of towel, but in its place . . .

Brimstone.

"I've found you now. You're mine!" And he was about to unleash a legion of doom on the boy.

I should have recognized the name. I should have known. How stupid was he not to see it? But then, he'd lived long enough to know how deceitful such things were.

The Malachai had been living in plain sight

of everyone. Flaunting his presence with careless abandon.

But no longer.

At last, Walter Devus would be human again.

And the Malachai would be no more.

CHAPTER 17

Y ou want me to do what? What part of stupid crawled up your sphincter and died?"

Angry and offended, Nick folded his arms over his chest as he faced Caleb in his run-down condo. While it was just the two of them in here, he'd had enough of the demon's attitude for one day.

What was wrong with him? Ever since Nick had been attacked in school, Caleb had been different toward him. It felt like the demon hated the very air he breathed.

Nick wasn't the one with a problem. Caleb was.

"We need to know what we're dealing with, Caleb. Otherwise, I wouldn't ask you to do this."

Caleb snarled at him. "What you're dealing with is one seriously pissed-off demon who keeps wondering why he's sticking his neck out for an idiot like you. I'm tired, Nick. Did you not get that from our earlier discussion?"

"I thought that was a fight we had."

"No, this is hell," he sneered, "and I'm trapped in it. And I'm sick of you. You hear me? Why don't you fight your own battles? You want information, get off your lazy butt and go get it."

Wishing he had the strength to lay into him and not get eviscerated, Nick gaped at his so-called protector, who had suddenly become a bad cross between a heckler and an abusive parent. "And you think something has crawled up *my*—"

"Get away from him, Nick."

Nick's eyes widened as Caleb manifested next to . . .

Caleb.

The two of them stood side by side in front of his makeshift bedroom. Same height. Same hair. Same eyes. Same black clothes and curled lips. The only difference was that the newcomer seemed to be in pain.

And bleeding at the corner of his mouth.

Ah yeah, this was just like that moment in *Terminator 2* when the evil chrome cyborg takes over the body of the nice security guard.

Except the real Caleb wasn't usually all that warm and fluffy either. Something that made them even harder to tell apart.

"Which of you's real?" Nick asked.

"The one limping, silly." Simi flashed in beside Nick and leaned against his shoulder. "Can't you tell the difference between the cute Malphas and the fugly fake one?"

Not really. If Caleb wasn't limping and bleeding, he'd have no clue.

Nick frowned at her. "What's going on?"

With her bright purple hair, which matched the color of her lipstick, pulled into pigtails, Simi let out an adorable sound that defied description. "Them nasty demons done found you. Kind of. See, there's a big bounty on your head—" She brushed her hand over his hair to emphasize her words. "—and if some mean nasty can find you and bring you in to have your brains eaten by their overlord, they get freed. So win–win. Well, not for you 'cause it would probably hurt to have your brains eaten. Though the Simi is pretty sure they'd kill you first." She paused to think about that with a strangely cute expression. "Then again, some don't, 'cause they like the sound of screams on the way down. I wonder if brains scream on their own. . . . Hmm. The Simi sees an expulsion coming on. Not ex . . ."

"Periment?"

"That's the word." Smiling, she touched him on the tip of his nose. "Experiment. Thank you, akri-Nicky. Good of you to use your brains while you still have some. The Simi's so proud for you."

"You're not helping my panic, Simi."

"Oh." She grinned at him. "Sorry. The Simi will be silent. Until it's not time to be silent anymore. Silent. I likes that word. Ever notice some words are just pretty to say?" She beamed like a beautiful doll. "Silent Simi." Her face fell as she touched her forefinger to her lower lip and pouted. "Oh, wait, no.

The Simi don't like the way that sounds at all. Blah! A silent Simi is not a good thing."

"Sim?" Caleb grunted. "A hand, please?" Good Caleb was trapped in a headlock by the other Caleb.

Nick started forward.

Good Caleb threw his hand out and stopped him. "Don't get hurt."

"I feel like a yo-yo."

"Better than what I feel like, buddy. Trust me."

The bad Caleb withdrew from the good one the moment Simi entered the fray. He started for the door, but Simi tossed her hand out and wrapped what appeared to be a sticky rope around him. She reeled him to her like a fisherman ready for some swordfish steak.

"Oh, no," Simi said. "We can't have that. Where you going, Mr. Meanie-Pants? You don't hurt people then run. That's just rude." She looked back at Caleb. "Can the Simi barbecue him, or is he on the 'No Simi' eat list?"

Caleb looked at the demon coldly. "*Bon appétit,* babe."

This time when Simi smiled, Nick saw that her

teeth were serrated and sharp. With a cry of delight, she vanished with the demon in tow.

Nick blinked several times as he tried to digest everything that was happening. "Simi's a demon."

"Yeah."

Simi was a demon. He kept repeating that in his head.

Well, that certainly explained a whole lot of her weirdness away. But still . . .

Nick was aghast. "For the record, do I know anyone not a demon or a freak?"

"Yes, you do. Not sure if Bubba and Mark go into the latter or not, though. I'm too tired to mentally categorize them. You figure it out, and I'll go with your Dewey decimal." Caleb collapsed on the sofa with a loud groan. "Are you all right?"

"Maybe, but my mom will kill you if she sees that blood on her couch."

Caleb looked down at the big stain that was spreading across the cushion where he lay. "I'll clean it before I go. I just need to lie here for a minute. You have no idea how much pain I'm in. And—" He narrowed his gaze on Nick. "—who told you?"

Um, that was random. "Told me what?"

"About your destiny."

Was he serious? "Dude. *You* did."

Caleb cursed, then winced. "It wasn't me, Nick. That stupid Fringer grabbed me and tossed me into Lataya."

Nick had no idea what he was talking about. "Who is that?"

"Not a person. It's a place. Think of it like a dungeon for demons where your powers get zapped."

A chill went over him as he realized that he'd been spending time with his enemies and he'd had no clue about it.

Yeah, that was terrifying and sobering.

"So when was the last time I spoke to you?"

Caleb licked the blood from his lips. "When I pulled you out of the locker and unwrapped you."

"Which really sucked, just so you know. You're the one who deserved to be tossed . . ." Nick changed his tone as he saw the deep gashes in Caleb's body. Wounds he'd taken for him. That put everything in perspective and made him feel both bad and grateful. "Okay, so you didn't deserve that, but still . . . I don't like being tossed inside lockers. For future reference, okay?"

"Duly noted."

Nervous over everything that had happened, Nick paced around the couch. "So what's going on with all of this?"

"This is what I was trying to tell you, kid. Fringe Hunters can take any form they want to. It's what makes them so deadly. For that matter, one shouldn't even be able to get into this condo, which is supposed to be protecting you from things like them and yet . . ." His eyes flashed to those freak show snake eyes. "Did you invite him in?"

"I thought I summoned *you*."

He leaned back with a groan. "Nick . . . we have got to get your powers honed. Your perspicacity is not where it needs to be. I swear I'm going to tie Simi to you until your eyes are opened to others. She has the best of anyone I've ever met. No one gets anything over on her."

He'd noticed that like Rémi and the rest of the bears, she hid in plain sight. "Where does she come from?"

"Her people are called Charonte, and they originated in Lemuria then moved to other places I can't talk about with you."

"Why?"

"I just can't, Nick, okay? Now, please give me a second to lie here in silence and bleed."

That was the least he could do, since he was the whole reason Caleb was hurt. "You want something to drink?"

"Human blood would be fabulous. But since I doubt you're donating, let me suffer for a minute longer."

Nick paced back and forth as he tried to understand just how scary his world was now.

"No, Nick," Caleb whispered from behind him. "The world has always been scary. You've just been lucky enough to be shielded from it. It's the saddest part of childhood, really. When that shimmery veil is ripped away by something horrible and you're left with the unvarnished truth. When the world no longer becomes safe and you see the ugly side of it. You, like most humans, fear us demons. But we're not the worst

predators out there. You know what we are. It's the
ones who lure you in with kindness or who attack
from the back. Those are monsters far worse than us.
All this time, you thought you knew. We all do. But
now you have *seen*."

"And I can't take that back."

Caleb shook his head.

Nick paused to look at him. "Were you ever a
child?"

"Very few creatures are lucky enough to be born
adult. We all suffer through childhood and adoles-
cence."

"Did you enjoy yours?" Nick asked, wanting to
know.

"Parts. But I grew up in a vastly different time and
place. You can't even begin to imagine it."

No, he guessed he couldn't.

Caleb's eyes returned to their human appearance.
"But there was one who was kind to me. Someone
who wasn't supposed to have kindness. What I know
of it, I learned from him. You should be glad that
you've met me after he did. I assure you the Shadow

Me you dealt with earlier was far kinder than I would have been before."

"But you don't want to be my protector."

"I never said that."

"Your expressions do."

Caleb laughed. "You haven't mastered your lessons, boy. You're misreading impatience. I have that with all creatures. I want my freedom. I make no bones about that. It's what I've yearned for these countless centuries. But my freedom would be wasted if I allowed you to be swallowed by darkness."

"You said prophecy couldn't be fought."

Caleb pushed himself up from the couch and cleaned the blood away with a swipe of his hand. "Since when do you pay attention in class? And especially *Moby Dick*?"

Nick shrugged. "Apparently I do. Who knew?" He sobered as he met Caleb's sinister gaze and the horrible reality of his future sank in with steely hooks. "Do you think I can be saved?"

"I wouldn't be here if I didn't. I'd be off building a really deep bunker."

"What if you're right, though. What if I can't fight it?"

"That's the wrong question, Nick. What if you can?"

CHAPTER 18

It wasn't many people who got inspirational speeches from demons. Nick counted himself lucky in that regard.

Or cursed.

"C'mon, Nick," he said to himself. "Concentrate." He supposedly had all these untapped powers just waiting to be carefully unleashed. It was time he learned to use them.

Barely one hour ago, another fourteen-year-old had been found murdered only three blocks north of Sanctuary—same style with the peculiar emblem around his body.

His coach was planning on delivering all their souls

up to his boss like the cherry on a special homemade chocolate sundae so that Devus could move on and repeat his offenses again and again.

Well, Nick Gautier was no cherry and he was no fool.

Honestly, he didn't know what he was anymore, but he couldn't stand by and let anyone else die or become a victim. Not if he could help it. It was time to fight, and fighting was the one thing he understood well.

"You can do this." He clenched his fist tight around the cord and thought as hard as he could.

It was useless. Grim's lessons were more aggravating than helpful. Frustrated, he started to lower his hand, only to feel a warm presence next to him. The room was bathed with a soft, glowing light that seemed to emanate the sensation of a mother's love and acceptance. It was so comforting, he wanted to lose himself in it.

Kody appeared by his side with her feet tucked up under her. "You *can* do this, Nick." She smiled at him, and his insides danced. Dog, if she wasn't the most beautiful girl he'd ever seen. She always looked so sweet and inviting.

"Hi," he whispered, half-afraid he was dreaming and that she'd vanish on him.

Her smile widened. "Hi."

Kody knew what her job was. Keep Nick straight or deliver his head on a platter to the powers who commanded her. But every time she looked into those dark blue eyes of his, she lost a part of herself to them.

A part of herself to him.

He was a hard man not to love. All that power wrapped in the body of someone who was still unsure and vulnerable. Someone who always put others' needs above his own. He wouldn't teach himself his powers to serve his own interests. It was to protect others that he sat here in utter frustration.

She closed her hands around his. "You're trying to force it."

"I need it to work. Don't have time for bull crap."

She gave him a chiding glance. Her brothers had always been like him, too, blindly forcing their way whenever they ran into opposition.

You see where that got them.

She forced her pain aside. This wasn't about them and the stupidity that had damned them both and ruined all their lives. A stupidity that had almost ended the world.

This was about Nick and his current idiocy. "And if you're building a bookcase and you break the nail in half because it won't obey you, what do you have?"

"Splinters."

She smiled. "Indeed."

Nick shivered as she leaned against him and held his hand in hers. She had the softest skin he'd ever felt. Like warm velvet.

"Close your eyes."

Her breath tickled his skin as he obeyed her.

"Now, picture in your mind what you want to know and then listen to the universe as it speaks to you."

He tried, but right now all he could really focus on was how good she felt against him. *Oh yeah, I'm twisted.*

"Are you getting anything?"

Um, yeah, but he wasn't about to go there. "I'm never going to make this work."

She dropped their entwined hands, then took the hematite into her palm as if to test its heft. "Maybe the pendulum isn't your thing."

"What do you mean?"

"Everyone's different. What works for one doesn't always work for another." She held her hands out in front of her and cupped them so that they formed a ball in her lap. She whispered in a beautiful language he couldn't decipher. But it was one he could listen to all day. Especially with the sweet musical cadence of her voice.

As he watched, a strange blue light emanated from her hands. It pulsed like electricity, then swirled around until it began to form a shape. After a minute, the mist became a dark gray, almost black mirror. But the surface wasn't glass. It appeared more iridescent and fluid.

She held it out to him. "It's a scrying mirror. Try it."

Still skeptical, he took it into his hands. "What do I do with it?"

"It's a window to the universe. Empty your mind and look into it. It'll show you everything you need to know and everything you seek."

His luck, the only thing it'd show him was that he had something stuck between his teeth.

Or worse. Something hanging out of his nose.

Cringing at the mere thought of *that* horror, he did as she said. The moment he did, he immediately saw the mirror begin to smoke. He started to drop it, but Kody wouldn't let him.

"It's okay, Nick. Watch it."

His skepticism faded as shapes began to take form and move. At first, he couldn't identify them, but one by one they clarified until he could hear voices in his head. Wow, it was like watching TV or a closed-circuit camera. He saw people he knew and some he didn't. One scene quickly blended into another, shifting and changing so fast, it was dizzying. "What am I looking at?"

"Your device." She put her hands over the images.

"This is the one you'll be strongest with. The one that spoke to you the moment you touched it. Your divination gift is scrying not dowsing."

Finally, he had something he could actually do. Grim's lessons had begun to make him feel defective and inadequate. But this . . .

This he understood. It was just like when he'd looked into Kyrian's car window.

The light in the room grew brighter.

Scowling, he met Kody's gaze. "Why is the room alive?"

"It's my shield around us. Since you're unused to your powers, every time you really tap them and they flow through you, you send out a homing beacon to others of our ilk. It's why Caleb threw you into the locker. Because you're so strong, preternatural beings are drawn to you. But you don't have the skills to protect yourself or fight them yet. Which means for now you're their yummy treat. If they kill you while you're weak, they can absorb those powers and use them for themselves."

Oh, goody. "That would be bad."

"Extremely bad, depending on who kills you."

Those words stabbed him again as his insecurities swallowed him whole. *I'm not ready for this. . . .* He looked at her and admitted to her the one thing he'd never admitted to another living soul. "I'm scared, Kody."

"You should be. But at the same time, you have me and Caleb and Simi, who will do anything to help you. We're not going to let you get hurt."

If only he had the same faith in himself. More than that, he didn't know whom he could really trust. Everyone told him to trust someone else. His gut had its own opinion.

And all of it confused him.

"How do you handle all of this?" he asked her, needing to know how long it would take for him to feel normal again.

"I was born knowing who and what I am. You're like an infant who just became self-aware. While you're talking and walking, you still don't know that the hot burner will scar you or that knives will cut you. You have to be taught the dangers of our world.

The predators and serpents who lie in wait, hoping for a chance to sink their fangs into you." She put both his hands on the mirror. "You're stronger than anyone I've ever known, Nick. And I believe in you."

When she talked like that, he could almost believe in himself, too.

Squeezing her hand, he took the mirror from her and studied it again. He saw his own reflection at first, and then the images returned. They appeared shadowy and ambiguous. Then more focused. With more clarity.

It took him a full minute to realize he was staring at the past. As Kody had said, it was as if he were watching through a window or like the proverbial fly on the wall.

He saw Devus in an old Victorian suit sitting at a large round table in what appeared to be an office of some sort with several men who were laughing at him.

"Second best is all you'll ever be, Walter. You might as well accept it."

Devus raked him with a sneer. "I assure you, Theodore, we'll win the game. You can bet your millions on it."

Theodore flicked his cigar ash toward Devus as he cast a scoffing glance at the others. "You were ever a dreamer, my boy. Ever a dreamer." The older man got up and motioned for the others to follow. Which they did. Their actions reminded him of a group of puppies following their leader.

Devus was so upset, he appeared on the verge of tears. All of a sudden, he began to throw things and overturn the furniture in the room. He ripped leatherbound books from their shelves and tore at his own hair. "I will win," he ground out between clenched teeth. "If I have to kill every player on the team to do it . . . I *will* win."

When he went to smash the mirror on the wall, he froze. There gazing at him was his own reflection, but with a calm expression, not the crazed one he currently wore.

"Did you mean what you said?" it asked him.

He set down the marble paperweight he'd intended to toss at the glass. "About what?"

"Will you kill every player to win?"

He sputtered for several seconds, his eyes truly panicked. "Who are you?"

"I'm someone who can make it happen. But I need to know if you're quite serious. Otherwise, I'm wasting my time, and that is one thing I will never do." The image started to fade.

"No! Wait!"

When it returned with an arched brow, Devus licked his lips. "I—I—I meant it."

"Then prove it."

"How?"

"If you are serious, I'll need a heart brought to me. One freshly carved from the body of a fourteen-year-old child."

Devus gasped in horror. "No. I can't."

"Too bad, then. The satisfaction of winning will go to another." The image went away.

"Come back!"

It didn't.

Devus sat there, shaking his head, pawing at the glass to see if maybe he'd imagined it. "I've gone crazy. I know it. And yet . . ."

Nick could see the gears working in Devus's mind as he debated what to do. He couldn't believe the coach would even consider it. Was the man insane?

He had to be.

The smoke from his scrying mirror swirled again as it showed other images. Horrific images.

Appalled and sickened, Nick turned his head as the coach stalked an innocent girl who was making her way home after work from a factory job. In a dark alley in downtown Atlanta, the coach cruelly strangled her, then removed her heart.

For a moment, Nick thought he'd vomit. How could anyone be so cold? So brutal? Any sympathy he might have had for Devus was gone, and in its place was a harsh, cold conviction.

Devus had taken his last life. This madness was going to stop here and now.

Kody watched as Nick struggled not to be sick. As he kept his head turned away from the grisly actions of the coach. That gave her hope. He wasn't curious or interested in the brutality at all. He was disgusted—as any normal person would be.

In fact, he didn't watch again until the coach had returned to the mirror with the girl's heart inside a wooden box. And even then, Nick cringed.

Please let me save you, Nick. Please. Stay like this so that I won't have to kill you. She had enough blood on her hands. She didn't want any more.

Kody turned her attention back to the coach as he made a bargain he should never have made.

Devus opened the lid to show his enchanted mirror what he'd done. There was no missing the proud glint in his eyes. The hopeful swagger of a man who would achieve his goal at any cost. "Is this good enough?"

The image in the mirror smiled. "Perfect. Better than I'd hoped."

"Then tell me what to do to win."

"You will have to gather a single, very personal item from each one of the players." The image in the mirror reached out with one hand to give Devus a red velvet bag. "Put their items into this."

Devus took it and nodded as the arm curled back into the mirror. "Then what?"

"You will burn wormwood and arsenic mixed with basil and cedar. Put those ashes in the bag with your players' personal items, and then at three a.m. on the morning when you're to play, you will spread them over the heart you took as a sacrifice. So long as you keep the box with you for the whole of the day, you will be invincible. Nothing can harm you, and no bad luck will befall you. Your team will play as they've never played before, and you will be victorious."

"You swear this to me?"

"I do, but don't be so happy, Coach. For this all comes with a steep price."

Devus's brow furrowed with confusion. "I've already killed a girl. What more is there?"

The mirror image *tsk*ed at him. "Her heart is only the catalyst for your players to do their best. That has nothing to do with your payment."

He swallowed in trepidation. "And that is?"

"Your life."

His face went completely white. "What?"

"You will have fame, Coach. Just as *you* wanted. A brilliant win over your opponents. I'll even be kind and give you an evening to bask in that victory. But come noon the next day, you and your players must die together. Imagine the news coverage then. Oh, the tragedy of champions dying on the heels of their great success. You'll be legendary. Over and over again."

Devus gulped heavily. "That's not what I want. I didn't sign on for that."

There was no pity in the mirror's eyes. "Yes, you did. You should have asked the terms before you made your contract. Have you never been told to read the fine print?"

Devus's hands shook uncontrollably. "It's not fair."

"Life never is. But don't despair. Unlike your players, you won't stay dead."

"What do you mean?"

"That is your bargain, Walter. So long as you gather souls for me, I won't take yours. However, if you fail to deliver the winning team to me by noon, you will suffer unimaginable torment for the rest of eternity. Do you understand?"

He nodded.

"Good. Now, be a good boy and don't lose your heart."

Nick pulled back from the scene with his stomach knotted and his fury hot. How dare the coach make a pact like that. And for what?

Vanity?

He'd never understand it.

Kody sighed, drawing his attention to her. "Well, now we know how it all began."

Nick opened his mouth to respond to that, but before he could, images started playing through his head. They came fast and furious, as they'd done in the mirror. And just as in the mirror, he had no control over them. It made him dizzy and nauseated.

Oh, the pain . . .

Gasping, he lay on the floor and pressed the heel of his hand to his eye, trying to alleviate some of misery. It felt as if his brain would literally explode.

"Nick?" Kody sucked her breath in sharply as she watched him convulse on the floor.

What was happening? What should she do?

She didn't sense him being under attack by anything, and yet that's what he acted like. Had she accidentally unleashed something on him? The very thought terrified her.

"Nick?" she tried again.

Again he didn't respond.

She thickened her protection in the room, just in case. It was so tight now, nothing could breach it. She pulled Nick's head into her lap and held him, hoping whatever had him would let go.

Nick heard the girl's voice in his head. Julianne . . . She was talking to him in a tone that sounded like Madaug's little brother. High-pitched and painful.

Free me, she begged him. *Please. I don't want to hurt anyone else. I want to go to my rest and be left alone. Why won't he go away? It's been so long, and I'm so very tired.*

It was the girl Devus had murdered. She . . .

Something thick and warm went through his veins. It wasn't like the other times when his powers had seized him. This was different. For once, he felt like he had control of it. Like he could channel and direct it.

Closing his eyes, he tried to focus.

Kody gasped and pulled away as she saw an orange aura engulf Nick's entire body. It was a demon's essence, and it made the hair on the back of her neck rise.

When he opened his eyes to look up at her, they were no longer blue. They were a vibrant lavender. The kind that didn't belong to a human.

"You have to teach me how to raise the dead." His voice was low and deep, and sounded nothing like the Nick she knew.

She blinked twice as her mind wrapped itself around his request. "It's forbidden."

His voice calmed down to its normal cadence as he pushed himself up to face her. "No, it's not. It's ill advised. But the only way to stop this is to let the girl confront her killer. She wants to be free, and I think we should let her."

Kody shook her head. "We can't do that, Nick. You're not strong enough, and you have no idea what doors that will open. Doors that don't shut easily."

She's lying to you.

Nick groaned as an unfamiliar voice filled his head. "Who are *you*?"

It didn't say.

But he'd felt it and honestly, he was tired of having Grand Central Station for a head. *People, things, animals. Keep out!* The station was closed for business. *Go haunt somewhere else.*

Kody put her hand on his forehead to check for a fever. "I'm Kody. Are *you* all right?"

He gave her a *no duh* look. "I wasn't talking to you. I hear voices in my head."

"What do they sound like?"

He struck himself against his ear in an effort to try to clear it. "I can't explain it exactly. I . . . My powers are slipping. I can feel them. They . . ." His words ended with a fierce groan as his insides twisted until he couldn't breathe.

Kody panicked as she saw his eyes changing again. His skin was marbling and swirling. She had to do something fast or she'd lose him.

"Look at me, Nick!"

He ignored her.

She had to calm him down and force those powers to recede. Get his thoughts to focus on something other than his pain. With no better thought, she kissed him.

Nick shuddered at the sensation of Kody's mouth on his. And as he tasted those full, soft lips, an inexplicable calm came over his entire being. He felt like he was floating. Cupping her face in his hands, he let the warmth of her mouth soothe him until he could think straight again.

In one act, she'd cured his headache and grounded him back in this reality.

Pulling back, he stared at her. "Thank you."

She inclined her head. "Anytime. Now, can you explain to me what you heard?"

"No. Not really. At first it was the murdered girl, Julianne."

She appeared less than convinced. "Are you sure it was her?"

"What do you mean?"

"It's extremely simple for a demon to appear as a dead person. It takes very little energy, and it's an

easy way to motivate people to do things. Go to someone in the guise of a loved one or child, and they'll do
most anything you bid them. Think of it like a cheat
code."

Nick didn't care for the thoughts of that, but at
least he understood what she was getting at. "You're
right. She could have been lying. But I don't think so.
One thing I've learned in my life is that nothing is
ever easy. And the mirror Devus thing even warned
him not to lose the girl's heart. I'm telling you, Kody.
The key to this is the girl whose death started it."

He could see the reluctance in her eyes before she
banished it. "You're right. In order to undo things,
you usually have to go to where they started. But . . ."

"But what?"

"You're talking about necromancy, Nick. That's
not something to play with, and it's not something
you learn in a few hours or days. Necromancers are a
different breed entirely."

"How so?"

"To do what they do, they lose a part of their soul
every time. And you are talking about the darkest

part of evil. It's not just the reanimation of the vessel—making the body move again. You have to reunite the soul, which means you're ripping that soul out of wherever it's gone to. And if it's been reborn . . . I don't think anything or anyone can touch it. But again, I don't know. I don't go there. For real good reasons."

He begged her with his eyes. "But you know someone who does—"

She remained firm in her conviction to avoid this catastrophe. "No, I don't."

"But you *know* someone who knows someone."

His persistence was as annoying as it was playful and cute. Ugh! She was the train derailing, and there was nothing she could do to stop it.

If she knew anything about Nick, it was that he was stubborn. There was no way she could sway him from this.

"We both know that someone. C'mon, grab your jacket and let's go to Caleb's."

Pacing in front of his giant marble foyer, which was so elaborate, it made Kyrian's look like a pauper's, Caleb glared at Nick and then Kody. "Are you out of your collective minds? I swear I can't leave you two alone for three seconds that you don't go off and hurt yourselves." He narrowed his gaze on Nick. "I expect stupid out of you, but *you*—" He turned on Kody then. "—know better."

She shrugged helplessly. "I tried to tell him that. He won't listen to me. Tag. You're it."

Facing Nick, Caleb gestured toward her. "Listen to her, Nick."

Nick wasn't trying to be difficult. He wasn't. He understood their panic and concerns, and he was grateful for it. But he knew what he'd seen and heard. "You two listen to me for once. While I may not be as well versed in this as you are, I do know what I saw. You two and everyone else keep telling me to learn my powers—*arr*, learn my powers—" He imitated a parrot before he continued on in his normal tone. "—and then when I do, you tell me I don't know what I'm talking about." He slung his hands out in surrender. "Fine. You win. I quit. You two deal with this. I'm going home. Packing up all my personal items, and when you, Caleb, end up dead because the coach has your jockstrap or something else I didn't steal but someone else did, don't call me. I'm done and I'm going to hide in a bunker until all of this is over with." He started for the door, but the moment he reached it, it locked in his face.

"I hate you, Nick," Caleb drawled.

"Feels mutual, Demon."

With a sigh of irritation, Caleb turned to Kody. "Do you really think this is wise?"

"Not at all. But I have no better idea. Do you?"

"I feel like I'm about to enter a Monty Python skit," Caleb muttered as he pulled out his phone and then dialed it. He glared at them while it rang and rang and rang.

Grimacing at the delay, Nick glanced toward Kody. "Do necromancers not have voice mail?"

She shrugged.

"Hey," Caleb said finally. "It's Malphas. . . . Yeah,

been a long time and I need a favor. How far are you from New Orleans?"

Nick could hear a deep voice on the other end, but he couldn't make out any individual words.

"All right. I'll see you then." Caleb hung up the phone and continued to grimace at them. "He'll be here in a few hours."

"Where's he coming from?" Nick asked.

"Wouldn't say and I know better than to pry." He rubbed the line of his eyebrow. "You two better know what you're doing."

Kody turned on Nick then. "For the record, Nick. Using the mirror shouldn't scare you. *This* should."

"Stop complaining," Nick said "I know, all right? I've either made a huge mistake or ended this. Instead of expending our energy on so much negativity, why don't we do something positive?"

"Like what? Pull the arms off Nick until he cries like a girl?"

Kody laughed.

Needless to say, Nick didn't find Caleb's sarcasm amusing. "Thanks for selling me out," he said to Kody.

She sobered. "I haven't done that yet, but the night's still young."

And they had school tomorrow. Nick checked his watch. "Crap. I need to head back home."

Caleb contradicted him. "I don't think that's a good idea. Any chance your mom would let you stay over for the night?"

"If I tell her we're studying, she might."

Caleb scoffed. "We are studying. Ways to survive the next few hours. It's a really important subject, too."

Nick couldn't agree more. Pulling out his phone, he called his mom, who was still on the clock at Sanctuary.

"Hey, baby, whatcha need?"

"Can I spend the night over at Caleb's house? We're working on a project together and I need more time."

"Nick." Her voice was full of suspicious irritation. "You know I don't like for you to do that on a school night."

"I know, Mom. And I wouldn't ask if it wasn't really, really, really important. Please?"

She made a noise at him. "Fine. Don't forget to brush your teeth."

"I won't."

"Call me if you need me."

"I will."

"All right. Tell me you love me, and I'll let you go."

His face turned red hot as he gave Caleb and Kody his back. "I love you," he whispered.

She made a kissing sound at him before she hung up.

Nick passed a sullen glare to Caleb. "Not one word."

"Wouldn't dream of it. And I have to say that I'm impressed."

"By what?"

"Your mom didn't grill us this time."

Nick snorted. "That's 'cause she already did that and you passed. Be grateful."

Kody swung her arms in front and behind her body so that she could clap her hands together. "So, gentlemen? What are we going to do for the next few hours?"

Nick smiled as he had a brilliant idea. "Hey, Caleb,

any chance you have a system and some games lying around in this sprawling mansion of yours?"

"You know it. Name it and I have it."

Nick was in the middle of pwning Caleb for the three thousandth time when the doorbell suddenly rang.

All three of them jumped out of their skins.

Kody covered her heart with her hand. "Guess that's our friend."

Caleb used his powers to flash himself downstairs to let him in.

Nick took the more human route and walked through the house until he reached the landing that looked down below. From the way Caleb and Kody had carried on, he'd expected some huge, hulking long-coat-wearing brute of a mountain man to appear.

But the guy who strode inside was anything but.

Dressed in a pair of loose-fitting olive green cargo pants, and a thin black T-shirt, he appeared extremely normal. His hair was a little long and a lot of shaggy, but the brown waves with the blond highlights were fashionable enough. He had his hands in his pockets, and a dark brown canvas messenger bag was hung across his body.

As Nick headed down the stairs, he realized that the guy also had on a pair of worn-out Birkenstocks. And a thin braided anklet of green and black thread.

While he had good muscle definition, he was more lean than beefy. Still, he was a typical man in his late twenties to early thirties with mirrored aviator sunglasses and an unassuming air about him.

At least until Nick drew closer. Then everything changed. You could feel the power emanating from him like an overcharged battery. Nick even swore he could hear the hum of it. And that wasn't the only thing to make a brave man run. He was covered with scars and burn marks and tattoos. Like a combat vet who'd been tortured by his enemies.

Nick hesitated.

Caleb cleared his throat before he introduced them. "Xenon, meet Nick Gautier."

Nick grimaced. "Xenon? What kind of name is that?"

"The only kind I answer to." His voice was deep and gravelly, like he didn't use it often. And as Nick closed the distance, Xenon approached him with a scowl. He raked his body slowly from top to bottom. Not in a rude way, but in a very thorough one. "Aren't you an enigma wrapped in a thick coating of contradictions."

Caleb snorted, "Don't eat the help, X. We need him."

"Pity." Xenon reached up and pulled his sunglasses off and then put them in a case inside his messenger bag. As he did that, Nick saw the tattoos on his hand. His left knuckles each carried one letter that spelled EASY. This right spelled HARD.

Nick laughed. "Cool tattoo. Does it have any special meaning?"

"Pray you never find out." Ignoring Nick, he turned his attention to Caleb. "What's the situation?"

Nick drifted back to where Kody stood on the

bottom stair. She had her arms crossed over her chest, letting him know how uncomfortable she was. She didn't say it, but he could hear it loud and clear in her body language.

He creeps me out.

"So how long will it take you to set up?" Caleb asked.

"Two days."

"You have one."

"You can't rush me, Malphas. It's more an art than a science. And if I screw this up . . . you know the consquences."

"Yeah. Still having flashbacks."

"Flashbacks? I'm still having therapy." Xenon's tone was flat and dry. "Where do I do this?"

Caleb led him to the study on the right side of the front door.

While they did whatever they were doing, Nick looked at Kody. "Are we . . . What exactly are we?"

She lifted a quizzical brow. "We who?"

"You and me. What exactly is going on between us?"

She fell silent for a few minutes as she thought it over. "I honestly don't know. I like you. A lot."

That was good to know. "But?" He dreaded her answer, even though he had to have one.

"We shouldn't be so familiar."

"You're the one who keeps kissing me."

Her face flamed bright red. "I know. I've got to stop tripping and falling on your mouth all the time."

"Ah . . . so that's what it was?"

She wrinkled her nose. "Of course it was."

He felt crushed by her words. "Glad you told me. Now I know."

As he started away from her, she pulled him to a stop. "Let's just take this one day at a time, okay? See where it takes us."

"I'm young. I'm good with that." He fell to his knees, and pretended to whimper and cry out in pain. "I'm going to die old and alone. Every loser in high school has a girl, but me. Why? Why?"

"Are you off your medication?"

Nick winked at her as he stood back up. "I must be 'cause I've been hallucinating all day long."

She shook her head and started for him. But she'd taken only a step when something slammed into the front door.

They exchanged a bemused scowl while Caleb came out of his study to answer it.

The moment the door was opened, a swarm of demons burst in and attacked.

CHAPTER 19

The demons came into Caleb's home like locusts, swarming them and pinning them to the floor. Nick couldn't move without being mobbed by them, and the same was true of Kody and Caleb.

"What kind of bachelor party are you throwing, Malphas?" Xenon asked as he came out of the study.

"Feel free to join us." Caleb was trying as hard to break free as Nick and Kody were.

It was useless.

Xenon vanished back into the room before they swarmed him, too.

"We're dead." Nick looked at Kody, wanting to

memorize the beauty of her face in case they didn't have women so lovely where he was headed.

Neither of them bothered to contradict his dire prediction. There was no need. The demons sat on his chest, banging his head against the floor so hard, he was amazed it didn't split open. Same for Kody and Caleb. They fought with everything they had, but it wasn't enough to even hurt their attackers.

The demons swarmed together and lifted them up as if they were about to fly them somewhere.

Just as Nick was convinced they wouldn't survive, Xenon came out of the study like the Terminator. He sprinkled something into the air that acted like acid, especially when he shot fireballs out of his hands that ignited it. As soon as it hit their attackers, they shrieked and flew off with their skin melting.

Chasing them out of the house and down the driveway, Xenon spoke in a calm, soothing voice while he attacked them. It was an impressive feat. One Nick would love to learn. But yelling out obscenities and sarcasm was more his style.

Once they were gone, Xenon came in and locked

the door. He grimaced at Caleb. "Thought you said this place was safe."

"Apparently, I was mistaken."

"Good job, Malphas."

Caleb flipped him off for the sarcasm. Then he looked over at Nick. "That was an assassination crew. Somehow they knew you were here."

That news made him sick to his stomach. "Do we need to go protect my mom?"

Xenon shook his head. "They don't follow like humans. They're more like basset hounds. We were attacked because they blood-tracked their target here. That would be *you*, by the way."

Crap. "What if my scent leads them to my house and my mom's there alone?"

"Calm down. Again, they don't work that way. They can track only a current scent, not a lingering one. Unless you've bathed in perfume so strong, it leaves a heavy, lasting impression, you're safe." He glanced over to Kody.

"I resent that look, and I don't wear perfume."

"Just checking."

Caleb limped over to Xenon. "Now you know why we have to hurry. Can you have us something by tomorrow?"

"I'll work on it all night. Not like I need sleep anyway with the crap in my head."

"Thanks."

Xenon gave a nod to Caleb before he went back to the office.

Caleb let out a weary sigh. "I'm going to bed. If anyone else attacks tonight, feed them Nick and tell them to go away."

"Hey!"

But Caleb ignored him as he left them alone.

"I think I'm going to turn in, too." She kissed his cheek. "Don't stay up too much later. Otherwise, I'll be worrying about you."

"I won't be long behind you."

"All right." She headed up the stairs to the guest wing. The fact that Caleb had wings said it all about how sick his house was.

Nick waited until they were gone before he went to the study to spy on their newcomer.

"You might as well come in, Nick. I can't stand someone at my back."

Nick pushed the door open wider and walked into the office that had wood paneling from floor to ceiling. Even though it had a desk and chair, it was sparsely decorated and had a lot of space in it.

Xenon had laid out all his supplies and was combining things into a small black iron pot in front of him.

In a strange way, he reminded Nick of a chef. Graceful and sure, as if the recipe was forever etched into his memory.

"So what are you doing?" Nick asked.

"I'm creating an elixir that will protect me when I summon this girl back for you."

"Do you think my plan will work?"

Xenon shrugged. "Not an expert on that kind of thing. You will either fail or succeed. One or the other is a given."

Hmmm . . .

Nick wandered closer. "So how did you get into this line of work, anyway?"

Xenon glanced askance at him as he added a green leafy thing to the pot. "Answered an ad in the paper."

"Did you?"

Xenon didn't respond. "Actually, kid, I need you for a second."

That made him cringe. "Why?"

"I have an ingredient I need from you."

Nick didn't like the sound of that at all. "Come again?"

"Get over here."

Not sure about that, he did what Xenon said, even though he felt like he should be running in the opposite direction. As soon as he was within arm's reach, Xenon grabbed him in a GI Joe kung fu death grip and laid open his hand with a blade Nick hadn't known Xenon had until he was bleeding.

"Don't pull back." He held Nick in place to let his blood drip into the pot.

"That's not sanitary. Ew!" And it burned like crazy.

"*Ew* is right, but trust me. You'll be glad you have this."

Not at the moment. As soon as he was free, Nick ran out of the room and retreated to the guest room Caleb had made for him. He practically jumped into the rice plantation bed that was elevated from the floor. Without pausing, he climbed under the covers and returned to nursing his throbbing hand.

He blew air across his palm, trying to stop the stinging.

Until the wound knitted itself closed.

His jaw slack, Nick stared at the scar that was right where his cut had been. Yeah, that was strange.

Go to sleep. Don't think about it.

But it was hard not to.

C'mon, body, cooperate. He had a busy day tomorrow, and he needed to be fresh and alert. Especially since he'd be taking down the coach . . .

Nick entered the school with Kody on his right and Caleb on his left. Heads turned as the three of them walked shoulder to shoulder to his locker. Dropping his backpack on the floor, Nick opened his padlock. "All right. The challenge is to find the box with the heart in it."

"We'll be looking." Kody headed off toward her homeroom.

Caleb clapped Nick on the back before he took off, too.

While Nick swapped out his books, Stone shouldered his way to him.

"What's that? A new shirt, Gautier? Don't tell me Goodwill's out of tacky." He was referring to the fact that Nick had been forced to borrow one of Caleb's black shirts for school today, since he hadn't packed an overnight bag.

"Grow up, Stone."

Stone went to shove him.

Nick dodged with a skill he'd never had before. In fact, he could see every blow Stone was going to make an instant prior to Stone's doing it.

He had to force himself not to strike the oaf. But if he did, he'd get suspended. "You're not worth the paperwork, Stone." Nick picked his backpack up and left him standing in the hallway to sputter.

Yeah, that felt good.

Real good. And he'd take longer to savor it, but right now he was on a quest. Something that had him skipping study hall so that he could search Devus's office while the coach taught his history class.

This time he was a lot more cautious about breaking in. He slipped into the room and pulled his pendulum out.

"All right, baby. Work for Daddy." He drew a quick sketch of the room on a page in his book. "Where is the heart box?"

At first nothing happened. Nick tightened his grip, ready to scream. When all of a sudden, the pendulum finally began to swing for him.

Ah, baby, thank you!

He watched as it formed a large circle around the room model. After a few seconds, it narrowed down to the desk.

"Right side?" he asked.

It swung to *yes*.

Delighted, he kissed the pendulum and slid it into his pocket. Nick opened drawers and . . .

Nothing was there.

The stupid thing had lied. He was so mad, he wanted to hurl it into the Pontchartrain. But he didn't.

Trust it. Ambrose's voice had never been louder. With a deep breath, Nick searched the drawers again.

And again there was nothing. Until he realized that the drawers looked a lot deeper on the outside than they did on the inside.

There was a false bottom.

His heart hammering, it didn't take long to find the panel and open it. Sure enough, there was the same box he'd seen in the mirror.

Excited and scared, he quickly put everything back the way it'd been and tucked the box inside his backpack. With ninjalike skills, he crept out and away from the office without being detected. As soon as he was clear, he called Caleb and Kody to update them on the status of Operation Payback.

Nick had barely reached his class when he heard his name being called over the intercom.

"Ms. Turtledove? Would you please have Nick Gautier report to the gym? Coach Devus wants to see him about an urgent matter."

Panic seized him. Did he know? Had Nick left something out of place?

I'm an idiot. And he was about to be a dead one.

Sweat broke out on his forehead as he returned to the coach's office. He pushed open the door to see Devus sitting with his hand in the drawer he'd just rifled through.

"You have it, Gautier?"

"Have what?"

He growled at him. "Don't play coy with me, you little punk. You know what I'm talking about. Hand it over. Now."

Nuh-huh. He wasn't about to return the box to him. Terrified, he glanced around, wondering if he could remember everything Xenon had taught him.

"Where is the next set of items?"

Oh *that* was what he was talking about. Nick let out a relieved breath as his fear subsided. "I didn't get anything else yet."

"What?"

Nick shrugged. "Sorry. Between class, homework, football practice, and work, I haven't had five minutes to myself."

Devus shot to his feet. "How dare you! You'll pay for this. By the end of the day—"

"Yeah . . . I don't think so." He used his thoughts to summon Kody and Caleb. "In fact, I want the items I stole back so that I can return them."

"You can't have them."

Trying not to be obvious, Nick attempted to make a circle on the floor with drops of the potion Xenon had given him.

The coach grabbed him and yanked him hard. "What are doing?"

"ADD. I have such a hard time holding still. Can't help myself."

"Maybe prison will be able to help you out with that."

"You think?" Nick asked sarcastically. "Tell you what. How about I send you where you belong, and you die quietly and leave us alone."

The coach grabbed him by the throat. "It's going to be a pleasure to ruin you, trailer park."

"It's going to be a pleasure to banish you, Bates Motel." Nick kneed him.

Releasing him, the coach doubled over to cup himself.

Kody popped in a heartbeat before Caleb joined the party. As soon as the coach saw Caleb, he cursed. "You? You're supposed to be dead."

Caleb appeared as confused as Nick felt. "What?"

The coach clapped his hands together and summoned his demons again.

Kody vanished.

"Hey." Caleb snapped. "Not a good time to get scared."

He and Nick put their backs together to battle the ugly winged beasts. Nick glanced over to the cameras. "How long do you think it'll take before the office sends security?"

"Eternity," Devus answered. "I made sure they can't see anything that goes on in here. Now I'm going to offer you both as a sacrifice to my master."

Caleb manifested his sword out of thin air. Nick pulled the one Ambrose had given him out of his pocket. No bigger than a pocketknife, it looked harmless. Until he closed his eyes and imagined it larger. It immediately shot to full size, and the moment it did, Devus gasped.

"You're the Malachai, not Caleb." He gestured to his demon army. "Get them both, but bring me the Malachai's sword!"

They descended on them in one fierce wave.

Nick sliced the first one to reach him in half. He ducked the blow from the next one, and went low to the ground. Popping to his feet, he was able to stab the next one who approached him. Nick trusted his sword, and it whispered to him what to do. With its help, he fought like he'd been born to it.

But they were still being overrun just by the sheer number of their attackers. He was growing weak, and Caleb wasn't much better.

Nick slipped on a bloodstain that forced him down to one knee. In this position, he was at a major disadvantage.

I'm going to die.

His sword was getting heavier and heavier. He wouldn't last much longer.

Just as he felt his arm give way, Cody appeared with Xenon at her side. She tossed the Necromancer the backpack with the heart box in it before she ran to them.

"Nice to leave us here," Caleb snapped.

"We needed a calvary."

Caleb glanced over at Xenon. "When's he going to help?"

Xenon yanked the box out of the backpack. "Right now." He started chanting.

Nick continued to fight as one demon caught him with a kick straight to his solar plexus. Ah, man, that hurt. If he didn't know better, he'd swear it just kicked his ribs out of his back.

More demons arrived.

"Something's not right."

Nick scowled in Xenon's direction. "Dude. Not a phrase I want to hear right now. Really."

"Want to or not," Xenon muttered in a calmness Nick's panic didn't warrant, "this isn't working."

"What do you mean, it's not working?" Caleb asked.

Xenon jerked Nick away from the next attack wave that Kody and Caleb engaged. "Are you sure you gave me something personal from the coach?"

"Yeah. It was a picture of him when he was human."

"I need something closer to him than that. Something that matters that is uniquely his."

The coach laughed at them. "There's nothing I care about. Nothing at all. You're all going to die."

Kody cried out as she went down and was swarmed. Caleb yelped as a demon sank its teeth into his shoulder.

Devus was right. They were about to lose.

Refusing to believe it, Nick cast his gaze around the office, looking for something, anything that was personal to the troll. Everyone cared about something.

Damn the stupid coach. Was it too much to ask that he at least make a grocery list?

Why couldn't—?

Nick's thought ended as he remembered an important detail. Smiling, he reached into his back pocket and jerked out the handwritten list of items the coach had wanted him to steal. That handwriting was as personal as it got. *Thank you, Grim for* that *lesson*. He handed it to Xenon.

"We're back in business." Xenon quickly shredded it and added it to the box. He started chanting again.

Devus finally took his attention off the fight to see what Xenon was doing. His face blanched as he saw the box.

"Nick?" Xenon called. "You're on."

Nick stabbed the demon in front of him, then rushed to the circle he'd created. Summoning his powers, he imagined the girl so that Xenon could pick her out.

Together they left the human realm and descended into an abyss so dark, it was painful to be there.

Xenon put a comforting hand on his shoulder. "What was her name again?"

"Julianne."

"Julianne?" Xenon shouted. "Can you hear us?"

Nick sensed her presence. Most of all, he sensed her fear. "It's me, Julianne. I'm here to help you."

She appeared in front of Nick. "Will you save me?"

He held his hand out to her. "Come with me, and we can take back your heart and free you, once and for all."

She placed her icy hand into his. The moment their skin touched, they were sucked through a vortex and dumped back into the coach's office. Nick caught

Julianne against him as they returned to keep her from falling over.

The moment she appeared, the demons shrieked as if in agony and disintegrated.

Devus shrank back as soon as he saw her. "No. It's not possible."

Julianne, whose skin was an iridescent gray, pointed an accusatory finger at him. "How dare you keep me trapped all these years. You had no right to do what you did. No right."

As she spoke, Nick felt his powers surge. He saw the fabric of the universe around him and smelled its sweet scent. He knew what the best punishment was. How to set all of this back to an even score. Changing the words of his chant, he didn't banish Devus like they'd intended. No not at all.

He swapped the coach's life force with Julianne's.

Devus screamed as he was sucked into the vortex. His screams, like him, were swallowed whole. Meanwhile Julianne was bathed in a bright yellow light. One that danced from her fingertips into the box where her heart lay. The heart glowed an instant and then dissolved.

Julianne threw her head back and gasped as it was magically put back inside her. Tears sprang to her eyes as her grayish ghost form turned human. Breathless, she stared at Nick in wonderment. "How did you do it?"

He swept his gaze around Kody, Caleb, and Xenon. "No idea whatsoever."

Laughing, she threw her arms around his neck and hugged him close. "You are my hero. Thank you. A thousand thank-yous."

A guy could get used to this. Minus the bloody nose and aching bruises that were making it hard to breathe while she held him like this. Not to mention he caught a venomous stare from Kody that said she didn't appreciate Julianne mauling him.

"Uh, Julianne? I can't breathe. Can you let go?"

She released him immediately and wiped away her tears.

But no sooner had she done that than a bright flash of thunder shook the windows of the office. It clapped so loud, it caused them to stagger.

Out of nowhere a huge . . .

Well, it had the body of a horse, face of a lion that

had met the business end of a shovel, and the tail of a goat. Man, that was some messed-up DNA there.

It snarled at them. "How dare you destroy my . . ." His words trailed off as he saw Nick. He started toward him.

Xenon stepped between them, cutting off his access to Nick. "Stand down, Trys. This one doesn't belong to you."

Trys spat on the ground at Xenon's feet. "We're not finished, you and I. I'll be back."

"I know. I can smell you already."

Trys vaporized.

Nick pointed to the lingering mist. "What was that?"

Xenon shrugged. "I'm not just a necromancer. I have a few other jobs, too."

Caleb held his hand out in that Jedi mindwipe manner. "Don't ask, Nick. He won't answer."

Nick held his hands up and ceded the point to Caleb. "Hey, we're all fed, and none of us are dead. It's a good day from where I'm standing."

Xenon shook his head, then glanced at Caleb over his shoulder. "I'll be expecting payment later."

"It'll be there. You're the one person I'd never dare cheat."

"Until next time." Xenon literally flashed out of the room.

Nick sputtered. "Where'd he go?"

"Not just a necromancer," Kody and Caleb said in unison.

"What an amazing world this is," Julianne breathed as she discovered the light switch and kept turning it off and on. Then, she ran back to hug Nick.

Kody put her hands on her hips as she curled her lip.

Caleb laughed. "Tuck your claws in, kitten. I'll take care of getting our girl home." He sighed heavily. "I better not get detention for this. If I do, Gautier, it's coming out of your hide."

"What else is new?"

Caleb and Julianne vanished.

"Where's he taking her?" Nick asked Kody.

"Back to where and when she lived before Devus killed her."

Nick widened his eyes as disbelief poured through him. "Can he do that?"

"Yes, he can."

Chalk up another wicked power for Caleb. Who knew?

Exhausted but relieved, Nick leaned back against the desk. Kody moved to stand by his side.

"Is this what I have to look forward to?" He dreaded the answer.

She laughed. "You know the Chinese have a curse."

"And that is?"

"May you live an interesting life."

Nick would laugh if he weren't so worried about just how interesting things were going to get. He used to look forward to the future. Now he wasn't so sure he was going to have one.

"Don't look so glum." Kody kissed the tip of his nose. Then she pulled a small leather band out of her pocket and tied it to his wrist.

Nick frowned at her actions. "What's this?" He turned it around until he saw that it had her name on it.

"You're no longer the only freshman without a girl-friend." And with that, she flounced out of the room.

Nick's heart thumped at what she'd just done. Holy snikes . . .

Well, if this was the reward, maybe getting pounded by demons wasn't so bad after all.

Yeah, I am definitely sick in the head.

Well? What news do you have?"

"Our corrupter is in place and is one the young Malachai now trusts."

"Are you sure?"

"Absolutely. Gautier will be turned, and soon, we will be free."

Free . . .

The most glorious of all words, and when they were free, the blood of man would flow down the paved streets like rivers.

EPILOGUE

Six Weeks Later

Nick sat on the stoop of their new home on Bourbon Street, taking a rest from helping his mom unpack their meager belongings. The scent of gumbo and crawfish wafted down from the restaurants along with the faint sounds of jazz and zydeco. Of tourists laughing and shouting.

While their new apartment could be considered huge only compared to their former condo, he at least had his own bedroom this time . . . one with actual walls and a real bed that Kyrian had given him as a birthday present. The new place was clean, with running hot water, and everything worked.

Best of all, the sadness was gone out of his mother's eyes. She had a pride to her now that he'd never seen in her before. That made everything worthwhile to him.

But he still wanted more.

His gaze went to the huge gray house across the street that had a wraparound porch trimmed with ornate black wrought iron. *That* was where he wanted to live.

"Don't worry, kid. You will."

He glanced to his right to see Ambrose walking toward him. He sneered at his uncle's appearance, still angry at him for the way he'd abandoned them when they needed him. "How do you know?" he asked belligerently.

Ignoring his venom, Ambrose smiled. "I just do. And it won't be long until you and your mom are hanging your baby pictures on the stairs of that very house."

Funny thing was, he could see it clear as a bell in his mind. Ever since Kody had given him his scrying mirror, his second sight kept getting better every day.

Not that it mattered right now. "I'm still angry with you for not helping us with the coach. That was so wrong of you."

"And yet you survived. You needed that experience, Nick. It gave you a confidence you didn't have before."

Yeah, right. That rated right up there with the old *This is going to hurt me more than it does you* bull crap. "Don't give me that psychobabble garbage about how it forced me to grow as an individual and that *that which doesn't kill you only makes you stronger*. I don't want to hear it. You tell me I can trust you, and then you're just as quick to walk out as my father was. Is this some inherited genetic defect I need to know about? Am I going to walk out on my kid, too?"

His expression turned dark. Deadly. "No. You'll never do that."

Nick rolled his eyes as Ambrose brushed back his hair from his face with his left hand. His heart stopped as he realized something.

No. No way.

It couldn't be.

Holding his breath, Nick reached up and took Ambrose's hand into his. *Oh my God.*

Ambrose had the same exact scar Xenon had given him when he'd cut his palm for blood.

A scar that Ambrose hadn't had the times he'd seen him before . . .

GO TO SCHOOL.
GET GOOD GRADES.
RAISE HELL.
SAVE THE WORLD.

BOOK 3

BOOK 2

BOOK 1